THE THREE
COFFINS

JOHN DICKSON CARR (1906-1977) was one of the greatest writers of the American Golden Age mystery and the only American author to be included in England's legendary Detection Club during his lifetime. Though he was born and died in the United States, Carr resided in England for nearly twenty years. Under his own name and various pseudonyms, he wrote more than seventy novels and numerous short stories and is best known today for his locked room mysteries.

OTTO PENZLER, the creator of American Mystery Classics, is also the founder of the Mysterious Press (1975); Mysterious-Press.com (2011), an electronic-book publishing company; and New York City's Mysterious Bookshop (1979). He has won a Raven, the Ellery Queen Award, two Edgars (for the *Encyclopedia of Mystery and Detection*, 1977, and *The Lineup*, 2010), and lifetime achievement awards from NoirCon and *The Strand Magazine*. He has edited more than seventy anthologies and written extensively about mystery fiction.

THE THREE COFFINS

JOHN DICKSON CARR

Introduction by
OTTO PENZLER

AMERICAN MYSTERY CLASSICS

Penzler Publishers
New York

Published in 2024 by Penzler Publishers
58 Warren Street, New York, NY 10007
penzlerpublishers.com

Distributed by W. W. Norton

Cover image: Andy Ross
Cover design: Mauricio Diaz

Paperback ISBN 978-1-61316-586-7
Hardcover ISBN 978-1-61316-585-0
eBook ISBN 978-1-61316-587-4

Library of Congress Control Number: 2024943987

Printed in the United States of America

9 8 7 6 5 4 3 2 1

INTRODUCTION

THE MYSTERY story has undergone incalculable developments since its creation. What had for many years been assumed to be a mystery—the detective story—was, in fact, merely one slice of the very large pie that also includes wedges of crime fiction, thrillers, police procedurals, espionage novels, and tales of suspense.

Of these sub-genres of the mystery, it is my contention that the most difficult to produce, or rather to produce well, is the novel of pure detection. There can be no slovenliness of plot here, or else there will be an element, however innocuous it may seem, upon which the astute reader will pounce and, when it remains unexplained or unremarked upon at the end of the book, the novel will be dismissed as being unfair, no matter how brilliantly executed all else may have been accomplished.

The greatest of the great names continue to be read today, coming on a hundred years, because they understood the rules, adhered to them, and had the talent, if not the outright genius, to produce works within the precise strictures of what was permitted. Who are the immortals who wrote these towering monuments of detection fiction? You know their names already: Agatha Christie, Dorothy L. Sayers, Ellery Queen, S.S. Van Dine, Philip MacDonald, Erle Stanley Gardner, R. Austin Freeman, Anthony Berkeley, Freeman Wills Crofts, A.E.W. Mason and, of course, John Dickson Carr. These were the first gods in the pantheon of detective fiction authors. Some are undoubtedly more readable than others. Try as I might, I could never make it from beginning to end of a Crofts novel without losing the battle against Morpheus. There are other greats who fail to make the list because the purity of their detective puzzles suffered by comparison, even though they created charming and often baffling plots which were sometimes transparent or left unexplained gaps. These include Arthur Conan Doyle, Rex Stout, Georges Simenon, and most writers of hard-boiled private eye stories.

Carr once provided his definition of a detective story, and it is a good one, however simple it may seem. "The detective story," he wrote in an introduction to *The Ten Best Detective Novels*, an anthology he prepared but which was never published, "is a conflict between criminal and detective in which the criminal, by means of some ingenious device—alibi, novel murder-method, or what you like—remains unconvicted, or even unsuspected, until the detective reveals his identity by means of evidence which has also been conveyed to the reader.

"This is the skeleton," he continues, "the framework, the Christmas tree on which all the ornaments are hung. If the skeleton has been badly hung, or the tree clumsily set in its base, no amount of glittering ornament will save it. It will fall over with a flop. Its fall may create a momentary sensation, especially among children; but adults are only depressed when they see the same sort of thing happen in fiction."

Although the majority of his books were set in England, Carr was born in the United States, in Pennsylvania, in 1906. His first detective novel, *It Walks by Night*, was published in 1930 when he was twenty-four years old. During an Atlantic crossing, he met an English woman, Clarice Cleaves, who he married in the United States but, deciding that England was the ideal place in which to write detective stories, settled there in 1933.

He was immediately successful and prolific, publishing thirty books by the end of 1939. Writing novels in such enormous quantities forced him to create a second identity, Carr Dickson, quickly changed to Carter Dickson when his original publisher, Harpers, protested that the name was too similar to the original.

After Henri Bencolin solved the crime in the first book, Carr created Dr. Gideon Fell, his best-known and most popular character. A voracious reader of detective stories as a child and young man, Carr greatly admired G.K. Chesterton's Father Brown stories and modeled Fell on the author.

Chesterton's girth was as prodigious as his ego, hence the estimable figure cut by Dr. Fell, who is described in a scene in *The Mad Hatter Mystery* thus: "There was the doctor, bigger and stouter than ever. He wheezed. His red face shone, and his small eyes twinkled over eye-glasses on a broad black ribbon. There was a grin under his bandit's moustache, and chuckling upheavals animated his several chins. On his head was the inevitable black shovel-hat; his paunch projected from a voluminous black cloak. Filling the stairs in grandeur, he leaned on an ash cane with one hand and flourished another cane with the other. It was like meeting Father Christmas or Old King Cole."

Under the Carter Dickson name, he produced a series of novels featuring Sir Henry Merrivale, who was often likened to Winston Churchill. Although not originally patterned after him, the curmudgeonly Merrivale acquired more and more of the future prime minister's characteristics as the series progressed.

When World War II erupted, Carr was summoned by the U.S. military and returned to America, only to have the BBC request his services and be promptly returned to London, where he produced propaganda programs and a popular weekly show titled *Appointment with Fear*.

After the war, he wrote the official biography of Sir Arthur Conan Doyle. When a left-wing government came into power, he took his wife and three daughters, as well as their English nurse, back to America to "escape Socialism," as he stated it. When the Labour Party was voted out in 1951, he and his family returned to England, staying until 1958 when he moved to Greenville, South Carolina, where he lived until his death in 1977.

The undisputed alcove he holds and will forever hold in the virtual Mystery Hall of Fame is as the creator of the most brilliant "locked room" mysteries ever written. While many writers tried their hands at producing "impossible" crimes, they were generally able to sustain the endeavor for a book or two, while the vast majority of Carr/Dickson titles were in this most demanding of all sub-genres.

These mysteries, as one would suspect, generally involve murder in a sealed room, often guarded, in which a hapless victim is executed, often at precisely a specific hour, as warned by the unsuspected killer. Secret doors, hidden panels, and other obvious devices are not permitted—especially not in Carr's books.

In a survey of mystery experts taken to determine the greatest of all locked room novels, it will come as a surprise to no one that first place was accorded to the fertile imagination of Carr for his most famous novel, *The Hollow Man* (titled *The Three*

Coffins in the United States). In addition to presenting one of the most baffling mysteries ever created, Carr courageously has his series detective, Gideon Fell, tell the Scotland Yard detective who has been baffled throughout the tale, and several suspects, that he is about to deliver a lecture regarding impossible crimes.

"But," asks one of the suspects, "if you're going to analyze impossible situations, why discuss detective fiction?"

"Because," Fell replies, "we're in a detective story, and we don't fool the reader by pretending we're not. . . . Let's candidly glory in the noblest pursuits possible to characters in a book."

He goes on to recite dozens of methods and variations by which apparently impossible murders may be accomplished—a tour de force of invention that has justly earned the plaudits of untold readers, scholars, and authors through the years. Carr offers and discards more plot devices and possible solutions in his fourteen-page chapter than have been thought of by a brigade of mystery authors who struggle mightily to conceive of one.

It is always a risk to tell too much about a book, in the off-chance that a reader will actually read an introduction, so I will simply quote from the first paragraph, which neatly sums up the hopeless task confronting Fell.

". . . Two murders were committed," Carr teases us, "in such fashion that the murderer must not only have been invisible, but lighter than air. According to the evidence, this person killed his first victim and literally disappeared. Again according to the evidence, he killed his second victim in the middle of an empty street, with watchers at either end; yet not a soul saw him, and no footprints appeared in the snow."

If you have an intellectual mind, one that enjoys being challenged by an author who openly dares you to be as clever as he is, all the early works of Carr and Dickson will give you all the mental gymnastics you can handle. So will the works of other authors who worked in the rarified atmosphere of impossible crimes. In addition to the works of the greatest of the greats, (though not many are impossible crimes) you might want to try any of the four novels about The Great Merlini, the stage magician created by Clayton Rawson; both novels by Hake Talbot, *Rim of the Pit* (number two in the poll mentioned above) and *The Hangman's Handyman*; *Too Many Magicians* by Randall Garrett, in which he establishes a parallel universe in which the laws of magic apply, yet writes a superb, fair-play locked room mystery; or Gaston Leroux's superb, if slightly slow-moving, *The Mystery of the Yellow Room*, in which the young police reporter Joseph Rouletabille discovers how someone in an hermetically sealed room could have been murdered.

THE DETECTIVE FICTION OF JOHN DICKSON CARR

1930 *It Walks By Night*, Harper (Henri Bencolin)

1931 *The Lost Gallows*, Harper (Henri Bencolin)

1931 *Castle Skull*, Harper (Henri Bencolin)

1932 *The Corpse in the Waxworks*, Harper (U.K. title: *The Waxworks Murder*) (Henri Bencolin)

1932 *Poison in Jest*, Harper (Patrick Rossiter)

1933 *Hag's Nook*, Harper (Gideon Fell)

1933 *The Bowstring Murders* by Carr Dickson, Morrow (John Gaunt)

1933 *The Mad Hatter Mystery*, Harper (Gideon Fell)

1934 *The Eight of Swords*, Harper (Gideon Fell)

1934 *The Plague Court Murders* by Carter Dickson, Morrow (Henry Merrivale)

1934 *The Blind Barber*, Harper (Gideon Fell)

1934 *Devil Kinsmere* by Roger Fairbairn, Harper (Historical)

1934 *The White Priory Murders* by Carter Dickson, Morrow (Henry Merrivale)

1935 *Death-Watch*, Harper (Gideon Fell)

1935 *The Red Widow Murders* by Carter Dickson, Morrow (Henry Merrivale)

1935 *The Three Coffins*, Harper (U.K. title: *The Hollow Man*) (Gideon Fell)

1935 *The Unicorn Murders* by Carter Dickson, Morrow (Henry Merrivale)

1936 *The Arabian Nights Murder*, Harper (Gideon Fell)

1936 *The Murder of Sir Edmund Godfrey*, Harper (Historical)

1937 *The Punch and Judy Murders* by Carter Dickson, Morrow (Henry Merivale)

1937 *The Burning Court*, Harper

1937 *The Peacock Feather Murders* by Carter Dickson, Morrow (Henry Merrivale)

1937 *The Four False Weapons*, Harper (Henri Bencolin)

1937 *The Third Bullet* by Carter Dickson (London, Hodder & Stoughton) (Colonel Marquis)

1937 *To Wake the Dead*, Hamish Hamilton (U.S. publication by Harper in 1938) (Gidcon Fcll)

1938 *The Judas Window* by Carter Dickson, Morrow (Henry Merrivale)

1938 *The Crooked Hinge*, Harper (Gideon Fell)

1938 *Death in Five Boxes* by Carter Dickson, Morrow (Henry Merrivale)

1939 *The Problem of the Green Capsule*, Harper (U.K. title: *The Black Spectacles*) (Gideon Fell)

1939 *Drop to His Death* by Carter Dickson and John Rhode (London, Heinemann; U.S. title: *Fatal Descent*, Dodd, Mead) (Dr. Horatio Glass and Inspector Hornbeam)

1939 *The Problem of the Wire Cage*, Harper (Gideon Fell)

1939 *The Reader Is Warned* by Carter Dickson, Morrow (Henry Merrivale)

1940 *And So to Murder* by Carter Dickson, Morrow (Henry Merrivale)

1940 *The Man Who Could Not Shudder*, Harper (Gideon Fell)

1940 *Nine–And Death Makes Ten* by Carter Dickson, Morrow (U.K. title: *Murder in the Submarine Zone*) (Henry Merrivale)

1940 *The Department of Queer Complaints* by Carter Dickson, Morrow (short stories; seven featuring Colonel March, four non-series)

1941 *The Case of the Constant Suicides*, Harper (Gideon Fell)

1941 *Seeing Is Believing* by Carter Dickson, Morrow (Henry Merrivale)

1941 *Death Turns the Tables*, Harper (Gideon Fell)

1942 *The Gilded Man* by Carter Dickson, Morrow (Henry Merrivale)

1942 *The Emperor's Snuff-Box*, Harper (Dr. Dermot Kinross)

1943 *She Died a Lady* by Carter Dickson, Morrow (Henry Merrivale)

1944 *Till Death Do Us Part*, Harper (Gideon Fell)

1944 *He Wouldn't Kill Patience* by Carter Dickson, Morrow (Henry Merrivale)

1945 *The Curse of the Bronze Lamp* by Carter Dickson, Morrow (U.K. title: *Lord of the Sorcerers)* (Henry Merivale)

1946 *He Who Whispers*, Harper (Gideon Fell)

1946 *My Late Wives* by Carter Dickson, Morrow (Henry Merrivale)

1947 *The Sleeping Sphinx*, Harper (Gideon Fell)

1947 *Dr. Fell, Detective and Other Stories*, American Mercury (short stories and radio plays)

1948 *The Skeleton in the Clock* by Carter Dickson, Morrow (Henry Merivale)

1949 *Below Suspicion*, Harper (Gideon Fell)

1949 *A Graveyard to Let* by Carter Dickson, Morrow (Henry Merrivale)

1950 *The Bride of Newgate*, Harper (Historical)

1950 *Night at the Mocking Widow* by Carter Dickson, Morrow (Henry Merrivale)

1951 *The Devil in Velvet*, Harper (Historical)

1952 *Behind the Crimson Blind* by Carter Dickson, Morrow (Henry Merrivale)

1952 *The 9 Wrong Answers*, Harper (Bill Dawson)

1953 *The Cavalier's Cup* by Carter Dickson, Morrow (Henry Merrivale)

1954 *The Third Bullet and Other Stories*, Harper (short stories, three featuring Gideon Fell, two with Henry Merrivale and two non-series)

1954 *The Exploits of Sherlock Holmes*, Random House (short stories, with Adrian Conan Doyle)

1955 *Captain Cut-Throat*, Harper (Historical)

1956 *Fear Is the Same* by Carter Dickson, Morrow (Historical)

1956 *Patrick Butler for the Defense*, Harper (Patrick Butler)

1957 *Fire Burn!*, Harper (Historical)

1958 *The Dead Man's Knock*, Harper (Gideon Fell)

1959 *Scandal at High Chimneys*, Harper (Historical)

1960 *In Spite of Thunder*, Harper

1961 *The Witch of the Low-Tide*, Harper (Historical)

1962 *The Demoniacs*, Harper (Historical)

1963 *The Men Who Explained Miracles*, Harper (short stories, two featuring Colonel March, two with Gideon Fell, one with Henry Merrivale and two non-series)

1964 *Most Secret*, Harper (Historical)

1965 *The House at Satan's Elbow*, Harper (Gideon Fell)

1966 *Panic in Box C*, Harper (Gideon Fell)

1967 *Dark of the Moon*, Harper (Gideon Fell)

1968 *Papa La-Bas*, Harper (Historical)

1969 *The Ghosts' High Noon*, Harper (Historical)

1971 *Deadly Hall*, Harper (Historical)

1972 *The Hungry Goblin*, Harper (Historical)

1980 *The Door to Doom and Other Detections*, Harper (short stories and radio plays)

1983 *The Dead Sleep Lightly*, Doubleday (radio plays)

1984 *Crime on the Coast* and *No Flowers by Request*, London, Gollancz (U.S. publication in 1987 by Berkley) (two round-robin novellas by various mystery writers; Carr wrote the first two chapters of the first)

1991 *Fell and Foul Play*, International Polygonics (short stories and radio plays)

1991 *Merrivale, March and Murder*, International Polygonics (short stories and a radio play)

1994 *Speak of the Devil*, Crippen & Landru (eight-part radio play)

2008 *13 to the Gallows* (four radio plays, two in collaboration with Val Gielgud)

2022 *The Kindling Spark: Early Tales of Mystery, Horror, and Adventure*, Crippen & Landru

1st
COFFIN:

THE PROBLEM OF THE
SAVANT'S STUDY

1

THE THREAT

To THE murder of Professor Grimaud, and later the equally in-credible crime in Cagliostro Street, many fantastic terms could be applied—with reason. Those of Dr. Fell's friends who like im-possible situations will not find in his casebook any puzzle more baffling or more terrifying. Thus: two murders were committed, in such fashion that the murderer must not only have been invis-ible, but lighter than air. According to the evidence, this person killed his first victim and literally disappeared. Again according to the evidence, he killed his second victim in the middle of an empty street, with watchers at either end; yet not a soul saw him, and no footprint appeared in the snow.

Naturally, Superintendent Hadley never for a moment be-lieved in goblins or wizardry. And he was quite right—unless you believe in a magic that will be explained naturally in this narrative at the proper time. But several people began to won-der whether the figure which stalked through this case might not be a hollow shell. They began to wonder whether, if you took away the cap and the black coat and the child's false-face, you might not reveal nothing inside, like a man in a certain famous romance by Mr. H. G. Wells. The figure was grisly enough, anyhow.

The words "according to the evidence" have been used. We must be very careful about the evidence when it is not given at first-hand. And in this case the reader must be told at the outset, to avoid useless confusion, on whose evidence he can absolutely rely. That is to say, it must be assumed that *somebody* is telling the truth—else there is no legitimate mystery, and, in fact, no story at all.

Therefore it must be stated that Mr. Stuart Mills at Professor Grimaud's house was not lying, was not omitting or adding anything, but telling the whole business exactly as he saw it in every case. Also it must be stated that the three independent witnesses of Cagliostro Street (Messrs. Short and Blackwin, and Police-constable Withers) were telling the exact truth.

Under these circumstances, one of the events which led up to the crime must be outlined more fully than is possible in retrospect. It was the keynote, the whiplash, the challenge. And it is retold from Dr. Fell's notes, in essential details exactly as Stuart Mills later told it to Dr. Fell and Superintendent Hadley. It occurred on the night of Wednesday, February 6th, three days before the murder, in the back parlour of the Warwick Tavern in Museum Street.

Dr. Charles Vernet Grimaud had lived in England for nearly thirty years, and spoke English without accent. Except for a few curt mannerisms when he was excited, and his habit of wearing an old-fashioned square-topped bowler hat and black string tie, he was even more British than his friends. Nobody knew much about his earlier years. He was of independent means, but he had chosen to be "occupied" and made a good thing of it financially. Professor Grimaud had been a teacher, a popular lecturer and writer. But he had done little of late, and occupied some vague unsalaried post at the British Museum which gave him access to what he called the low-magic manuscripts. Low magic was the hobby of which he had made capital: any form of picturesque supernatural devilry from vampirism to the Black Mass, over which he nodded and chuckled with childlike amusement—and got a bullet through the lung for his pains.

A sound common-sense fellow, Grimaud, with a quizzical twinkle in his eye. He spoke in rapid, gruff bursts, from deep down in his throat; and he had a trick of chuckling behind closed teeth. He was of middle size, but he had a powerful chest and enormous physical stamina. Everybody in the neighbourhood of the Museum knew his black beard, trimmed so closely that it looked only like greying stubble, his shells of eye-glasses, his upright walk as he moved along in quick short steps, raising his hat curtly or making a semaphore gesture with his umbrella.

He lived, in fact, just round the corner at a solid old house on the west side of Russell Square. The other occupants of the house were his daughter Rosette, his housekeeper, Mme Dumont, his secretary, Stuart Mills, and a broken-down ex-teacher named Drayman, whom he kept as a sort of hanger-on to look after his books.

But his few real cronies were to be found at a sort of club they had instituted at the Warwick Tavern in Museum Street. They met four or five nights in a week, an unofficial conclave, in the snug back room reserved for that purpose. Although it was not officially a private room, few outsiders from the bar ever blundered in there, or were made welcome if they did. The most regular attendants of the club were fussy baldheaded little Pettis, the authority on ghost stories; Mangan, the newspaperman; and Burnaby, the artist; but Professor Grimaud was its undisputed Dr. Johnson.

He ruled. Nearly every night in the year (except Saturdays and Sundays, which he reserved for work), he would set out for the Warwick accompanied by Stuart Mills. He would sit in his favourite cane armchair before a blazing fire, with a glass of hot rum and water, and hold forth autocratically in the fashion he enjoyed. The discussions, Mills says, were often brilliant, although nobody except Pettis or Burnaby ever gave Professor Grimaud serious battle. Despite his affability, he had a violent temper. As a rule they were content to listen to his storehouse of knowledge about witchcraft and sham witchcraft, wherein trickery hoaxed the credulous; his childlike love of mystification and drama, wherein he would tell a story of mediaeval sorcery, and, at the end, abruptly explain all the puzzles in the fashion of a detective story. They were amusing evenings, with something of the rural-inn flavor about them, though they were tucked away behind the gas-lamps of Bloomsbury. They were amusing evenings—until the night of February 6th, when the premonition of terror entered as suddenly as the wind blowing open a door.

The wind was blowing shrewdly that night, Mills says, with a threat of snow in the air. Besides himself and Grimaud, there were present at the fireside only Pettis and Mangan and Burnaby. Professor Grimaud had been speaking, with pointed gestures of his cigar, about the legend of vampirism.

"Frankly, what puzzles me," said Pettis, "is your attitude towards the whole business. Now, I study only fiction; only ghost stories that never happen. Yet in a way I believe in ghosts. But you're an authority on attested happenings—things that we're forced to call facts unless we can refute 'em. Yet you don't believe a word of what you've made the most important thing in your life. It's as though Bradshaw wrote a treatise to prove that steam-locomotion was impossible, or the editor of the Encyclopaedia Britannica inserted a preface saying that there wasn't a reliable article in the whole edition."

"Well, and why not?" said Grimaud, with that quick, gruff bark of his wherein he hardly seemed to open his mouth. "You see the moral, don't you?"

" 'Much study hath made him mad,' perhaps?" suggested Burnaby.

Grimaud continued to stare at the fire. Mills says that he seemed more angry than the casual gibe would have warranted. He sat with the cigar exactly in the middle of his mouth, drawing at it in the manner of a child sucking a peppermint-stick.

"I am the man who knew too much," he said, after a pause. "And it is not recorded that the temple priest was ever a very devout believer. However, that is beside the point. I am interested in the causes behind these superstitions. How did the superstition start? What gave it impetus, so that the gullible could believe? For example! We are speaking of the vampire legend. Now, that is a belief which prevails in Slavonic lands. Agreed? It got its firm grip on Europe when it swept in a blast out of Hungary between 1730 and 1735. Well, how did Hungary get its proof that dead men could leave their coffins, and float in the air in the form of straw or fluff until they took human shape for an attack?"

"Was there proof?" asked Burnaby.

Grimaud lifted his shoulders in a broad gesture.

"They exhumed bodies from the churchyards. They found some corpses in twisted positions, with blood on their faces and hands and shrouds. That was their proof. . . . But why not? Those were plague years. Think of all the poor devils who were buried alive though believed to be dead. Think how they struggled to get out of the coffin before they really died. You see, gentlemen? That's what I mean by the causes behind superstitions. That's what I am interested in."

"*I also*," said a new voice, "*am interested in it.*"

Mills says that he had not heard the man come in, although he thought he felt a current of air from the opened door. Possibly they were startled by the mere intrusion of a stranger, in a room where a stranger seldom intruded and never spoke. Or it may have been the man's voice, which was harsh, husky, and faintly foreign, with a sly triumph croaking in it. Anyhow, the suddenness of it made them all switch round.

There was nothing remarkable about him, Mills says. He stood back from the firelight, with the collar of his shabby black overcoat turned up and the brim of his shabby soft hat pulled down. And what little they could see of his face was shaded by the gloved hand with which he was stroking his chin. Beyond the fact that he was tall and shabby and of gaunt build, Mills could tell nothing. But in his voice or bearing, or maybe a trick of gesture, there was something vaguely familiar while it remained foreign.

He spoke again. And his speech had a stiff, pedantic quality, as though it were a burlesque of Grimaud.

"You must forgive me, gentlemen," he said, and the triumph grew, "for intruding into your conversation. But I should like to ask the famous Professor Grimaud a question."

Nobody thought of snubbing him, Mills says. They were all intent; there was a kind of wintry power about the man, which disturbed the snug firelit room. Even Grimaud, who sat dark

and solid and ugly as an Epstein figure, with his cigar halfway
to his mouth and his eyes glittering behind the thin glasses, was
intent. He only barked:

"Well?"

"You do not believe, then," the other went on, turning his
gloved hand round from his chin only far enough to point with
one finger, "that a man can get up out of his coffin; that he can
move anywhere invisibly; that four walls are nothing to him; and
that he is as dangerous as anything out of hell?"

"I do not," Grimaud answered, harshly. "Do you?"

"Yes. I have done it. But more! I have a brother who can do
much more than I can, and is very dangerous to you. *I* don't want
your life; he does. But if *he* calls on you . . ."

The climax of this wild talk snapped like a piece of slate exploding in the fire. Young Mangan, an ex-footballer, jumped to
his feet. Little Pettis peered round nervously.

"Look here, Grimaud," said Pettis, "this fellow's stark mad.
Shall I—" He made an uneasy gesture in the direction of the
bell, but the stranger interposed.

"Look at Professor Grimaud," he said, "before you decide."

Grimaud was regarding him with a heavy, graven contempt.
"No, no, no! You hear me? Let him alone. Let him talk about his
brother and his coffins—"

"Three coffins," interposed the stranger.

"Three coffins," agreed Grimaud, with bristling suavity, "if you
like. As many as you like, in God's name! Now perhaps you'll tell
us who you are?"

The stranger's left hand came out of his pocket and laid a
grubby card on the table. Somehow the sight of that prosaic
visiting-card seemed to restore sane values; to whirl the whole

delusion up the chimney as a joke; and to make of this harsh-voiced visitor nothing but a scarecrow of an actor with a bee under his shabby hat. For Mills saw that the card read: *Pierre Fley. Illusionist.* In one corner was printed *2B Cagliostro Street W.C. 1.,* and over it was scribbled *Or c/o Academy Theatre.* Grimaud laughed. Pettis swore and rang the bell for the waiter.

"So," remarked Grimaud, and ticked the card against his thumb. "I thought we should come to something like that. You are a conjuror, then?"

"Does the card say so?"

"Well, well, if it's a lower professional grade, I beg your pardon," nodded Grimaud. A sort of asthmatic mirth whistled in his nostrils. "I don't suppose we might see one of your illusions?"

"With pleasure," said Fley, unexpectedly.

His movement was so quick that nobody anticipated it. It looked like an attack, and was nothing of the kind—in a physical sense. He bent across the table toward Grimaud, his gloved hands twitching down the collar of his coat, and twitching it back up again before anybody else could get a glimpse of him. But Mills had an impression that he was grinning. Grimaud remained motionless and hard. Only his jaw seemed to jut and rise, so that the mouth was like a contemptuous arc in the clipped beard. And his color was a little darker, though he continued to tick the card quietly against his thumb.

"And now, before I go," said Fley, curtly, "I have a last question for the famous professor. Some one will call on you one evening soon. I also am in danger when I associate with my brother, but I am prepared to run that risk. Some one, I repeat, will call on you. Would you rather I did—or shall I send my brother?"

"Send your brother," snarled Grimaud, getting up suddenly, "and be damned!"

The door had closed behind Fley before anybody moved or spoke. And the door also closes on the only clear view we have of the events leading up to the night of Saturday, February 9th. The rest lies in flashes and glimpses, to be interpreted in jig-saw fashion as Dr. Fell later fitted together the charred fragments between the sheets of glass. The first deadly walking of the hollow man took place on that last-named night, when the side streets of London were quiet with snow and the three coffins of the prophecy were filled at last.

2
THE DOOR

THERE WAS roaring good-humour that night round the fire in Dr. Fell's library at Number 1 Adelphi Terrace. The doctor sat ruddy-faced and enthroned in his largest, most comfortable, and decrepit chair, which had sagged and cracked across the padding in the only way a chair can be made comfortable, but which for some reason makes wives go frantic. Dr. Fell beamed with all his vastness behind the eye-glasses on the black ribbon, and hammered his cane on the hearth rug as he chuckled. He was celebrating. Dr. Fell likes to celebrate the arrival of his friends; or, in fact, anything else. And tonight there was double cause for revelry.

For one thing, his young friends, Ted and Dorothy Rampole, had arrived from America in the most exuberant of good spirits. For another his friend Hadley—now Superintendent Hadley of the C.I.D., remember—had just concluded a brilliant piece of work on the Bayswater forgery case, and was relaxing. Ted Rampole sat at one side of the hearth, and Hadley at the other, with the doctor presiding between over a steaming bowl of punch.

Upstairs the Mesdames Fell, Hadley, and Rampole were conferring about something, and down here the Messieurs Fell and Hadley were already engaged in a violent argument about something else, so Ted Rampole felt at home.

Sitting back lazily in the deep chair, he remembered old days. Across from him Superintendent Hadley, with his clipped moustache and his hair the colour of dull steel, was smiling and making satiric remarks to his pipe. Dr. Fell flourished the punch ladle in thunder.

They seemed to be arguing about scientific criminology, and photography in particular. Rampole remembered hearing echoes of this, which had roused the ribald mirth of the C.I.D. During one of his absent-minded intervals of pottering about after a hobby, Dr. Fell had been snared by his friend the Bishop of Mappleham into reading Gross, Jesserich, and Mitchell. He had been bitten. Now Dr. Fell has not, it may be thankfully stated, what is called the scientific brain. But his chemical researches left the roof on the house, since, fortunately, he always managed to smash the apparatus before the experiment had begun; and, beyond setting fire to the curtains with a Bunsen burner, he did little damage. His photographic work (he said) had been very successful. He had bought a Davontel microscopic camera, with an achromatic lens, and littered the place with what resembled X-ray prints of a particularly dyspeptic stomach. Also, he claimed to have perfected Dr. Gross' method of deciphering the writing on burnt paper.

Listening to Hadley jeer at this, Rampole let his mind drift drowsily. He could see the firelight moving on crooked walls of books, and hear fine snow ticking the window panes behind drawn curtains. He grinned to himself in sheer amiability. He had nothing in the excellent world to irk him—or had he? Shifting, he stared at the fire. Little things popped up like a jack-in-the-box to jab you when you were most comfortable.

Criminal cases! Of course there was nothing to it. It had been Mangan's ghoulish eagerness to enrich a good story. All the same—

"I don't give a hoot *what* Gross says," Hadley was declaring, with a flap of his hand on the chair-arm. "You people always seem to think a man is accurate just because he's thorough. In most cases the letters against burnt paper don't show up at all . . ."

Rampole cleared his throat pacifically. "By the way," he said, "do the words 'three coffins' mean anything to you?"

There was an abrupt silence, as he had hoped there would be. Hadley regarded him suspiciously. Dr. Fell blinked over the ladle with a puzzled air, as though he vaguely associated the words with a cigarette or a pub. Then a twinkle appeared in his eye.

"Heh," he said, and rubbed his hands. "Heh-heh-heh! Making peace, hey? Or do you by any chance mean it? What coffins?"

"Well," said Rampole, "I shouldn't exactly call it a criminal case—" Hadley whistled.

"—but it's a queer business, unless Mangan was stretching things. I know Boyd Mangan quite well; he lived on the other side for a couple of years. He's a damned good fellow who's knocked about the world a lot and has a too-Celtic imagination." He paused, remembering Mangan's dark, slovenly, rather dissipated good looks; his slow-moving ways despite his excitable temperament; his quick generosity and homely grin. "Anyhow, he's here in London working for the *Evening Banner* now. I ran into him this morning in the Haymarket. He dragged me into a bar and poured out the whole story. Then," said Rampole, laying it on with a trowel, "when he learned I knew the great Dr. Fell—"

"Rats," said Hadley, looking at him in that sharp, watchful way of his. "Get down to cases."

"Heh-heh-heh," said Dr. Fell, highly delighted. "Shut up, will you, Hadley? This sounds interesting, my boy. Well?"

"Well, it seems that he's a great admirer of a lecturer or writer named Grimaud. Also he has fallen hard for Grimaud's daughter, and that makes him a still greater admirer of the old man. The old man and some of his friends have a habit of visiting a pub near the British Museum, and a few nights ago something happened which seems to have shaken up Mangan more than the antics of a casual lunatic would warrant. While the old man was talking about corpses getting up out of their graves, or some such cheerful subject, in walked a tall queer-looking bird who began babbling some nonsense about himself and his brother really being able to leave their graves and float in the air like straw." (Here Hadley made a disgusted noise and relaxed his attention, but Dr. Fell continued to look curiously at Rampole.) "Actually, it seems to have been some sort of threat against this Professor Grimaud. At the end this stranger made a threat that his brother would call on Grimaud before long. The odd part was that, though Grimaud didn't turn a hair, Mangan swears he was actually scared green."

Hadley grunted. "That's Bloomsbury for you. But what of it? Somebody with a scary old-womanish mind—"

"That's the point," growled Dr. Fell, scowling. "He isn't. I know Grimaud quite well. I say, Hadley, you don't know how queer it is unless you know Grimaud. H'mf. Ha. Go on, son. How did it end?"

"Grimaud didn't say anything. In fact, he turned it into a joke and an anti-climax that punctured the lunacy pretty well. Just after this stranger had gone, a street musician came up against the door of the pub and struck up 'The Daring Young Man on the Flying Trapeze.' The whole crowd of them burst out laughing, and sanity was restored. Grimaud smiled and said, 'Well, gentlemen, our revived corpse will have to be even nimbler than that if he expects to float down from *my* study window.'

"They dismissed it at that. But Mangan was curious to find out who this visitor, this 'Pierre Fley,' was. Fley had given Grimaud a card with the name of a theatre on it. So the next day Mangan followed it up in the guise of getting a newspaper story. The theatre turned out to be a rather broken-down and disreputable music-hall in the East End, staging nightly variety. Mangan didn't want to run into Fley. He got into talk with the stage-door keeper, who introduced him to an acrobat in the turn before Fley. This acrobat calls himself—Lord knows why—'Pagliacci the Great,' although he's actually an Irishman and a shrewd one. He told Mangan what he knew.

"Fley is known at the theatre as 'Loony.' They know nothing about him; he speaks to nobody and ducks out after every show. But—this is the point—he is *good*. The acrobat said he didn't understand why some West End manager hadn't tumbled to it long before, unless Fley was simply unambitious. It's a sort of super-conjuring, with a specialty in vanishing-tricks. . . ."

Hadley grunted again, derisively.

"No," insisted Rampole, "so far as I can gather it isn't just the old, old stuff. Mangan says he works without an assistant, and that all his props together can go into a box the size of a coffin. If you know anything about magicians, you'll know what a whale of an incredible thing that is. In fact, the man seems hipped on the subject of coffins. Pagliacci the Great once asked him why, and got a jump he didn't expect. Fley turned round with a broad grin and said: 'Three of us were once buried alive. Only one escaped.' Pagliacci said: 'And how did you escape?' To which Fley answered, calmly: 'I didn't, you see. I was one of the two who did not escape.'"

Hadley was tugging at the lobe of his ear. He was serious now.

"Look here," he said, rather uneasily, "this may be a little more important than I'd thought. The fellow's crazy, right enough. If he's got any imaginary grudge— You say he's an alien? I might give the Home Office a call and have him looked up. Then, if he tries to make trouble for your friend . . ."

"*Has* he tried to make trouble?" asked Dr. Fell.

Rampole shifted. "Some sort of letter has come for Professor Grimaud in every post since Wednesday. He has torn 'em up without saying anything, but somebody told his daughter about the affair at the pub, and she has begun to worry. Finally, to cap the whole business, yesterday Grimaud himself began to act queerly."

"How?" asked Dr. Fell. He took away the hand with which he had been shading his eyes. His little eyes blinked at Rampole in startling sharpness.

"He phoned Mangan yesterday, and said: 'I want you to be at the house on Saturday evening. Somebody threatens to pay me a visit.' Naturally, Mangan advised warning the police, which Grimaud wouldn't hear of. Then Mangan said: 'But hang it, sir, this fellow's stark mad and he may be dangerous. Aren't you going to take *any* precautions to defend yourself?' To which the professor answered: 'Oh yes, by all means. I am going to buy a painting.'"

"A what?" demanded Hadley, sitting up.

"A painting to hang on the wall. No, I'm not joking. It seems he did buy it: it was a landscape of some sort, weird business showing trees and gravestones, and a devil of a huge landscape that it took two workmen to carry upstairs. I say 'devil of a landscape' advisedly; I haven't seen it. It was painted by an artist named Burnaby, who's a member of the club and an amateur criminologist. . . . Anyhow, that's Grimaud's idea of defending himself."

To Hadley, who was again eyeing him suspiciously, he repeated his words with some violence. They both turned to look at Dr. Fell. The doctor sat wheezing over his double chins, his big mop of hair rumpled and his hands folded on his cane. He nodded, staring at the fire. When he spoke, the room seemed to grow less comfortable.

"Have you got the address of the place, my boy?" he asked, in a colourless voice. . . . "Good. Better warm up your car, Hadley."

"Yes, but look here—!"

"When an alleged lunatic threatens a sane man," said Dr. Fell, nodding again, "then you may or may not be disturbed. But when a sane man begins to act exactly like the lunatic, then I know *I'm* jolly well disturbed. It may be nothing at all. But I don't like it." Wheezing, he hoisted himself up. "Come on, Hadley. We'll go and have a look at the place, even if we only cruise past."

A sharp wind bit through the narrow streets of the Adelphi; the snow had stopped. It lay white and unreal on the terrace, and in the Embankment gardens below.

In the Strand, bright and deserted during the theatre hour, it was churned to dirty ruts. A clock said five minutes past ten as they turned up into Aldwych. Hadley sat quiet at the wheel, his collar turned up. At Dr. Fell's roar for more speed, Hadley looked first at Rampole and then at the doctor piled into the rear seat.

"This is a lot of nonsense, you know," he snapped. "And it's none of our business. Besides, if there has been a visitor, he's probably gone by now."

"I know," said Dr. Fell. "That's what I'm afraid of."

The car shot into Southampton Row. Hadley kept hooting the horn as though to express his own feelings—but they gathered speed. The street was a bleak canyon, opening into the bleaker canyon of Russell Square. On the west side ran few foottracks and even fewer wheelmarks. If you know the telephone box at the north end, just after you pass Keppel Street, you will have seen the house opposite even if you have not noticed it. Rampole saw a plain, broad, three-storied front, the ground floor of stone blocks painted dun, and red brick above. Six steps led up to a big front door with a brass-edged letter-slot and brass knob. Except for two windows glowing behind drawn blinds on the ground floor over the areaway, the whole place was dark. It seemed the most prosaic house in a prosaic neighbourhood. But it did not remain so.

A blind was torn aside. One of the lighted windows went up with a bang just as they idled past. A figure climbed on the sill, outlined against the crackling blind, hesitated, and leaped. The leap carried him far over beyond the spiked area rails. He struck the pavement on one leg, slipped in the snow, and pitched out across the kerb nearly under the wheels of the car.

Hadley jammed on his brakes. He was out of the car as it skidded against the kerb, and had the man by the arm before the latter had got to his feet. But Rampole had caught a glimpse of the man's face in the headlights.

"Mangan!" he said. "What the devil—!"

Mangan was without a hat or overcoat. His eyes glittered in the light like the glassy bits of snow streaking his arms and hands.

"Who's that?" he demanded, hoarsely. "No, no, I'm all right!

Let go, damn it!" He yanked loose from Hadley and began to wipe his hands on his coat. "Who—*Ted!* Listen. Get somebody. Come along yourself. Hurry! He locked us in—there was a shot upstairs; we just heard it. He'd locked us in, you see. . . ."

Looking behind him, Rampole could see a woman's figure silhouetted against the window. Hadley cut through these incoherent words.

"Steady on. Who locked you in?"

"*He* did. Fley. He's still in there. We heard the shot, and the door's too thick to break. Well, are you coming on?"

He was already running for the front steps, with Hadley and Rampole after him. Neither of the latter had expected the front door to be unlocked, but it swung open when Mangan wrenched the knob. The high hallway inside was dark except for a lamp burning on a table far at the rear. Something seemed to be standing back there, looking at them, with a face more grotesque than any they might have imagined on Pierre Fley; and then Rampole saw it was only a suit of Japanese armour decked out in its devil mask. Mangan hurried to a door at the right, and turned the key that was in the lock. The door was opened from inside by the girl whose silhouette they had seen at the window, but Mangan held her back with his arm extended. From upstairs they could hear a heavy banging noise.

"It's all right, Boyd!" cried Rampole, feeling his heart rise in his throat. "This is Superintendent Hadley—I told you about him. Where is it? What is it?"

Mangan pointed at the staircase. "Carry on. I'll take care of Rosette. He's still upstairs. He can't get out. For God's sake be careful!"

He was reaching after a clumsy weapon on the wall as they went up thick-carpeted stairs. The floor above was dark and seemed deserted. But a light shone down from a niche in the staircase to the next floor, and the banging had changed to a series of thuds.

"Dr. Grimaud!" a voice was crying. "Dr. *Gri*maud! Answer me, will you?"

Rampole had no time to analyze what seemed the exotic, thick atmosphere of this place. He hurried after Hadley up the second staircase, under an open archway at its top, and into a broad hallway which ran the breadth of the house instead of the length. It was panelled to the ceiling in oak, with three curtained windows in the long side of this oblong opposite the staircase, and its thick black carpet deadened every footstep. There were two doors—facing each other from the narrow ends of the oblong. The door far down at their left was open; the door at their right, only about ten feet from the staircase, remained closed despite the man who was beating on it with his fists.

This man whirled round at their approach. Although there was no illumination in the hallway itself, a yellow light streamed through the arch from the niche on the staircase—from the stomach of a great brass Buddha in the niche—and they could see everything clearly. Full in the glow stood a breathless little man who was gesturing uncertainly. He had a big goblin-like shock of hair on his big head, and peered behind big spectacles.

"Boyd?" he cried. "Drayman? I say, is that you? Who's there?"

"Police," said Hadley, and strode past him as he jumped back.

"You can't get in there," said the little man, cracking the joints of his fingers.

"But we've got to get in. The door's locked on the inside. Somebody's in there with Grimaud. A gun went off— He won't answer. Where's Madame Dumont? Get Madame Dumont! That fellow's still in there, I tell you!"

Hadley turned round snappishly.

"Stop dancing and see if you can find a pair of pliers. The key's in the lock; we'll turn it from the outside. I want a pair of *pliers.* Have you got 'em?"

"I—I really don't know where—"

Hadley looked at Rampole. "Hop down to the toolbox in my car. It's under the back seat. Get the smallest pliers you can find, and you might bring along a couple of heavy spanners. If this fellow is armed—"

Rampole turned round to see Dr. Fell emerge through the arch, wheezing heavily. The doctor did not speak, but his face was not so ruddy as before. Going downstairs three at a time, Rampole blundered for what seemed hours before he found the pliers. As he returned he could hear Mangan's voice behind the closed door in the downstairs room, and the hysterical tones of a girl. . . .

Hadley, still impassive, eased the pliers gently into the keyhole. His powerful hands clamped, and began to turn towards the left.

"There's something moving in there—" said the little man.

"Got it," said Hadley. "Stand back!" He drew on a pair of gloves, braced himself, and threw the door inward. It flapped back against the wall with a crash that shook tinglings from the chandelier inside. Nothing came out, although something was trying to come out. Except for that, the bright room was empty. Something, on which Rampole saw a good deal of blood, was painfully trying to drag itself on hands and knees across the black carpet. It choked, rolled over on its side, and lay still.

3
THE FALSE FACE

"STAY IN the door, two of you," Hadley said, curtly. "And if anybody's got weak nerves, don't look."

Dr. Fell lumbered in after him, and Rampole remained in the doorway with his arm extended across it. Professor Grimaud was heavy, but Hadley did not dare wrench. In that effort to crawl to the door there had been a hemorrhage which was not altogether internal, although Grimaud kept his teeth clenched against the blood. Hadley raised him up against one knee. His face had a bluish tinge under the mask of blackish-grey stubble; his eyes were closed and sunken; and he was still trying to press a sodden handkerchief to the bullet hole in his chest. They heard his breath sink thinly. Despite a draught, there was still a sharp mist of powder-smoke.

"Dead?" muttered Dr. Fell.

"Dying," said Hadley. "See the colour? He got it through the lung." He whirled round towards the little man In the doorway. "Phone for an ambulance. Quick! There's not a chance, but he may be able to say something before—"

"Yes," said Dr. Fell, with a kind of fierce sombreness; "that's the thing we're most interested in, isn't it?"

"If it's the only thing we can do," Hadley answered, coolly, "yes. Get me some sofa pillows from over there. Make him as comfortable as we can." When Grimaud's head lolled on one pillow, Hadley bent close. "Dr. Grimaud! *Dr. Grimaud!* Can you hear me?"

The waxy eyelids fluttered. Grimaud's eyes, only half open, moved in a queer, helpless, puzzled way, like a small child's in a face that you would have described as "knowing" or "civilized." He could not seem to understand what had happened. His glasses hung down on a cord from the dressing-gown; he made a weak twitching of his fingers as though he would try to raise them. His barrel chest still rose and fell slightly.

"I am from the police, Dr. Grimaud. Who did this? Don't try to answer if you can't. Nod your head. Was it the man Pierre Fley?"

A faint look of comprehension was succeeded by an even more puzzled expression. Then, distinctly Grimaud shook his head.

"Who was it, then?"

Grimaud was eager; too eager, for it defeated him. He spoke for the first and last time. His lips stuttered in those words whose interpretation, and even the exact wording itself, was so puzzling afterwards. Then he fainted.

The window in the left-hand wall was a few inches up, and a chill draught blew through. Rampole shivered. What had been a brilliant man lay inert on a couple of pillows, spilled and torn like a sack; with something rattling like clockwork inside it to show that it lived, but no more. There was too much blood in the bright, quiet room.

"My God!" Rampole said, uncontrollably, "isn't there anything we can *do?*"

Hadley was bitter. "Nothing, except get to work. 'Still in the house?' Fine lot of dummies!—oh, myself included." He pointed to the partly open window. "Of course the fellow was out of there before we were even inside the house. He certainly isn't here now."

Rampole looked round. The sharp tang of powdersmoke was blowing away, from his vision as well as from the room. He saw the place for the first time in focus.

It was a room some fifteen feet square, with walls panelled in oak and thick black carpet on the floor. In the left-hand wall (as you stood at the door) was the window with its brown velvet draperies blowing. On either side of the window stretched high bookshelves with marble busts along the top. Just out from the window, so as to get the light from the left, stood a great flat-topped desk heavy in claw-footed carving. A padded chair was pushed back from it; at the extreme left was a lamp of mosaic glass, and a bronze ash-tray over which a dead cigar had smoldered to long ash. The blotter, on which a closed calfskin book had been put down, was clean except for a tray of pens and a pile of note-slips held down by a curious little figure—a buffalo carved in yellow jade.

Rampole looked across the room at the side directly opposite the window. In that wall was a great stone fireplace, flanked also by shelves and busts. Above the fireplace, two fencing-foils hung crossed behind a blazoned shield of arms which Rampole did not (then) examine. Only on that side of the room had furniture been disarranged. Just before the fire, a long brown-leather sofa had been knocked awry, and a leather chair rolled back in a twisted-up hearth rug. There was blood on the sofa.

And finally, towards the rear wall of the room facing the door, Rampole saw the painting. Between the bookshelves in this wall there was a vast cleared space where cases had recently been removed; removed within the last few days, for the marks of their bases were still indented in the carpet. A place on the wall had been made for the painting which Grimaud would now never hang. The painting itself lay face upwards on the floor not far from where Grimaud himself lay—and it had been slashed across twice with a knife. In its frame it was fully seven feet broad by four feet high: a thing so big that Hadley had to trundle it out and switch it round in the cleared space down the centre of the room before he could prop it up for a look.

"And that," said Hadley, propping it against the back of the sofa, "is the painting he bought to 'defend himself' with, is it? Look here, Fell, do you think Grimaud was just as mad as this fellow Fley?"

Dr. Fell, who had been owlishly contemplating the window, lumbered round. "As Pierre Fley," be rumbled, and pushed back his shovel-hat, "who *didn't* commit the crime. H'm. I say, Hadley, do you see any weapon?"

"I do not. First there isn't any gun—a high-calibre automatic is what we want—and now there isn't any knife with which this thing was cut to blazes. Look at it! It looks like an ordinary landscape to me."

It was not, Rampole thought, exactly ordinary. There was a sort of blowing power about it, as though the artist had painted in a fury and caught in oils the wind that whipped those crooked trees. You felt bleakness and terror. Its motif was sombre, with a greenish tint underlying greys and blacks, except for low white mountains rising in the background. In the foreground, through the branches of a crooked tree, you could see three headstones in rank grass. Somehow it had an atmosphere like this room, subtly foreign, but as hard to identify as a faint odour. The headstones were toppling; in one way you looked at it, there was an illusion that this was because the grave mounds had begun to heave and crack across. Even the slashes did not seem to disfigure it.

Rampole started a little as he heard a trampling of feet up the staircase in the hall. Boyd Mangan burst in, thinner and more dishevelled than Rampole remembered. Even his black hair, which clung to his head in wirelike scrolls, looked rumpled. He took a quick look at the man on the floor, the heavy brows shading his eyes, and then began to rub a parchment-like cheek. Actually he was about Rampole's age, but the slanting lines drawn under his eyes made him look ten years older.

"Mills told me," he said. "Is he——?" He nodded quickly at Grimaud.

Hadley ignored this. "Did you get the ambulance?"

"Chaps with a stretcher—coming now. The whole neighbourhood's filthy with hospitals, and nobody knew where to telephone. I remembered a friend of the professor's who's got a nursing-home round the corner. They're——" He stood aside to admit two uniformed attendants, and behind them a placid little clean-shaven man with a bald head. "This is Dr. Peterson—er—the police. And that's your—patient."

Dr. Peterson sucked in his cheek and hurried over. "Stretcher, boys," he said, after a brief look. "I won't dig for it here. Take him easy." He scowled and stared curiously round as the stretcher was carried out.

"Any chance?" asked Hadley.

"He might last a couple of hours; not more, and probably less. If he hadn't had the constitution of a bull he'd be dead already. Looks as though he's made a further lesion in the lung trying to exert himself—torn it across." Dr. Peterson dived into his pocket. "You'll want to send your police surgeon round, won't you? Here's my card. I'll keep the bullet when I get it. I should guess a thirty-eight bullet, fired from about ten feet off. May I ask what happened?"

"Murder," said Hadley. "Keep a nurse with him, and if he says anything have it taken down word for word." As the doctor hurried out, Hadley scribbled on a leaf of his notebook and handed it to Mangan. "Got your head about you? Good. I wish you'd phone the Hunter Street police station with these instructions; they'll get in touch with the Yard. Tell 'em what happened if they ask. Dr. Watson is to go to the address of this nursing-home, and the rest are to come on here. . . . Who's that at the door?"

The man at the door was the small, thin, top-heavy youth who had been pounding there to begin with. In full light Rampole saw a big goblin-like shock of dark red hair. He saw dull brown eyes magnified behind thick gold-rimmed glasses, and a bony face sloping outwards to a large and loose mouth. This mouth wriggled with a sonorous precision of utterance, showing wide-spaced teeth with an upward movement of the lip like a fish. The mouth looked flexible from much speaking. Every time he spoke, in fact, he had the appearance of thinly addressing an audience, raising and lowering his head as though from notes, and speaking in a penetrating sing-song towards a point over his listeners' heads. You would have diagnosed a Physics B.Sc. with Socialist platform tendencies, and you would have been right. His clothes were of a reddish-check pattern, and his fingers were laced together before him. His earlier terror had changed to inscrutable calm. He bowed a little, and replied without expression:

"I am Stuart Mills. I am, or was, Dr. Grimaud's secretary." His big eyes moved round. "May I ask what has happened to the—culprit?"

"Presumably," said Hadley, "he escaped through the window while we were all so sure he couldn't get out. Now, Mr. Mills—"

"Pardon me," the sing-song voice interposed, with a sort of aerial detachment about it. "He must have been a very extraordinary man if he did that. Have you examined the window?"

"He's right, Hadley," said Dr. Fell, wheezing heavily. "Take a look! This business is beginning to worry me. I tell you in all sincerity that, if our man didn't leave here by way of the door . . ."

"He did not. I am not," announced Mills, and smiled, "the only witness to that. I saw it all from start to finish."

". . . then he must have been lighter than air to leave by the window. Open the window and have a look. H'mf, wait! We'd better search the room first."

There was nobody hidden in the room. Afterwards, growling under his breath, Hadley eased the window up. Unbroken snow—stretching flat up to the window-frame itself—covered all the wide sill outside. Rampole bent out and looked round.

There was a bright moon in the west, and every detail stood out sharp as a wood-cut. It was a good fifty feet to the ground; the wall fell away in a drop of smooth, wet stone. Just below there was a back yard, like that of all the houses in this row, surrounded by a low wall. The snow lay unbroken in this courtyard, or any other as far as they could look, and along the tops of the walls. Below in the whole side of the house there were no windows whatever. The only windows were on this top floor; and the nearest one to this room was in the hallway to the left, a good thirty feet away. To the right, the nearest window would have been in the adjoining house, an equal distance away. Ahead there lay a vast chessboard of adjoining back yards from houses lining the square, so that the nearest house was several hundred yards away. Finally, there stretched above this window a smooth upward run of stone for some fifteen feet to the roof—whose slope afforded neither hold for the fingers nor for the attaching of a rope.

But Hadley, craning his neck out, pointed malevolently.

"All the same, that's it," he declared. "Look there! Suppose he first hitched a rope to a chimney or something, and had it dangling outside the window when he paid his visit. Then he kills Grimaud, swings out, climbs up over the edge of the roof, crawls up to untie the rope from the chimney, and gets away. There will be plenty of tracks of *that*, right enough. So—"

"Yes," said Mills' voice. "That is why I must tell you that there aren't any."

Hadley looked round. Mills had been examining the fireplace, but now he regarded them with his wide-spaced teeth showing in an impassive smile, though his eyes looked nervous and there was sweat on his forehead.

"You see," he continued, lifting his hand with the forefinger raised, "as soon as I perceived that the man in the false face had disappeared—"

"The *what?*" said Hadley.

"The false face. Do I make myself clear?"

"No. We must see whether we can't extract some sense presently, Mr. Mills. In the meantime, what is this business about the roof?"

"There are no tracks or marks of any nature on it, you see," the other answered, with a bright expression of his eyes as he opened them wide. This was another trick of his, smiling and staring as though with inspiration, even if it sometimes seemed rather a half-witted inspiration. He raised his forefinger again. "I repeat, gentlemen: when I saw that the man in the false face had evidently disappeared, I foresaw difficulties for myself—"

"Why?"

"Because I myself had this door under observation, and I should have been compelled to asseverate that the man had not come out. Very well. It was therefore deducible that he must have left (a) by way of a rope to the roof, or (b) by means of climbing up inside the chimney to the roof. This was a simple mathematical certainty. If $PQ = pq$, it is therefore quite obvious that $PQ = pq + p\beta + qa + a\beta$."

"Is it indeed?" said Hadley, with restraint. "Well?"

"At the end of this hallway which you see—that is to say, which you could see if the door were open," pursued Mills, with unshakable exactitude, "I have my workroom. From there a door leads to the attic, and thence to a trap-door opening out on the roof. By raising the trap-door I could see clearly both sides of the roof over this room. The snow was not marked in any fashion."

"You didn't go out there?" demanded Hadley.

"No. I could not have kept my footing if I had. In fact, I do not at the moment see how this could be done even in dry weather."

Dr. Fell turned a radiant face. He seemed to resist a desire to pick up this phenomenon and dangle him in the air like an ingenious toy.

"And what then, my boy?" he enquired, affably. "I mean, what did you think when your equation was shot to blazes?"

Mills remained smiling and inflexibly profound. "Ah, that remains to be seen. I am a mathematician, sir. I never permit myself to think." He folded his arms. "But I wished to call this to your attention, gentlemen, in spite of my firm statement that he did not leave by the door."

"Suppose you tell us exactly what did happen here tonight," urged Hadley, passing a hand across his forehead. He sat down at the desk and took out his notebook. "Easy, now! We'll lead up to it gradually. How long have you worked for Professor Grimaud?"

"For three years and eight months," said Mills, clicking his teeth. Rampole saw that, in the legal atmosphere of the notebook, he was compressing himself to give brief answers.

"What are your duties?"

"Partly correspondence and general secretarial duties. In greater ratio to assist him in preparing his new work, *The Origin and History of Middle-European Superstitions, Together with* . . ."

"Quite so. How many people live in this house?"

"Besides Dr. Grimaud and myself, four."

"Yes, yes, well?"

"Ah, I see! You wish their names. Rosette Grimaud, his daughter. Madame Dumont, who is housekeeper. An elderly friend of Dr. Grimaud, named Drayman. A general maid whose last name I have never yet been told, but whose first name is Annie."

"How many were here tonight when this happened?"

Mills brought the toe of his shoe forward, balanced himself, and studied it, another trick of his. "That, obviously, I cannot say with certainty. I will tell you what I know." He rocked back and forth. "At the conclusion of dinner, at seven-thirty, Dr. Grimaud came up here to work. This is his custom on Saturday evenings. He told me he did not wish to be disturbed until eleven o'clock; that is also the inviolable custom. He said, however,"—quite suddenly beads of sweat appeared on the young man's forehead again, though he remained impassive—"he said, however, that he might have a visitor about half-past nine."

"Did he say who this visitor might be?"

"He did not."

Hadley leaned forward. "Come, now, Mr. Mills! Haven't you heard of any threat to him? Didn't you hear what happened on Wednesday evening?"

"I—er—I had previous information of it, certainly. In fact, I was at the Warwick Tavern myself. I suppose Mangan told you?"

Uneasily, but with startling vividness, he sketched out the story. Meanwhile, Dr. Fell had stumped away and was going through an examination he several times made that night. He seemed most interested in the fireplace. Since Rampole had already heard an outline of the tavern incident, he did not listen to Mills; he watched Dr. Fell. The doctor inspected the bloodstains splashing the top and right arm of the disarranged sofa. There were more bloodstains on the hearth, though they were difficult to follow against the black carpet. A struggle there? Yet, Rampole saw, the fire-irons were upright in their rack, in such a position that a struggle before the hearth must have sent them clattering. A very small coal fire had been nearly smothered under a drift of charred papers.

Dr. Fell was muttering to himself. He reared up to examine the escutcheon. To Rampole, no student of heraldry, this presented itself as a divided shield in red and blue and silver: a black eagle and crescent moon in the upper part, and in the lower a wedge of what looked like rooks on a chessboard. Though its colours were darkened, it glowed with barbaric richness in a queerly barbaric room. Dr. Fell grunted.

But he did not speak until he began to examine the books in the shelves at the left of the fireplace. After the fashion of bibliophiles, he pounced. Then he began to yank out book after book, glance at the title-page, and shoot it back in again. Also, he seemed to have pounced on the most disreputable-looking volumes in the shelves. He was raising some dust, and making so much noise that it jarred across Mills' sing-song recital. Then he rose up and waved books at them in excited intentness.

"I say, Hadley, I don't want to interrupt, but this is very rummy and very revealing. Gabriel Dobrentei, 'Yorick és Eliza levelei,' two volumes. 'Shakspere Minden Munkái,' nine volumes in different editions. And here's a name—" He stopped. "H'mf. Ha. Do you know anything about these, Mr. Mills? They're the only books in the lot that haven't been dusted."

Mills was startled out of his recital. "I—I don't know. I believe they are from a batch that Dr. Grimaud meant for the attic. Mr. Drayman found them put away behind others when we removed some bookcases from the room last night to make room for the painting to be hung. . . . Where was I, Mr. Hadley? Ah yes! Well, when Dr. Grimaud told me that he might have a visitor tonight, I had no reason to assume it was the man of the Warwick Tavern. He did not say so."

"What, exactly, did he say?"

"I—you see, after dinner I was working in the big library downstairs. He suggested that I should come upstairs to my workroom at half-past nine, sit with my door open, and—and 'keep an eye on' this room, in case . . ."

"In case?"

Mills cleared his throat. "He was not specific."

"He told you all this," snapped Hadley, "and you still did not suspect who might be coming?"

"I think," interposed Dr. Fell, wheezing gently, "that I may be able to explain what our young friend means. It must have been rather a struggle. He means that in spite of the sternest convictions of the youngest B.Sc., in spite of the stoutest buckler emblazoned with $x^2 + 2xy + y^2$, he still had enough imagination to get the wind up over that scene at the Warwick Tavern. And he didn't want to know any more than it was his duty to know. Is that it, hey?"

"I do not admit it, sir," Mills returned, with relief, nevertheless. "My motives have nothing to do with the facts. You will observe that I carried out my orders exactly. I came up here at precisely half-past nine—"

"Where were the others then? Steady, now!" urged Hadley. "Don't say you can't reply with certainty; just tell us where you *think* they were."

"To the best of my knowledge, Miss Rosette Grimaud and Mangan were in the drawing-room, playing cards. Drayman had told me that he was going out; I did not see him."

"And Madame Dumont?"

"I met her as I came up here. She was coming out with Dr. Grimaud's after-dinner coffee; that is to say, with the remnants of it. . . . I went to my workroom, left my door open, and drew out the typewriter desk so that I could face the hallway while I worked. At exactly"—he shut his eyes, and opened them again—"at exactly fifteen minutes to ten I heard the front-door bell ring. The electric bell is on the second floor, and I heard it plainly.

"Two minutes later, Madame Dumont came up from the staircase. She was carrying one of those trays on which it is customary to place visiting-cards. She was about to knock at the door when I was startled to see the—er—the tall man come upstairs directly after her. She turned round and saw him. She then exclaimed certain words which I am unable to repeat verbatim, but whose purport was to ask why he had not waited downstairs;

and she seemed agitated. The—er—tall man made no reply. He walked to the door, and without haste turned down the collar of his coat and removed his cap, which he placed in his overcoat pocket. I think that he laughed, and that Madame Dumont cried out something, shrank back against the wall, and hurried to open the door. Dr. Grimaud appeared on the threshold in some evident annoyance; his exact words were, 'What the devil is all this row about?' Then he stood stockstill, looking up at the tall man; and his exact words were, 'In God's name, who are *you?*'"

Mills' sing-song voice was hurling the words faster; his smile had become rather ghastly, although he tried to make it merely bright.

"Steady, Mr. Mills. Did you get a good look at this tall man?"

"A fairly good look. As he came up under the arch from the staircase, he glanced down in my direction."

"Well?"

"The collar of his overcoat was turned up, and he wore a peaked cap. But I am endowed with what is called 'long sight,' gentlemen, and I could distinctly observe the conformation and colour of the nose and mouth. He was wearing a child's false face, a species of mask in papier-mâché. I have an impression that it was long, of a pinkish colour, and had a wide-open mouth. And, so far as my observation went, he did not remove it. I think I am safe in asserting—"

"You are generally right, are you not?" asked a cold voice from the doorway. "It was a false face. And, unfortunately, he did not remove it."

4
THE IMPOSSIBLE

SHE STOOD in the doorway, looking from one to the other of them. Rampole received the impression of an extraordinary woman without knowing why he felt it. There was nothing remarkable about her, except a certain brilliance and vividness of the black eyes, which had a sanded, reddish look as though of smart without tears. She seemed all contradiction. She was short, and of sturdy figure, with a broad face, rather high cheekbones, and a shiny skin: yet Rampole had a curious impression that she could have been beautiful if she had tried. Her dark brown hair was coiled loosely over her ears, and she wore the plainest of dark dresses slashed with white across the breast: yet she did not look dowdy.

Poise, strength, carriage, what? The word "electric" is meaningless, yet it conveys the wave that came with her; something of crackle and heat and power, like a blow. She moved towards them, her shoes creaking. The prominent dark eyes, turned a little upwards at the outer corner, sought Hadley. She was rubbing the palms of her hands together before her, up and down. Rampole was conscious of two things—that the killing of Professor

Grimaud had struck her with a hurt from which she would never recover, and would have left her stunned and crying if it had
not been for one other wish.

"I am Ernestine Dumont," she said, as though interpreting
the thought. "I have come to help you find the man who shot
Charles."

She spoke almost without accent, but with a certain slur and
deadness. The palms of her hands continued to brush up and
down.

"When I heard, I could not come up—at first. Then I wished
to go with him in the ambulance to the nursing-home, but the
doctor would not let me. He said the police would wish to speak
with me. Yes, I suppose that was wise."

Hadley rose and moved out for her the chair in which he had
been sitting.

"Please sit down, madame. We should like to hear your own
statement in a moment. I must ask you to listen carefully to
what Mr. Mills is saying, in case you should be required to cor-
roborate . . ."

She shivered in the cold from the open window, and Dr. Fell,
who had been watching her sharply, lumbered over to close it.
Then she glanced at the fireplace, where the fire had smoul-
dered nearly out under the mass of burnt papers. Realizing
Hadley's words over the gap, she nodded. She looked at Mills
absent-mindedly, with a sort of vacant affection which showed
almost in a smile.

"Yes, of course. He is a nice poor fool boy, and he means well.
Do you not, Stuart? You must go on, by all means. I will—look."

Mills showed no anger, if he felt any. His eyelids flickered a
few times, and he folded his arms.

"If it gives the Pythoness any pleasure to think so," he sang, imperturbably, "I have no objection. But perhaps I had better continue. Er—where was I?"

"Dr. Grimaud's words when he saw the visitor, you told us, were, 'In God's name, who are *you?*' Then?"

"Ah yes! He was not wearing his eye-glasses, which were hanging down by their cord; his sight is not good without them, and I am under the impression that he mistook the mask for a real face. But before he could raise the glasses, the stranger made so quick a movement that I was rather confused, and he darted in at the door. Dr. Grimaud made a movement to get in front of him, but he was too quick, and I heard him laughing. When he got inside—" Mills stopped, apparently puzzled. "This is most extraordinary. I am under the impression that Madame Dumont, although she was shrinking back against the wall, closed the door after him. I recall that she had her hand on the knob."

Ernestine Dumont blazed.

"What do you wish to be understood by that, little boy?" she asked. "You fool, be sure you know what you are saying. Do you think I would willingly have had that man alone with Charles?— He kicked the door shut behind him. Then he turned the key in the lock."

"One moment, madame. . . . Is that true, Mr. Mills?"

"I wish it clearly understood," Mills sang, "that I am merely trying to give *every* fact and even every impression. I meant nothing. I accept the correction. He did, as the Pythoness says, turn the key in the lock."

"That is what he calls his little joke, 'the Pythoness,'" Mme Dumont said, savagely. "Ah, bah!"

Mills smiled. "To resume, gentlemen: I can well believe that the Pythoness was agitated. She began to call Dr. Grimaud's Christian name, and to shake the knob of the door. I heard voices inside, but I was some distance away, and you will perceive that the door is thick." He pointed. "I could distinguish nothing until, after an interval of about thirty seconds, during which it is deducible that the tall man removed his mask, Dr. Grimaud called out, to the Pythoness, rather angrily: '*Go* away, you fool. I can handle this.'"

"I see. Did he seem—afraid, or anything of the sort?"

The secretary reflected. "On the contrary, I should have said that he sounded in a sense relieved."

"And you, madame: you obeyed and went away without further—?"

"Yes."

"Even though," said Hadley, suavely, "I presume it is not usual for practical jokers to call at the house in false faces and act in such a wild way? You knew, I suppose, of the threat to your employer?"

"I have obeyed Charles Grimaud for over twenty years," said the woman, very quietly. The word "employer" had stung her hard. Her reddish, sanded eyes were intent. "And I have never known a situation which he could *not* handle. Obey! Of course I did; I would always obey. Besides, you do not understand. You have asked me nothing." The contempt changed to a half-smile. "But this is interesting—psychologically, as Charles would say. You have not asked Stuart why *he* obeyed, and caused no fuss. That is merely because you think he would have been afraid. I thank you for the implied compliment. Please go on."

Rampole had a sensation of watching a supple wrist on a swordsman. Hadley seemed to feel this, too, although he addressed the secretary.

"Do you remember, Mr. Mills, the time at which this tall man went into the room?"

"It was at ten minutes to ten. There is a clock on my typewriter desk, you see."

"And when did you hear the shot?"

"At exactly ten minutes past ten."

"You mean to say that you watched the door all that time?"

"I did, most assuredly." He cleared his throat. "In spite of what the Pythoness describes as my timidity, I was the first to reach the door when the shot was fired. It was still locked on the inside, as you gentlemen saw—you yourselves arrived very shortly afterwards."

"During the twenty minutes while these two were together, did you hear any voices, movements, sounds of any kind?"

"At one point I was under the impression that I heard voices raised, and something which I can only describe as resembling a bumping sound. But I was some distance away. . . ." He began to rock again, and stare, as he met Hadley's cold eye. The sweat broke out again. "Now I am aware, of course, that I am under the necessity of telling what must seem an absolutely incredible story. Yet, gentlemen, I *swear* . . . *!*" Quite suddenly he lifted a plump fist and his voice went high.

"That is all right, Stuart," the woman said, gently. "I can confirm you."

Hadley was suavely grim. "That would be just as well, I think. One last question, Mr. Mills. Can you give an exact outward description of this caller you saw? . . . In a moment, madame!" he broke off, turning quickly. "In good time. Well, Mr. Mills?"

"I can state accurately that he wore a long black overcoat, and a peaked cap of some brownish material. His trousers were darkish. I did not observe his shoes. His hair, when he took off the cap—" Mills stopped. "This is extraordinary. I do not wish to be fanciful, but now that I recall it, his hair had a dark, painted, *shiny* look, if you understand me, almost as though his whole head were made of papier-maché."

Hadley, who had been pacing up and down past the big picture, turned on him in a way that brought a squeak from Mills.

"Gentlemen," cried the latter, "you asked me to tell you what I saw. And that is what I saw. It is true."

"Go on," said Hadley, grimly.

"I believe he was wearing gloves, although he put his hands in his pockets and I cannot be absolutely certain. He was tall, a good three or four inches taller than Dr. Grimaud, and of a medium—er—anatomical structure. That is all I can definitely assert."

"Did he look like the man Pierre Fley?"

"Well—yes. That is to say, in one way yes, and another no. I should have said this man was even taller than Fley, and not quite so thin, but I would not be prepared to swear it."

During this questioning, Rampole had been watching Dr. Fell out of the tail of his eye. The doctor, his big cloak humped and his shovel-hat under one arm, had been lumbering about the room with annoyed digs of his cane at the carpet. He bent down to blink at things until his eye-glasses tumbled off his nose. He looked at the painting, along the rows of books, at the jade buffalo on the desk. He went down wheezingly to look at the fireplace, and hoisted himself up again to study the coat of arms over it. Toward the last he seemed to become blankly amiable—and yet always, Rampole saw, he was watching Mme Dumont. She seemed to fascinate him. There was something rather terrible in that small bright eye, which would swing round the second he had finished looking at something. And the woman knew it. Her hands were clenched in her lap. She tried to ignore him, but her glance would come round again. It was as though they were fighting an intangible battle.

"There are other questions, Mr. Mills," said Hadley, "particularly about this Warwick Tavern affair and that painting. But they can wait until we get things in order. . . . Would you mind going down and asking Miss Grimaud and Mr. Mangan to come up here? Also Mr. Drayman, if he has returned? . . . Thanks. Stop a bit! Er—any questions, Fell?"

Dr. Fell shook his head with broad amiability. Rampole could see the woman's white knuckles tighten.

"Must your friend walk about in that way?" she cried, abruptly, and in the shrillness of the voice she pronounced the *w* as v. "It is maddening. It is—"

Hadley studied her. "I understand, madame. Unfortunately, that is his way."

"Who are you, then? You walk into my house—"

"I had better explain. I am the superintendent of the Criminal Investigation Department. This is Mr. Rampole. And the other man, of whom you may have heard, is Dr. Gideon Fell."

"Yes. Yes, I thought so." She nodded, and then slapped the desk beside her. "Well, well, well! Even so, must you forget your manners? Must you make the room freezing with your open windows, even? May we not at least have a fire to warm us?"

"I don't advise it, you know," said Dr. Fell. "That is, until we see what papers have already been burnt there. It must have been rather a bonfire."

Ernestine Dumont said, wearily: "Oh, why must you be such fools? Why do you sit here? You know quite well who did this. It was the fellow Fley, and you know it. Well, well, well? Why don't you go after him? Why do you sit here when I tell you he did it?"

There was a look about her, a trance-like and gypsyish look of hatred. She seemed to see Fley go down a trap on a gallows.

"Do you know Fley?" Hadley snapped.

"No, no, I never saw him! I mean, before this. But I know what Charles told me."

"Which was what?"

"Ah, *zut!* This Fley is a lunatic. Charles never knew him, but the man had some insane idea that he made fun of the occult, you understand. He has a brother who is"—she gestured—"the same, you understand? Well, Charles told me that he might call here tonight at half-past nine. If he did, I was to admit him. But when I took down Charles' coffee-tray at half-past nine, Charles laughed and said that if the man had not arrived by then he would not come at all. Charles said: 'People with a grudge are prompt.'" She sat back, squaring her shoulders. "Well, he was wrong. The door bell rang at a quarter to ten. I answered it. There was a man standing on the step. He held out a visiting-card, and said, 'Will you take this to Professor Grimaud and ask if he will see me?'"

Hadley leaned against the edge of the leather sofa and studied her.

"What about the false face, madame? Didn't you think that a little odd?"

"I did not *see* the false face! Have you noticed there is only one light in the downstairs hall? Well! There was a street lamp behind him, and all I could see was his shape. He spoke so courteously, you understand, and handed in the card, that for a second I did not realize . . ."

"One moment, please. Would you recognize that voice if you heard it again?"

She moved her shoulders as though she were shifting a weight on her back, "Yes! I don't know—yes, yes! But it did not sound right, you see; muffled up in that mask, I think now. Ah, why are men such—!" She leaned back in the chair, and for no apparent reason tears brimmed over her eyes. "I do not see such things! I am real, I am honest! If some one does you a hurt, good. You lie in wait for him and kill him. Then your friends go into court and swear you were somewhere else. You do not put on a painted mask, like old Drayman with the children on Guy Fawkes night; you do not hand in visiting-cards like this horror of a man, and go upstairs and kill a man and then vanish out of a window. It is like the legends they told us when I was a girl. . . ." Her cynical poise cracked across in hysteria. "Oh, my God, Charles! My poor Charles!"

Hadley waited, very quietly. She had herself in hand in a moment; she also was as still, and as foreign and inexplicable, as the big painting which faced her in tortured sombreness across the room. The gust of emotion left her relieved and watchful, though she breathed hard. They could hear the scraping noise of her finger nails on the chair-arms.

"The man said," Hadley prompted, "'Will you take this to Professor Grimaud and ask if he will see me?' Very well. Now at this time, we understand, Miss Grimaud and Mr. Mangan were downstairs in the drawing-room near the front door?"

She looked at him curiously.

"Now that is a strange thing to ask. I wonder why you ask it? Yes—yes, I suppose they were. I did not notice."

"Do you remember whether the drawing-room door was open or shut?"

"I don't know. But I should think it was shut, or I should have seen more light in the hall."

"Go on, please."

"Well, when the man gave me the card, I was going to say, 'Step in, please, and I will see,' when I *did* see. I could not be faced with him alone—a lunatic? I wished to go up and get Charles to come down. So I said, 'Wait there and I will see.' And I very quickly slammed the door in his face, so that the spring-lock caught and he could not get in. Then I went back to the lamp and looked at the card. I still have it; I had no chance to deliver it. And it was blank."

"Blank?"

"There was no writing or printing on it at all. I went up to show it to Charles, and plead with him to come down. But the poor little Mills has told you what happened. I was going to knock at the door, when I heard somebody come upstairs be-hind me. I looked round, and there he was coming big and thin behind me. But I will swear, I will swear on the Cross, that I had locked that door downstairs. Well, I was not afraid of him! No! I asked him what he meant by coming upstairs.

"And still, you understand, I could not see the false face, be-cause his back was to that bright light on the stairs, which shows up all this end of the hall and Charles's door. But he said, in French, *'Madame, you cannot keep me out like that,'* and turned down his collar and put his cap in his pocket. I opened the door because I knew he would not dare face Charles, just as Charles opened it from inside. Then I saw the mask, which was a pinkish colour like flesh. And before I could do anything he made a hor-rible jump inside, and kicked the door shut, and turned the key in the lock."

She paused, as though she had got through the worst part of the recital, and could breathe more easily now.

"And then?"

She said, dully: "I went away, as Charles ordered me to do. I made no fuss or scene. But I did not go far. I went a little way down the stairs, where I could still see the door to this room, and I did not leave my post any more than poor Stuart did. It was—horrible. I am not a young girl, you understand. I was there when the shot was fired; I was there when Stuart ran forward and began to pound the door; I was even there when you people began to come upstairs. But I could not stand it. I *knew* what had happened. When I felt myself going faint, I had just time to get to my room at the foot of that flight when I was—ill. Women sometimes are." The pale lips cracked across her oily face in a smile, shakily. "But Stuart was right; nobody left that room. God help us both, we are telling the truth. However else that horror left the room, he did not leave by the door. . . . And now please, please, will you let me go to the nursing-home to see Charles?"

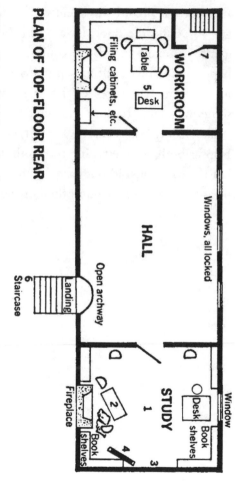

PLAN OF TOP-FLOOR REAR

1. Where Grimaud's body was found.
2. Disarranged sofa, chairs, and hearth rug.
3. Cleared space against wall, where painting was to have been hung.
4. Painting itself, propped up lengthwise against bookshelves.
5. Where Mills sat.
6. Where Mme Dumont stood.
7. Door leading to staircase communicating with trap in roof.

5

THE JIG-SAW WORDS

It was Dr. Fell who answered. He was standing with his back to the fireplace, a vast black-caped figure under the fencing-foils and shield of arms. He seemed to fit there, like a baron out of feudalism, with the bookshelves and white busts towering on either side of him. But he did not look like a very terrible Front de Bœuf. His eye-glasses were corning askew on his nose as he bit off the end of a cigar, turned, and expectorated it neatly into the fireplace.

"Ma'am," he said, turning back with a long challenging sound in his nose, like a battle cry, "we shall not detain you very long. And it is only fair to say that I don't in the least doubt your story, any more than I doubt Mills'. Before getting down to business, I will prove that I believe you. . . . Ma'am, do you remember what time tonight it stopped snowing?"

She was looking at him with hard, bright, defensive eyes. She had evidently heard of Dr. Fell.

"Does it matter? I think it was about half-past nine. Yes! I remember, because when I came up to collect Charles's coffee-tray

I looked out of the window and I noticed that it had stopped. Does it matter?"

"Oh, very much, ma'am. Otherwise we have only half an impossible situation. . . . And you are quite right. H'mf. Remember, Hadley? Half-past nine is about the time it stopped. Right, Hadley?"

"Yes," admitted the superintendent. He also looked at Dr. Fell suspiciously. He had learned to distrust that blank stare over the several chins. "Granting that it was half-past nine, what then?"

"Not only had it stopped snowing a full forty minutes before the visitor made his escape from this room," pursued the doctor, with a meditative air, "but it had stopped fifteen minutes before the visitor even arrived at this house. That's true, ma'am? Eh? He rang the door-bell at a quarter to ten? Good. . . . Now, Hadley, do you remember when *we* arrived at this house? Did you notice that, before you and Rampole and young Mangan went charging in, *there wasn't a single footprint on the flight of steps leading up to the front door, or even the pavement leading up to the steps?* You see, I did. I remained behind to make sure."

Hadley straightened up with a kind of muffled roar. "By God! that's right! The whole pavement was clean. It—" He stopped, and swung slowly round to Mme Dumont. "So this, you say, is your evidence of why you believe madame's story? Fell, have you gone mad, too? We hear a story of how a man rang the door-bell and walked through a locked door fifteen minutes after the snow had stopped, and yet—"

Dr. Fell opened his eyes. Then a series of chuckles ran up the ridges of his waistcoat.

"I say, son, why are you so flabbergasted? Apparently he sailed out of here without leaving a footprint. Why should it upset you to learn that he also sailed in?"

"I don't know," the other admitted, stubbornly. "But, hang it, it does! In my experience with locked-room murders, getting in and getting out are two very different things. It would throw my universe off balance if I found an impossible situation that worked sensibly both ways. Never mind! You say—"

"Please listen. I say," Mme Dumont interposed, pale but with the bunched muscles standing out at the corners of her jaws, "that I am telling the absolute truth, so help me God!"

"And I believe you," said Dr. Fell. "You mustn't let Hadley's stern Scotch common-sense overawe you. He will believe it, too, before I'm through with him. But my point is this. I have shown you, haven't I, that I have strong faith in you—if I can credit what you have said? Very well. I only want to warn you not to upset that faith. I should not dream of doubting what you have already told me. But I fancy I shall very strongly doubt what you are going to tell me in a moment."

Hadley half-closed one eye. "I was afraid of that. I always dread the time when you begin to trot out your damned paradoxes. Seriously, now—"

"Please go on," the woman said, stolidly.

"Humph. Harrumph. Thanks. Now, ma'am, how long have you been Grimaud's housekeeper? No, I'll change that. How long have you been with him?"

"For over twenty-five years," she answered. "I was more than his housekeeper—once."

She had been looking at her interlocked fingers, which she moved in and out; but now she lifted her head. Her eyes had a fierce, steady glaze, as though she wondered how much she dared tell. It was the expression of one peering round a corner at an enemy, ready for instant flight.

"I tell you that," she went on quietly, "in the hope that you will give me your word to keep silent. You will find it in your alien records at Bow Street, and you may make unnecessary trouble that has nothing to do with this matter. It is not for myself, you understand. Rosette Grimaud is my daughter. She was born here, and there had to be a record. But she does not know it—nobody knows it. Please, please, can I trust you to keep silent?"

The glaze over her eyes was changing to a different one. She had not raised her voice, but there was a terrible urgency in it.

"Why, ma'am," said Dr. Fell, a wrinkle in his forehead, "I can't see that it's any of our business. Can you? We shall certainly say nothing about it."

"You mean that?"

"Ma'am," the doctor said, gently, "I don't know the young lady, but I'll bet you a tanner you're worrying yourself unnecessarily, and that you've both been worrying yourselves unnecessarily for years. She probably knows already. Children do. And she's trying to keep it from *you*. And the whole world goes skew-whiff because we like to pretend that people under twenty will never have any emotions, and people over forty never had. Humph. Let's forget it. Shall we?" He beamed. "What I wanted to ask you, Where did you first meet Grimaud? Before you came to England?"

She breathed hard. She answered, but vaguely, as though she were thinking of something else.

"Yes. In Paris."

"You are a Parisienne?"

"Er—what—? No, no, not by birth! I am of the provinces. But I worked there when I met him. I was a costumier."

Hadley looked up from jotting in his notebook. "'Costumier'?" he repeated. "Do you mean a dressmaker, or what?"

"No, no, I mean what I say. I was one of the women who made

costumes for the opera and the ballet. We worked in the Opéra itself. You can find record of that! And, if it will save you time, I will tell you that I was never married and my maiden name was Ernestine Dumont."

"And Grimaud?" Dr. Fell asked, sharply. "Where was he from?"

"From the south of France, I think. But he studied at Paris. His family are all dead, so that will not help you. He inherited their money."

There was an air of tension which these casual questions did not seem to warrant. Dr. Fell's next three questions were so extraordinary that Hadley stared up from his notebook, and Ernestine Dumont, who had recovered herself, shifted uneasily, with a wary brilliance in her eyes.

"What is your religious faith, ma'am?"

"I am a Unitarian. Why?"

"H'm, yes. Did Grimaud ever visit the United States, or has he any friends there?"

"Never. And he has no friends that I know of there."

"Do the words 'seven towers' mean anything to you, ma'am?"

"No!" cried Ernestine Dumont, and went oily white.

Dr. Fell, who had finished lighting his cigar, blinked at her out of the smoke. He lumbered out from the hearth and round the sofa, so that she shrank back. But he only indicated the big painting with his cane, tracing out the line of the white mountains in the background of the picture.

"I won't ask you whether you know what this represents," he continued, "but I will ask you whether Grimaud told you why he bought it. What sort of charm was it supposed to contain, anyhow? What power did it have to ward off the bullet or the evil eye? What sort of weight could its influ . . ." He stopped, as though recalling something rather startling. Then he reached out, wheezing, to lift the picture off the floor with one hand and turn it curiously from side to side. "Oh, my hat!" said Dr. Fell, with explosive absent-mindedness. "O Lord! O Bacchus! Wow!"

"What is it?" demanded Hadley, jumping forward. "Do you see anything?"

"No, I don't see anything," said Dr. Fell argumentatively. "That's just the point. Well, madame?"

"I think," said the woman, in a shaky voice, "that you are the strangest man I ever met. No. I do not know what that thing is. Charles would not tell me. He only grunted and laughed in his throat. Why don't you ask the artist? Burnaby painted it. He should know. But you people will never do anything sensible. It looks like a picture of a country that does not exist."

Dr. Fell nodded sombrely. "I am afraid you are right, ma'am. I don't think it does exist. And if three people were buried there, it might be difficult to find them—mightn't it?"

"Will you stop talking this gibberish?" shouted Hadley; and then Hadley was taken aback by the fact that this gibberish had struck Ernestine Dumont like a blow. She got to her feet to conceal the effect of those meaningless words.

"I am going," she said. "You cannot stop me. You are all crazy. You sit here raving while—while you let Pierre Fley escape. Why don't you go after him? Why don't you *do* something?"

"Because you see, ma'am . . . Grimaud himself said that Pierre Fley did not do this thing." While she was still staring at him, he let the painting fall back with a thump against the sofa. The scene out of a country which did not exist, and yet where three gravestones stood among crooked trees, brought Rampole's mind to an edge of terror. He was still looking at the painting when they heard footsteps on the stairs.

It was a heartening thing to see the prosaic, earnest, hatchet face of Sergeant Betts, whom Rampole remembered from the Tower of London case. Behind him came two cheerful plain-clothes men carrying the photographic and fingerprint apparatus. A uniformed policeman stood behind Mills, Boyd Mangan, and the girl who had been in the drawing-room. She pushed through this group into the room.

"Boyd told me you wanted me," she said, in a quiet but very unsteady voice. "But I insisted on going over with the ambulance, you see. You'd better get over there as quick as you can, Aunt Ernestine. They say he's—going."

She tried to be efficient and peremptory, even in the way she drew off her gloves; but she could not manage it. She had those decided manners which come in the early twenties from lack of experience and lack of opposition. Rampole was rather startled to see that her hair was a heavy blond colour, bobbed and drawn behind the ears. Her face was squarish, with somewhat high cheekbones; not beautiful, but disturbing and vivid in the way that makes you think of old times even when you do not know what times. Her rather broad mouth was painted dark red, but in contrast to this, and to the firm shape of the whole face, the long hazel eyes were of an uneasy gentleness. She looked round quickly, and shrank back towards Mangan with her fur coat drawn tightly round. She was not far from sheer hysteria.

"Will you please hurry and tell me what you want?" she cried. "Don't you realize he's *dying?* Aunt Ernestine . . ."

"If these gentlemen are through with me," the woman said, stolidly, "I will go. I meant to go, as you know."

She was docile all of a sudden. But it was a heavy docility, with a half challenge in it—as though there were limits. Some-thing bristled between these two women, something like the uneasiness in Rosette Grimaud's eyes. They looked at each other quickly, without a direct glance; they seemed to burlesque each other's movements, to become abruptly conscious of it, and stop. Hadley prolonged the silence, as though he were confronting two suspects with each other at Scotland Yard. Then:

"Mr. Mangan," he said, briskly, "will you take Miss Grimaud down to Mr. Mills' room at the end of the hall? Thank you. We shall be with you in a moment. Mr. Mills, just a second! Wait. . . . Betts!"

"Sir?"

"I want you to do some important work. Did Mangan tell you to bring ropes and a flashlight? . . . Good. I want you to go up on the roof of this place and search every inch of it for a footprint or a mark of any kind, especially over this room. Then go down to the yard behind this place, and both adjoining yards, and see if you can find any marks there. Mr. Mills will show you how to get to the roof. . . . Preston! Is Preston here?"

A sharp-nosed young man bustled in from the hall—the Sergeant Preston whose business it was to poke for secret places and who had discovered the evidence behind the panel in the Death Watch case.

"Go over this room for any secret entrance whatever, understand? Tear the place to bits if you like. See if anybody could get up the chimney. . . . You fellows carry on with the prints and pictures. Mark out every blood stain in chalk before you photograph. But don't disturb that burnt paper in the fireplace. . . . Constable! Where the hell's that constable?"

"Here, sir."

"Did Bow Street phone through the address of a man named Fley—Pierre Fley? . . . Right. Go to wherever he lives and pick him up. Bring him here. If he's not there, wait. Have they sent a man to the theatre where he works? . . . All right. That's all. Hop to it, everybody."

He strode out into the hall, muttering to himself. Dr. Fell, lumbering after him, was for the first time imbued with a ghoul-ish eagerness. He poked at the superintendent's arm with his shovel-hat.

"Look here, Hadley," he urged, "you go down and attend to the questioning, hey? I think I can be of much more service if I stay behind and assist those duffers with their photographs . . ."

"No, I'm hanged if you spoil any more plates!" said the other, with heat. "Those film packs cost money, and, besides, we need the evidence. Now, I want to talk to you privately and plain-ly. What's all this wild mumbo-jumbo about seven towers, and people buried in countries that never existed? I've seen you in these fits of mystification before, but never quite so bad. Let's compare notes. What did you . . . yes, yes. What is it?"

He turned irascibly as Stuart Mills plucked at his arm.

"Er—before I conduct the sergeant up to the roof," said Mills, imperturbably, "I think I had better tell you that in case you wish to see Mr. Drayman, he is here in the house."

"Drayman? Oh yes! When did he get back?"

Mills frowned. "So far as I am able to deduce, he did not get back. I should say he had never left. A short time ago I had occa-sion to look into his room . . ."

"Why?" enquired Dr. Fell, with sudden interest.

The secretary blinked impassively. "I was curious, sir. I dis-covered him asleep there, and it will be difficult to rouse him; I believe he has taken a sleeping draught. Mr. Drayman is fond of taking them. I do not mean that he is an inebriate or a drug-us-er, but quite literally that he is very fond of taking sleeping draughts."

"Rummiest household *I* ever heard of," declared Hadley, after a pause, to nobody in particular. "Anything else?"

"Yes, sir. There is a friend of Dr. Grimaud's downstairs. He has just arrived, and he would like to see you. I do not think it is anything of immediate importance, but he is a member of the circle at the Warwick Tavern. His name is Pettis—Mr. Anthony Pettis."

"Pettis, eh?" repeated Dr. Fell, rubbing his chin. "I wonder if that's the Pettis who collects the ghost stories and writes those excellent prefaces? H'm, yes. I dare say. Now, how would he fit into this?"

"I'm asking you how anything fits into it," insisted Hadley. "Look here. I can't see this fellow now, unless he's got something important to tell. Get his address, will you, and say I'll call on him in the morning? Thanks." He turned to Dr. Fell. "Now carry on about the seven towers and the country that never existed."

The doctor waited until Mills had led Sergeant Betts down the big hall to the door at the opposite end. A subdued mutter of voices from Grimaud's room was the only noise. The bright yellow light still streamed from the great arch of the staircase, illuminating the whole hall. Dr. Fell took a few lumbering steps round the hall, looking up and down and then across at the three brown-draped windows. He pulled back the drapes and made certain that these three windows were all firmly locked on the inside. Then he beckoned Hadley and Rampole towards the staircase.

"Scrum," he said. "A little comparing of notes, I admit, will be advisable before we tackle the next witnesses. But not for a second about the seven towers. I'll lead up to those gradually, like Childe Roland. Hadley, a few disjointed words—the only real evidence we have, because it comes from the victim—may be the most important clue of all. I mean those few mutterings from Grimaud just before he fainted. I hope to heaven we all heard 'em. Remember, you asked him whether Fley had shot him. He shook his head. Then you asked him who had done it. What did he say?— I want to ask each of you in turn what you thought you heard."

He looked at Rampole. The American's wits were muddled. He had a strong recollection of certain words, but the whole was confused by a too-vivid picture of a blood-soaked chest and a writhing neck. He hesitated.

"The first thing he said," Rampole answered, "sounded to me like *hover*—"

"Nonsense," interrupted Hadley. "I jotted it all down right away. The first thing he said was *Bath* or 'the bath,' though I'm hanged if I see—"

"Steady now. Your own gibberish," said Dr. Fell, "is a little worse than mine. Go on, Ted."

"Well, I wouldn't swear to any of it. But then I did hear the words *not suicide,* and *he couldn't use rope.* Next there was some reference to a *roof* and to *snow* and to a *fox.* The last thing I heard sounded like *too much light.* Again, I wouldn't swear it was all in consecutive order."

Hadley was indulgent. "You've got it all twisted, even if you have got one or two of the points." He seemed uneasy, nevertheless. "All the same, I'm bound to admit that my notes don't make much better sense. After the word *bath,* he said *salt and wine.* You're right about the rope, although I heard nothing about suicide. Roof and snow are correct; *too much light* came afterwards; then *got gun.* Finally, he did say something about a fox, and the last thing—I barely heard it because of that blood—was something like *Don't blame poor . . .* And that's all."

"O Lord!" groaned Dr. Fell. He stared from one to the other. "This is terrible. Gents, I was going to be very triumphant over you. I was going to explain what he said. But I am beaten by the staggering size of your respective ears. I never heard all that out of the gabble, although I dare say you're within some distance of the truth. Wow!"

"Well, what's your version?" demanded Hadley.

The doctor stumped up and down, rumbling. "I heard only the first few words. They make tolerably good sense if I'm right—*if* I'm right. But the rest is a nightmare. I have visions of foxes running across roofs in the snow, or—"

"Lycanthropy?" suggested Rampole. "Did anybody mention werewolves?"

"No, and nobody's going to!" roared Hadley. He struck his notebook. "To put everything in order, Rampole, I'll write down what you thought you heard for comparison. . . . So. We now have:

"Your list. *Hover. Not suicide. He couldn't use rope. Roof. Snow. Fox. Too much light.*

"My list. *Bath. Salt. Wine. He couldn't use rope. Roof. Snow. Too much light. Got gun. Don't blame poor—*

"There we are. And, as usual, with your own brand of cussedness, Fell, you're most confident about the most senseless part. I might rig up an explanation that could fit together all the latter part, but how the devil does a dying man give us a clue by talking about baths and salt and wine?"

Dr. Fell stared at his cigar, which had gone out.

"H'mf, yes. We'd better clear up a little of that. There are puzzles enough as it is. Let's go gently along the road. . . . First, my lad, what happened in that room after Grimaud was shot?"

"How the hell should I know? That's what I'm asking you. If there's no secret entrance—"

"No, no, I don't mean how the vanishing-trick was worked. You're obsessed with that business, Hadley; so obsessed that you don't stop to ask yourself what *else* happened. First let's get clear the obvious things for which we can find an explanation, and go on from there. Humph. Now, then, what clearly did happen in that room after the man was shot? First, all the marks centred round the fireplace—"

"You mean the fellow climbed up the chimney?"

"I am absolutely certain he didn't," said Dr. Fell, testily. "That flue is so narrow that you can barely get your fist through. Control yourself and think. First, a heavy sofa was pushed away from in front of the fireplace; there was a good deal of blood on the top, as though Grimaud had slipped or leaned against it. The hearth rug was pulled or kicked away; there was blood on that; and a fireside chair was shoved away. Finally, I found spots of blood on the hearth and even in the fireplace. They led us to a huge mass of burnt papers that had nearly smothered the fire.

"Now, consider the behaviour of the faithful Madame Dumont. As soon as she came into that room, she was very terribly concerned about that fireplace. She kept looking at it all the time, and nearly grew hysterical when she saw I was doing so, too. She even, you recall, made the foolish blunder of asking us to light a fire—even though she must have known that the police wouldn't go fooling about with coals and kindling to make witnesses comfortable on the very scene of a crime. No, no, my boy. Somebody had tried to burn letters or documents there. She wanted to be certain they had been destroyed."

Hadley said, heavily: "So she knew about it, then? And yet you said you believed her story?"

"Yes. I did and do believe her story—about the visitor and the crime. What I don't believe is the information she gave us about herself and Grimaud. . . . Now think again what happened! The intruder shot Grimaud. Yet Grimaud, although he is still conscious, does not shout for help, try to stop the killer, make a row of any kind, or even open the door when Mills is pounding there. But he does do something. He does do something, with such a violent exertion that he tears wide open the wound in his lung: as you heard the doctor say.

"And I'll tell you what he did do. He knew he was a goner and that the police would be in. He had in his possession a mass of things that *must be* destroyed. It was more vital to destroy them than to catch the man who shot him or even save his own life. He lurched back and forth from that fireplace, burning this evidence. Hence the sofa knocked away, the hearth rug, the stains of blood. . . . You understand now?"

There was a silence in the bright bleak hall.

"And the Dumont woman?" Hadley asked, heavily.

"She knew it, of course. It was their joint secret. And she happens to love him."

"If this is true, it must have been something pretty damned important that he destroyed," said Hadley, staring. "How the devil do you know all this? What secret could they have had, anyway? And what makes you think they had any dangerous secret at all?"

Dr. Fell pressed his hands to his temples and ruffled his big mop of hair. He spoke argumentatively.

"I may be able to tell you a little of it," he said, "although there are parts that puzzle me beyond hope. You see, neither Grimaud nor Dumont is any more French than I am. A woman with those cheekbones, a woman who pronounces the silent 'h' in honest, never came from a Latin race. But that's not important. They're both Magyar. To be precise: Grimaud came originally from Hungary. His real name is Károly, or Charles, or Grimaud Horváth. He probably had a French mother. He came from the principality of Transylvania, formerly a part of the Hungarian kingdom but annexed by Rumania since the war. In the late 'nineties or early nineteen hundreds, Károly Grimaud Horváth and his two brothers were all sent to prison. Did I tell you he had two brothers? One we haven't seen, but the other now calls himself Pierre Fley.

"I don't know what crime the three brothers Horváth had committed, but they were sent to the prison of Siebenturmen, to work in the salt-mines near Tradj in the Carpathian Mountains. Charles probably escaped. Now, the rather deadly 'secret' in his life can't concern the fact that he was sent to prison or even that he escaped before finishing the sentence; the Hungarian kingdom is broken up, and its authority no longer exists. More probably he did some black devilry that concerned the other two brothers; something pretty horrible concerning those three coffins, and people buried alive, that would hang him even now if it were discovered. . . . That's all I can hazard at the moment. Has anybody got a match?"

6
THE SEVEN TOWERS

In the long pause after this recital, Hadley tossed a matchbox to the doctor and eyed him malevolently.

"Are you joking?" he asked. "Or is this black magic?"

"Not about a thing like this. I wish I could. Those three coffins . . . Dammit, Hadley!" muttered Dr. Fell, knocking his fists against his temples, "I wish I could see a glimmer—something . . ."

"You seem to have done pretty well. Have you been holding out information, or how do you know all that? Stop a bit!" He looked at his notebook. "'Hover.' 'Bath.' 'Salt.' 'Wine.' In other words, you're trying to tell us that what Grimaud really said was, 'Horváth,' and 'salt-mine'? Take it easy, now! If that's your basis, we're going to have a lot of star-gazing on our hands to twist round the rest of those words."

"This assumption of rage," said Dr. Fell, "shows that you agree with me. Thankee. As you yourself shrewdly pointed out, dying men do not commonly mention bath salts. If your version is correct, we might as well all retire to a padded cell. He really said it, Hadley. I heard him. You asked him for a name, didn't you? Was it Fley? No. Who was it, then? And he answered, Horváth."

"Which *you* say is his own name."

"Yes. Look here," said Dr. Fell. "If it will salve your wounds, I will cheerfully admit that it wasn't fair detective work, and that I didn't show you the sources of my information from that room. I'll show you them presently, although Lord knows I tried to show them to you at the time.

"It's like this. We hear from Ted Rampole about a queer customer who threatens Grimaud, and significantly talks about people 'buried alive.' Grimaud takes this seriously; he has known that man before and knows what he is talking about, since for some reason he buys a picture depicting three graves. When you ask Grimaud who shot him, he answers with the name 'Horváth' and says something about salt-mines. Whether or not you think that's odd of a French professor, it is rather odd to find up over his mantelpiece the device of a shield graven thus: *coupé, a demi-eagle issuant sable, in chief a moon argent* . . ."

"I think we may omit the heraldry," said Hadley, with a sort of evil dignity. "What is it?"

"It's the arms of Transylvania. Dead since the war, of course, and hardly very well known in England (or France) even before that. First a Slavic name, and then Slavic arms. Next those books I showed you. Know what they were? They were English books translated into the Magyar. I couldn't pretend to read 'em—"

"Thank God."

"—but I could at least recognize the complete works of Shakespeare, and Sterne's *Letters from Yorick to Eliza,* and Pope's *Essay on Man.* That was so startling that I examined 'em all."

"Why startling?" asked Rampole. "There are all sorts of funny books in anybody's library. There are in your own."

"Certainly. But suppose a scholarly Frenchman wants to read English. Well, he reads it in English, or he gets it translated into

French. But he very seldom insists on getting its full flavour by first having it translated into Hungarian. In other words, they weren't *Hungarian* books; they weren't even French books on which a Frenchman might have been practising his Magyar; they were English. It meant that whoever owned those books, his native language was Hungarian. I went through all of 'em, hoping to find a name. When I found *Károly Grimaud Horváth, 1898* faded out on one flyleaf, it seemed to put the tin hat on it.

"If Horváth was his real name, why had he kept up this pretence for so long? Think of the words 'buried alive,' and 'saltmines,' and there is a gleam. But, when you ask him who shot him, he said Horváth. A moment like that is probably the only time when a man isn't willing to talk about himself; he didn't mean himself, but somebody else named Horváth. While I was thinking of that, our excellent Mills was telling you about the man called Fley at the public house. Mills said that there seemed something very familiar about Fley, although he had never seen him before, and that his speech sounded like a burlesque of Grimaud's. Was it Grimaud he suggested? Brother, brother, brother! You see, there were three coffins, but Fley mentioned only two brothers. It sounded like a third.

"While I was thinking about this, there entered the obviously Slavic Madame Dumont. If I could establish Grimaud as coming from Transylvania, it would narrow down our search when we tried to find out his history. But it had to be done delicately. Notice that carved figure of a buffalo on Grimaud's desk? What does that suggest to you?"

"It doesn't suggest Transylvania, I can tell you that," the superintendent growled. "It's more like the Wild West—Buffalo Bill—Indians. Hold on! Was that why you asked her whether Grimaud had ever been in the United States?"

Dr. Fell nodded guiltily. "It seemed an innocent question, and she answered. You see, if *he'd* got that figure in an American curio shop— H'm. Hadley, I've been in Hungary. I went in my younger and lither days, when I'd just read *Dracula*. Transylvania was the only European country where buffaloes were bred; they used 'em like oxen. Hungary was full of mixed religious beliefs; but Transylvania was Unitarian. I asked Madame Ernestine, and she qualified. Then I threw my hand grenade. If Grimaud had been innocently associated with salt-mines, it wouldn't matter. But I named the only prison in Transylvania where convicts were used to work the salt-mines. I named the Siebenturmen—or the Seven Towers—without even saying it was a prison. It almost finished her. Now perhaps you will understand my remark about the seven towers and the country that does not now exist. And for God's sake will somebody give me a match?"

"You've got 'em," said Hadley. He took a few strides round the hall, accepted a cigar from the now bland and beaming Dr. Fell, and muttered to himself: "Yes—so far as it goes, it seems reasonable enough. Your long shot about the prison worked. But the whole basis of your case, that these three people are brothers, is pure surmise. In fact, I think it's the weakest part of the case...."

"Oh, admitted. But what then?"

"Only that it's the crucial joint. Suppose Grimaud didn't mean that a person named Horváth had shot him, but was only referring to himself in some way? Then the murderer might be anybody. But if there are three brothers, and he did mean that, the thing is simple. We come back to the belief that Pierre Fley *did* shoot him, after all, or Fley's brother did. We can put our hands on Fley at any time, and as for the brother—"

"Are you sure you'd recognize the brother," said Dr. Fell, reflectively, "if you met him?"

"How do you mean?"

"I was thinking of Grimaud. He spoke English perfectly, and also passed perfectly for a Frenchman. I don't doubt he did study at Paris, and that the Dumont woman did make costumes at the Opéra. Anyhow, there he went stumping round Bloomsbury for nearly thirty years, gruff, good-natured, harmless, with his clipped beard and his square bowler, keeping a check on a savage temper and placidly lecturing in public. Nobody ever saw a devil in him—though somehow I fancy it must have been a wily, brilliant devil. Nobody ever suspected. He could have shaved, cultivated tweeds and a port-wine complexion, and passed for a British squire, or anything else he liked. . . . Then what about this third brother? He's the one who intrigues me. Suppose he's right here somewhere in our midst, in some guise or other, and nobody knows him for what he really is?"

"Possibly. But we don't know anything about the brother."

Dr. Fell, struggling to light his cigar, peered up with extraordinary intentness.

"I know. That's what bothers me, Hadley." He rumbled for a moment, and then blew out the match with a vast puff. "We have two theoretical brothers who have taken French names: Charles and Pierre. Then there's a third. For the sake of clearness and argument, let's call him Henri—"

"Look here. You're not going to tell me you know something about him also?"

"On the contrary," returned Dr. Fell, with a sort of ferocity, "I'm going to emphasize just how little we know about him. We know about Charles and Pierre. But we haven't even the merest hint about Henri, *although* Pierre appears to be forever talking about him and using him as a threat. It is, 'My brother who can do much more than I can.' 'My brother who wants your life.' 'I am in danger when I associate with him.' And so on. But no shape comes out of the smoke, neither man nor goblin. Son, it worries me. I think that ugly presence is behind the whole business, controlling it, using poor half-crazy Pierre for his own ends, and probably as dangerous to Pierre as to Charles. I can't help feeling that this presence staged the whole scene at the Warwick Tavern; that he's somewhere close at hand and watchful; that—" Dr. Fell stared round, as though he expected to see something move or speak in the empty hall. Then he added: "You know, I hope your constable gets hold of Pierre and keeps hold of him. Maybe his usefulness is over."

Hadley made a vague gesture. He bit at the end of his clipped moustache. "Yes, I know," he said; "but let's stick to the facts. The facts will be difficult enough to dig out, I warn you. I'll cable the Rumanian police tonight. But if Transylvania's been annexed, in the fuss and uproar there may be few official records left. The Bolshies were storming through there just after the war, weren't they? Um. Anyhow, we want facts! Come on and let's get after Mangan and Grimaud's daughter. I'm not entirely satisfied with *their* behaviour, by the way. . . ."

"Eh? Why?"

"I mean, always provided the Dumont woman is telling the truth," Hadley amended. "You seem to think she is. But, as I've heard the thing, wasn't Mangan here tonight at Grimaud's request, in case the visitor should drop in? Yes. Then he seems to have been rather a tame watch-dog. He was sitting in a room near the front door. The door-bell rings—if Dumont's not lying—and enter the mysterious visitor. All this time Mangan doesn't show any curiosity; he sits in the room with the door shut, pays no attention to the visitor, and only kicks up a row when he hears a shot and suddenly finds that the door has been locked. Is that logical?"

"Nothing is logical," said Dr. Fell. "Not even— But that can wait."

They went down the long hall, and Hadley assumed his most tactful and impassive manner when he opened the door. It was a room somewhat smaller than the other, lined with orderly books and wooden filing cabinets. It had a plain rag carpet on the floor, hard business-like chairs, and a sickly fire. Under a green-shaded hanging-lamp, Mills' typewriter desk was drawn up directly facing the door. On one side of the machine neat manuscript sheets lay clipped in a wire basket; on the other side stood a glass of milk, a dish of dried prunes, and a copy of Williamson's *Differential and Integral Calculus.*

"I'll bet he drinks mineral water, too," said Dr. Fell, in some agitation. "I'll swear by all my gods he drinks mineral water and reads that sort of thing for fun. I'll bet—" He stopped at a violent nudge from Hadley, who was speaking to Rosette Grimaud across the room. Hadley introduced the three of them.

"Naturally, Miss Grimaud, I don't wish to distress you at this time—"

"Please don't say anything," she said. She was sitting before the fire, so tense that she jumped a little. "I mean—just don't say anything about *that.* You see, I'm fond of him, but not so fond that it hurts terribly unless somebody begins to talk about it. Then I begin to think."

She pressed her hands against her temples. In the firelight, with her fur coat thrown back, there was again a contrast between eyes and face. But it was a changing contrast. She had her mother's intense personality shaped into blond, square-faced, rather barbaric Slavic beauty. Yet in one moment the face would be hard and the long hazel eyes gentle and uneasy, like the curate's daughter. And in the next moment the face would be softened and the eyes brilliantly hard, like the devil's daughter. Her thin eyebrows turned a little upwards at the outer corners, but she had a broad humorous mouth. She was restless, sleek, and puzzling. Behind her stood Mangan in gloomy helplessness.

"One thing, though," she went on, pounding her fist slowly on the arm of the chair—"one thing I've got to know, though, before you start your third degree." She nodded towards a little door across the room, and spoke breathlessly. "Stuart's showing that detective of yours up to the roof. Is it true, *is* it true what we hear about a man getting in—and out—and killing my father— without—without—?"

"Better let me handle this, Hadley," said Dr. Fell, very quietly.

The doctor, Rampole knew, was firmly under the impression that he was a model of tact. Very often this tact resembled a load of bricks coming through a skylight. But his utter conviction that he was doing the thing handsomely, his vast good-nature and complete naïveté, had an effect that the most skilled tact could never have produced. It was as though he had slid down on the bricks himself to offer sympathy or shake hands. And people instantly began to tell him all about themselves.

"Harrumph!" he snorted. "Of course it's not true, Miss Grimaud. We know all about how the blighter worked his trick, even if it was done by somebody you never heard of." She looked up quickly. "Furthermore, there'll be no third degree, and your father has a fighting chance to pull through. Look here, Miss Grimaud, haven't I met you somewhere before?"

"Oh, I know you're trying to make me feel better," she said, with a faint smile. "Boyd has told me about you, but—"

"No, I mean it," wheezed Dr. Fell, seriously. He squinted at memory. "H'm, yes. Got it! You're at London University, aren't you? Of course. And you're in a debating circle or something? It seems to me I officiated as chairman when your team debated Woman's Rights in the World, wasn't it?"

"That's Rosette," assented Mangan, gloomily. "She's a strong feminist. She says—"

"Heh-heh-heh," said Dr. Fell. "I remember now." He was radiant, and pointed with a vast flipper. "She may be a feminist, my boy, but she has startling lapses. In fact, I remember that debate as ending in the most beautiful and appalling row I ever heard outside a Pacifist meeting. You were on the side for Women's Rights, Miss Grimaud, and against the Tyranny of Man. Yes, yes. You entered very pale and serious and solemn, and stayed like that until your own side began to present their case. They went on something awful, but you didn't look pleased. Then one lean female carried on for twenty minutes about what woman needed for an ideal state of existence, but you only seemed to get madder and madder. So when your turn came, all you did was rise to proclaim in silvery ringing tones that what woman needed for an ideal existence was less talking and more copulation."

"Good God!" said Mangan, and jumped.

"Well, I felt like it—then," said Rosette, hotly. "But you don't need to think . . ."

"Or perhaps you didn't say copulation," ruminated Dr. Fell. "Anyway, the effect of that terrible word was beyond description. It was as though you had whispered, 'Asbestos!' to a gang of pyromaniacs. Unfortunately, I tried to keep a straight face by swallowing water. This, my friends, is a practice to which I am unaccustomed. The result had the general aspect, to eye and ear, of a bomb exploding in an aquarium. But I was wondering whether you and Mr. Mangan often discussed these subjects. They must be enlightening talks. What was the argument about this evening, for instance?"

Both of them began to speak at once, chaotically. Dr. Fell beamed, and they both stopped with a startled expression.

"Yes," nodded the doctor. "You understand now, don't you, that there's nothing to be afraid of in talking to the police? And that you can speak as freely as you like? It'll be better, you know. Let's face the thing and clear it up sensibly now, among ourselves, hey?"

"Right," said Rosette. "Has somebody got a cigarette?"

Hadley looked at Rampole. "The old blighter's done it," he said.

The old blighter was again lighting his cigar while Mangan fumbled in his haste to produce cigarettes. Then Dr. Fell pointed.

"Now, I want to know about a very rummy thing," he continued. "Were you two kids so engrossed in each other that you didn't notice anything tonight until the rumpus started? As I understand it, Mangan, Professor Grimaud asked you here tonight to be on the lookout for possible trouble. Why didn't you? Didn't you hear the door-bell?"

Mangan's swarthy face was clouded. He made a fierce gesture.

"Oh, I admit it's my fault. But at the time I never gave it a thought. How was I going to know? Of course I heard the door-bell. In fact, we both spoke to the fellow—"

"You *what?*" interrupted Hadley, striding past Dr. Fell.

"Certainly. Otherwise you don't think I'd have let him get past me and upstairs, do you? But he said he was old Pettis—Anthony Pettis, you know."

7
THE GUY FAWKES VISITOR

"Of course we know now that it wasn't Pettis," Mangan pursued, lighting the girl's cigarette with an angry snap of his lighter, "Pettis must be all of five feet four inches tall. Besides, now that I think back on it, it wasn't even a very exact imitation of his voice. But he sang out and spoke in words Pettis always uses. . . ."

Dr. Fell scowled. "But didn't it strike you as queer that even a collector of ghost stories should walk about dressed up like a Fifth of November Guy? Is he addicted to pranks?"

Rosette Grimaud looked up with a startled expression. She held out her cigarette level and motionless, as though she were pointing, and then twitched to look at Mangan. When she turned back again there was a narrow flash of those long eyes, a deepness of breathing like anger or cruelty, or enlightenment. They had shared a thought—and Mangan was much the more disturbed by it. He had the air of one who is trying to be a good fellow and at peace with the world, if the world would only let him. Rampole had a feeling that this secret thought did not concern Pettis at all, for Mangan stumbled before he could recapture Dr. Fell's question.

"Pranks?" he repeated, and passed a hand nervously over his wiry black hair. "Oh! Pettis? Good Lord, no! He's as correct and fussy as they make 'em. But, you understand, we didn't see his face. It was like this:

"We'd been sitting in that front room since just after dinner—"

"Stop a bit," interrupted Hadley. "Was the door to the hall open?"

"No. Hang it all," said Mangan in a defensive tone, and shifted, "you don't sit in a draughty room on a snowy night with the door standing open; not without central heating, you don't. I knew we could hear the bell ring if it did ring. Besides—well, honestly, I didn't expect anything to happen. The professor gave us the impression at dinner that it was a hoax, or that it had been adjusted somehow; anyway, that he had been inclined to get the wind up over nothing. . . ."

Hadley was looking at him with hard, bright eyes. "You got that impression, too, Miss Grimaud?"

"Yes, in a way. . . . I don't know! It's always hard to tell," she answered, with a faint anger (or rebellion?), "whether he's annoyed or amused or just pretending both. My father has a queer sense of humour, and he loves dramatic effects. He treats me as a child. I don't think I ever in my life saw him frightened, so I don't know. But for the past three days he's been acting so dashed queerly that when Boyd told me about the man in that pub—" She lifted her shoulders.

"In what way was he acting queerly?"

"Well, muttering to himself, for instance. And suddenly roaring out over trifles, which he seldom does. And then again he would laugh too much. But most of all it was those letters. He began to get them in every post. Don't ask me what was in them; he burnt all of them. They were in plain penny envelopes. . . . I shouldn't have noticed at all if it hadn't been for a habit of his." She hesitated. "Maybe you'll understand. My father is one of those people who can never get a letter in your presence without your instantly knowing what it's about or even who it's from. He'll explode, 'Damned swindler!' or, 'Now, there's impudence for you!' or, genially, 'Well, well, here's a letter from old So-and-so!'—in rather a surprised tone, as though he expected somebody in Liverpool or Birmingham to be at the other side of the moon. I don't know if you understand . . . ?"

"We understand. Please go on."

"But when he got these notes, or whatever they were, he didn't say anything at all. He didn't move a muscle. Yet, you see, he never openly destroyed one except yesterday morning at the breakfast table. After he'd glanced at it he crumpled it up, got up from his chair, and went over in a thoughtful sort of way and threw it in the fire. Just at that second Au—" Rosette glanced quickly at Hadley, seemed to discover her own hesitation, and blundered into confusion. "Mrs.—Madame—oh, I mean Aunt Ernestine! Just at that second she asked him if he would have some more bacon. Suddenly he whirled round from the fire and yelled, 'Go to hell!' It was so unexpected that before we had recovered our wits he'd stamped out of the room, muttering that a man couldn't have any peace. He looked devilish. That was the day he came back with that painting. He was good-humoured again; he banged about, chuckling, and helped the cabman and somebody else cart it upstairs. I—I don't want you to think—" Evidently the memories were crowding back again to this complex Rosette; she began to think, and that was bad. She added, shakily, "I don't want you to think I don't like him."

Hadley ignored the personal. "Did he ever mention this man at the public house?"

"Off-handedly, when I asked him. He said it was one of the quacks who often threatened him for jeering at—the history of magic. Of course I knew it wasn't merely that."

"Why, Miss Grimaud?"

During a pause she looked at him unwinkingly.

"Because I felt that this was the real thing. And because I have often wondered whether there was anything in my father's past life which might bring something like that on him."

It was a direct challenge. During a long silence they could hear muffled creakings and flat, heavy footsteps shaking on the roof. Some change moved and played like firelight on her face—fear, or hatred, or pain, or doubt. That illusion of the barbaric had returned—as though the mink coat should have been a leopard-skin coat. Crossing her legs, she leaned back voluptuously, wriggling into the chair. She tilted her head against the back of the chair, so that the firelight gleamed on her throat and in her half-shut eyes. She regarded them with a faint, fixed smile; the cheekbones were outlined in shadow. All the same, Rampole saw that she was trembling. Why, incidentally, should her face seem broader than it was long?

"Well?" she prompted.

Hadley appeared mildly surprised. "Bring something on him? I don't quite understand. Had you any reason to think so?"

"Oh, no reason! I don't think so, really. Just these fancies—" The denial was quick, but the sharp rise and fall of her breast had quietened. "Probably it's living with my father's hobby. And then my mother—she's dead, you know; died when I was quite a kid—my mother was supposed to have second-sight." Rosette raised her cigarette again. "But you were asking me . . . ?"

"About tonight, first of all. If you think it would be helpful to go into your father's past, the Yard will certainly act on your suggestion."

She jerked the cigarette away from her lips.

"But," pursued Hadley in the same colourless voice, "let's get on with the story Mr. Mangan was telling. You two went to the drawing-room after dinner, and the door to the hall was shut. Now, did Professor Grimaud tell you what time he expected a dangerous visitor?"

"Er—yes," said Mangan. He had taken out a handkerchief and was mopping his forehead. Seen sideways in the firelight, there were many small wrinkles across the forehead of the thin, hollowed, sharp-angled face. "That was another reason why I didn't tumble to who it might be. He was too early. The professor said ten o'clock, and this fellow arrived at a quarter to."

"Ten o'clock. I see. You're sure he said that?"

"Well—yes! At least, I think so. About ten o'clock. Wasn't it, Rosette?"

"I don't know. He didn't say anything to me."

"I—see. Go on, Mr. Mangan."

"We had the radio on. That was bad, because the music was loud. And we were playing cards in front of the fire. All the same, I heard the door-bell, I looked up at the clock on the mantel, and it said a quarter to ten. I was getting up when I heard the front door open. Then I heard Mrs. Dumont's voice saying something like, 'Wait, I'll see,' and a sound as though the door slammed. I called out, 'Ahoy there! Who is it?' But the radio was making such a row that I naturally stepped over and shut it off.

And just afterwards we heard Pettis—naturally we both thought it was Pettis—call out: 'Hullo, children! It's Pettis. What's all this formality about seeing the Governor? I'm going up and break in on him.'"

"Those were his exact words?"

"Yes. He always called Dr. Grimaud the Governor; nobody else had the nerve to; except Burnaby, and he calls him Pop. . . . So we said, 'Righto,' as you do, and didn't bother any more about it. We both sat down again. But I noticed that it was getting near ten o'clock and I began to be watchful and jumpy, now that it was coming towards ten o'clock . . ."

Hadley drew a design on the margin of his notebook.

"So the man who called himself Pettis," he mused, "spoke to you through the door without seeing you? How did he know you two were there, do you think?"

Mangan frowned. "He saw us through the window, I suppose. As you come up the front steps you can see straight into the front room through the nearest window. I always notice it myself. In fact, if I see anybody in the front room I usually lean across and tap on the window instead of ringing the bell."

The superintendent was still drawing designs, meditatively. He seemed about to ask a question, but checked himself. Rosette regarded him with a sharp, unwinking gaze. Hadley merely said:

"Go on. You were waiting for ten o'clock—"

"And nothing happened," Mangan insisted. "But, a funny thing, every minute past ten o'clock I got more nervous instead of more relieved. I told you I didn't really expect the man would come, or that there would be any trouble. But I kept picturing that dark hall, and the queer suit of armour with the mask out there, and the more I thought of it the less I liked it. . . ."

"I know exactly what you mean," said Rosette. She looked

at him in a strange, rather startled manner. "I was thinking the same thing. But I didn't want to talk about it in case you called me a fool."

"Oh, I have these psychic fits, too. That," Mangan said bitterly, "is why I get the sack so often, and why I shall probably get the sack for not phoning in this story tonight. News editor be damned. I'm no Judas." He shifted. "Anyway, it was nearly ten past ten when I felt I couldn't stand it any longer. I slammed down the cards and said to Rosette, 'Look here, let's get a drink and turn on all the lights in the hall—or do something.' I was going to ring for Annie, when I remembered it was Saturday and her night out. . . ."

"Annie? That's the maid? Yes. I'd forgotten her. Well?"

"So I went over to open the door, and it was locked on the outside. It was like . . . like this! You have some conspicuous object in your bedroom, like a picture or an ornament, that's so common you never fully notice it. Then one day you walk in and have a vague feeling that there's something wrong with the room. It irritates and disturbs you, because you can't imagine why. Then all of a sudden a gap jumps up, and you see with a shock that the object has been removed. Understand? I felt just like that. I *knew* something was wrong, I felt it ever since that fellow had sung out from the hall, but it never hit me with a smash until I found that door locked. Just as I began idiotically yanking at the knob, we heard the shot.

"A firearm indoors makes a devil of a noise, and we heard it even up at the top of the house. Rosette screamed—"

"I did not!"

"Then she pointed at me and said what I'd been thinking, too. She said, "That wasn't Pettis at all. He's got in.'"

"Can you fix the time of that?"

"Yes. It was just ten minutes past ten. Well, I tried to break the door down." In spite of staring at that memory, a wry and mocking gleam of mirth twinkled in Mangan's eyes. It was as though he hated to speak, but could not help commenting. "I say, have you ever noticed how easy it is to break down doors in the stories? Those stories are a carpenter's paradise. They're an endless trail of doors smashed down on the slightest pretext, even when somebody inside won't answer a casual question. But try it on one of these doors! . . . That's about all. I banged my shoulder-bone against it for a while, and then I thought about getting out through the window and in again through the front door or the area door. I ran into you, and you know what happened."

Hadley tapped the notebook with his pencil. "Was it customary for the front door to be unlocked, Mr. Mangan?"

"O Lord! I don't know! But it was the only thing I could think of. Anyhow, it *was* unlocked."

"Yes, it was unlocked. Have you anything to add to that, Miss Grimaud?"

Her eyelids drooped. "Nothing—that is, not exactly. Boyd has told you everything that happened just as it happened. But you people always want all kinds of queer things, don't you? Even if they don't seem to bear on the matter? This probably has nothing to do with the matter at all, but I'll tell you. . . . A little while before the door-bell rang, I was going over to get some cigarettes from a table between the windows. The radio was on, as Boyd says. But I heard from somewhere out in the street, or on the pavement in front of the door, a loud sound like—like a thud, as though a heavy object had fallen from a big height. It wasn't an ordinary street noise, you see. Like a man falling."

Rampole felt himself stirring uneasily. Hadley asked:

"A thud, you say? H'm. Did you look out to see what it was?"

"Yes. But I couldn't see anything. Of course, I only pulled the blind back and peeped round the side of it, but I can swear the street was empt—" She stopped in full flight. Her lips fell open a little and her eyes were suddenly fixed. "Oh, my *God!*" she said.

"Yes, Miss Grimaud," said Hadley without inflection, "the blinds were all down, as you say. I especially noticed that, because Mr. Mangan got entangled with one when he jumped out. That was why I wondered how the visitor could have seen you through any window in that room. But possibly they weren't drawn down all the time?"

There was a silence, except for faint noises on the roof. Rampole glanced at Dr. Fell, who was propped back against one of the unbreakable doors with his chin in his hand and his shovel-hat tilted over his eyes. Then Rampole looked at the impassive Hadley, and back to the girl.

"He thinks we're lying, Boyd," said Rosette Grimaud, coolly. "I don't think we'd better say anything more."

And then Hadley smiled. "I don't think anything of the kind, Miss Grimaud. I'm going to tell you why, because you're the only person who can help us. I'm even going to tell you what did happen. —Fell!"

"Eh?" boomed Dr. Fell, looking up with a start.

"I want you to listen to this," the superintendent pursued, grimly. "A while ago you were having a lot of pleasure and mystification out of saying that you believed the stories—apparently incredible—told by Mills and Mrs. Dumont; without giving any reasons why you believed them. I'll return the compliment. I'll say that I believe not only their story, but the story told by these two also. And, in explaining why, I'll also explain the impossible situation."

This time Dr. Fell did come out of his abstraction with a jerk.

He puffed out his cheeks and peered at Hadley as though prepared to leap into battle.

"Not all of it, I admit," pursued Hadley, "but enough to narrow down the field of suspects to a few people, and to explain why there were no footprints in the snow."

"Oh, *that!*" said Dr. Fell, contemptuously. He relaxed with a grunt. "You know, for a second I hoped you had something. But that part is obvious."

Hadley kept his temper with a violent effort. "The man we want," he went on, "made no footprints on the pavement or up the steps because he never walked on the pavement or up the steps—after the snow had stopped. He was in the house all the time. He had been in the house for some time. He was either (a) an inmate; or (b) more probably somebody who had concealed himself there, using a key to the front door earlier in the evening. This would explain all the inconsistencies in everybody's story. At the proper time he put on his fancy rig, stepped outside the front door on the swept doorstep, and rang the door-bell. It explains how he knew Miss Grimaud and Mr. Mangan were in the front room when the blinds were drawn— he had seen them go in. It explains how, when the door was slammed in his face and he was told to wait outside, he could simply walk in—he had a key."

Dr. Fell was slowly shaking his head and rumbling to himself. He folded his arms argumentatively.

"H'mf, yes. But why should even a slightly cracked person indulge in all that elaborate hocus-pocus? If he lived in the house, the argument isn't bad: he wanted to make the visitor seem an outsider. But if he really came from outside, why take the dangerous risk of hanging about inside long before he was ready to act? Why not march straight up at the right time?"

"First," said the methodical Hadley, checking it off on his fingers, "he had to know where people were, so as to have no interference. Second, and more important, he wanted to put the finishing touches on his vanishing-trick by having no footprints whatever, anywhere, in the snow. The vanishing-trick would be everything to the crazy mind of—brother Henri, let's say. So he got in while it was snowing heavily, and waited until it had stopped."

"Who," Rosette asked in a sharp voice, "is brother Henri?"

"He's a name, my dear," Dr. Fell returned, affably. "I told you that you didn't know him. . . . Now, Hadley, here's where I enter a mild, firm objection to this whole rummy affair. We've talked glibly about snow starting and stopping, as though you could regulate it like a tap. But I want to know how in blazes a man can tell WHEN snow is going to start or stop? That is, a man seldom says to himself, 'Aha! On Saturday night I will commit a crime. On that night, I think, it will commence to snow at exactly 5:00 P.M., and leave off at exactly 9:30 P.M. This will afford me ample time to get into the house, and be prepared with my trick when the snowfall ends.' Tut, tut! Your explanation is rather more staggering than your problem. It's much easier to believe that a man walked on snow without leaving a footprint than to believe he knew precisely when he would have it to walk on."

The superintendent was irritable. "I am trying," he said, "to get to the main point of all this. But if you must fight about that— Don't you see it explains away the last problem?"

"What problem?"

"Our friend Mangan here says that the visitor threatened to pay his visit at ten o'clock. Mrs. Dumont and Mills say nine-thirty. Wait!" He checked Mangan's outburst. "Was A lying, or B? First, what sane reason could either have for lying af-

terwards about the time he *threatened* to come? Second, if A says ten o'clock and B says nine-thirty, then, innocent or guilty, one of the two should have learned beforehand the time at which the visitor really would arrive. And which was right about the time he did arrive?"

"Neither," said Mangan, staring. "It was between 'em. At 9:45."

"Yes. That's a sign that neither lied. It's a sign that the visitor's threat to Grimaud was not definite; it was 'nine-thirty or ten o'clock or thereabouts.' And Grimaud, who was trying pretty desperately to act as though the threat hadn't scared him, nevertheless took very good care to mention both times in order to make sure everybody was there. My wife does the same thing with invitations to bridge parties. . . . Well, but *why* couldn't brother Henri be definite? Because, as Fell says, he couldn't turn off the snow like a tap. He could risk a long gamble on there being snow tonight, as there's been for several nights; but he had to wait until it stopped even if he waited until midnight. He didn't have to wait so long. It stopped at half-past nine. And then he acted exactly as such a lunatic would—he waited fifteen minutes so that there could be no argument afterwards, and rang the bell."

Dr. Fell opened his mouth to speak, looked shrewdly at the intent faces of Rosette and Mangan, and stopped.

"Now, then!" said Hadley, squaring his shoulders. "I've shown you two that I believe everything you say, because I want your help on the most important thing this tells us. . . . The man we want is no casual acquaintance. He knows this house inside out—the rooms, the routine, the habits of the occupants. He knows your phrases and nicknames. He knows how this Mr. Pettis is accustomed to address not only Dr. Grimaud, but *you;* hence he's no casual business friend of the professor whom you haven't seen. So I want to know all about everybody who's a frequent enough visitor to this house, everybody who is close enough to Dr. Grimaud, to answer the description."

She moved uneasily, startled. "You think—somebody like that. . . . Oh, it's impossible! No, no, no!" (It was a queer echo of her mother's voice.) "Not anybody like that, anyhow!"

"Why do you say that?" Hadley asked, sharply. "Do you know who shot your father?"

The sudden crack of the words made her jump. "No, of course not!"

"Or have any suspicion?"

"No. Except," her teeth gleamed, "I don't see why you should keep looking outside the house. That was a very nice little lesson in deduction you gave, and thanks awfully. But if the person had come from *inside* the house, and acted as you said, then it would really be reasonable, wouldn't it? It would apply much better."

"To whom?"

"Let's see! Well . . . that's your business, isn't it?" (He had somehow stirred a sleek tiger cat, and she was enjoying it.) "Of course, you haven't met the whole household. You haven't met Annie—or Mr. Drayman, come to think of it. But your other idea is utterly ridiculous. In the first place, my father has very few friends. Outside of the people in this house, there are only two who fit the qualifications, and neither of them could possibly be the man you want. They couldn't be in the mere matter of their physical characteristics. One is Anthony Pettis himself; he's no taller than I am, and I'm no Amazon. The other is Jerome Burnaby, the artist who did that queer picture. He has a deformity; a slight one, but it couldn't be disguised and anybody could spot it a mile away. Aunt Ernestine or Stuart would have known him instantly."

"All the same, what do you know about them?"

She lifted her shoulders. "Both are middle-aged, well-to-do, and potter after their hobbies. Pettis is bald-headed and fastidious. . . . I don't mean he's old-womanish: he's what the men call a good fellow, and he's clever as sin. Bah! Why won't they *do* something with themselves!" She clenched her hands. Then she glanced up at Mangan, and a slow, calculating, drowsily pleasant expression came into her look. "Burnaby—yes, Jerome has done something with himself, in a way. He's fairly well known as an artist, though *he'd* rather be known as a criminologist. He's big and bluff; he likes to talk about crime and brag about his athletic prowess of old. Jerome is attractive in his way. He's very fond of me, and Boyd is horribly jealous." Her smile widened.

"I don't like the fellow," said Mangan, quietly. "In fact, I hate him like poison—and we both know it. But at least Rosette's right about one thing. He'd never do a thing like that."

Hadley scribbled again. "What is this deformity of his?"

"A club foot. You can see how he couldn't possibly conceal it."

"Thank you. For the moment," said Hadley, shutting up his notebook, "that will be all. I should suggest that you go along to the nursing-home. Unless . . . er—any questions, Fell?"

The doctor stumped forward. He towered over the girl, peering down at her with his head a little on one side.

"Just one last question," he said, brushing aside the black ribbon of his eye-glasses as he would a fly. "Harrumph! Ha! Now! Miss Grimaud, why are you so certain that the guilty person is this Mr. Drayman?"

8
THE BULLET

He never received any answer to that question, although he received some illumination. It was all over before Rampole realized what had happened. Since the doctor had spoken with the greatest casualness, the name "Drayman" had made no impression on Rampole, and he was not even looking at Rosette. Uneasily, he had been wondering for some time what had happened to change the gusty, garrulous, beaming Mangan he used to know into this shuffling figure who backed and deprecated and talked like a fool. In the past Mangan had never talked like a fool, even when he talked like an idiot. But now—

"You *devil!*" cried Rosette Grimaud.

It was like a screech of chalk on a blackboard. Rampole whirled round to see high cheekbones gone still higher as her mouth widened, and a blaze that seemed to take the colour from her eyes: It was only a glimpse; she had flung herself past Dr. Fell, the mink coat flying, and out into the hall, with Mangan after her. The door slammed. Mangan reappeared for a moment, said to them, "Er—sorry!" and quickly closed the door once more. He looked almost grotesque in the doorway, his back bent and his head lowered, so that it seemed all wrinkled forehead and nervous dark eyes shining intensely. His hands were extended, with palms turned down, as though he were trying to quiet an audience. "Er—sorry!" he said, and closed the door.

Dr. Fell remained blinking at it.

"She's her father's daughter, Hadley," he wheezed, and shook his head slowly. "Harrumph, yes. She goes just so far under hard emotional pressure; very quiet, powder packed into a cartridge; then some little thing jars the hair trigger, and—h'm. I'm afraid she's morbid in the real sense, but maybe she thinks she has reason to be. I wonder how much she knows?"

"Oh, well, she's a foreigner. But that's not the point. It seems to me," said Hadley, with some asperity, "that you're always making a wild shot like a trick rifleman and knocking the cigarette out of somebody's mouth. What was that business about Drayman, anyhow?"

Dr. Fell seemed bothered.

"In a minute, in a minute. . . . What did you think of her, Hadley? And Mangan?" He turned to Rampole. "My ideas are a little mixed. I'd got the impression, from what you said, that Mangan was a wild Irishman of the type I know and like."

"He was," said Rampole. "Understand?"

"As to what I think of her," Hadley said, "I think she could sit here as cool as you please, analyzing her father's life (she's got a damned good head on her, by the way); and yet at this moment I'll bet she's in tears and hysterics, rushing across there, because she didn't show him enough consideration. I think she's fundamentally sound. But she's got the Old Nick in her, Fell. She wants a master in both senses. She and Mangan will never hit it off until he has sense enough to punch her head or take her own advice at the London University debate."

"Ever since you have become superintendent of the C.I.D.," declared Dr. Fell, squinting at him, "I have detected in you a certain raffish air which pains and surprises me. Listen, you old satyr. Did you honestly believe all that rubbish you talked, about the murderer sneaking into this house to wait until the snowstorm had stopped?"

Hadley permitted himself a broad grin. "It's as good an explanation as any," he said, "until I can think of a better. And it keeps their minds occupied. Always keep witnesses' minds occupied. At least I believe their story. . . . We're going to find something in the way of footprints on that roof, don't you worry. But we'll talk about that later. What about Drayman?"

"To begin with, I had stuck in my mind an odd remark made by Madame Dumont. It was so odd that it jumped out of the sentence. Not a calculated remark; she cried it out at the time she was most hysterical, when she could not understand why even murderers acted out so silly a charade. She said (if you wish to kill somebody), 'You do not put on a painted mask, like old Drayman with the children on Guy Fawkes night.' I filed away the suggestion of this Guy Fawkes spectre, wondering what it meant. Then, all unintentionally, I phrased a question about Pettis—when speaking to Rosette—with the words, 'dressed up like a Fifth of November Guy?' Did you notice her expression, Hadley? Just my suggestion that the visitor was dressed like that gave her the hint, but it startled her as much as it pleased her. She didn't say anything; she was thinking. She hated the person she was thinking of. What person?"

Hadley stared across the room. "Yes, I remember. I could see she was hinting at somebody she suspected or wanted us to suspect; that was why I asked her flat out. She practically made me see it was somebody in this house. But to tell you the truth,"—he rubbed his hand across his forehead—"this is such a rum crowd that for a second I thought she was hinting at her own mother."

"Not by the way she dragged in Drayman. 'You haven't met Annie—or Mr. Drayman, come to think of it.' The important news was in the postscript. . . ." Dr. Fell stumped round the type-writer desk, peering malevolently at the glass of milk. "We must rout him out. He interests me. Who is this Drayman, this old friend and hanger-on of Grimaud, who takes sleeping draughts and wears Fifth of November masks? What's his place in the household; what's he doing here, anyway?"

"You mean—blackmail?"

"Rubbish, my boy. Did you ever hear of a schoolmaster be-ing a blackmailer? No, no. They're much too worried about what people might find out about *them*. The academic profession has its faults, as I know for my sins; but it doesn't produce blackmail-ers. . . . No, it was probably only a kindly impulse of Grimaud to take him in, but—"

He paused as a rush of cold air blew his cloak. A door across the room, evidently communicating with a staircase to the attic and the roof, opened and shut. Mills popped in. His mouth was bluish and a large wool muffler was wound round his neck; but he looked warm with satisfaction. After refreshing himself with a pull at the glass of milk (impassively, with head thrown back in a way which somehow suggested a sword-swallower), he put out his hands to the fire.

He chattered: "I have been watching your detective, gentle-men, from a point of vantage at the top of the trap-door. He has caused a few landslides, but. . . . Excuse me! Didn't you have a commission of some description for me to execute? Ah yes. I am anxious to lend assistance, but I fear I forgot—"

"Wake up Mr. Drayman," the superintendent said, "if you

have to slosh him with water. And . . . Hullo! Pettis! If Mr. Pettis is still here, tell him I want to see him. What did Sergeant Betts discover up there?"

Betts answered for himself. He looked as though he had taken a header in a ski-jump; he breathed hard, stamped and slapped the snow from his clothes as he shook his way towards the fire.

"Sir," he announced, "you can take my word for it that not even a bird's lit on that roof anywhere. There's no mark of any kind in any place. I've covered every foot of it." He stripped off his sodden gloves. "I had myself tied on a rope to each of the chimneys, so I could get down and crawl straight along the gutters. Nothing round the edges, nothing round the chimneys, nothing anywhere. If anybody got up on that roof tonight, he must have been lighter than air. Now I'll go down and have a look at the back garden . . ."

"But—!" cried Hadley.

"Quite so," said Dr. Fell. "Look here, we'd better go down and see what your bloodhounds are doing in the other room. If the good Preston—"

Sergeant Preston, fuming a little, pulled open the door to the hall as though he had been summoned. He looked at Betts and back to Hadley.

"It's taken me a little time, sir," he reported, "because we had to pull out all those bookcases and shove 'em back again. The answer is nothing! No secret entrance of any kind. Chimney's solid and no funny business about it; flue's only about two or three inches wide, and goes up on an angle at that. . . . Is that all, sir? The boys have finished."

"Fingerprints?"

"Plenty of prints, except— You raised and lowered that window yourself, didn't you, sir? With your fingers on the glass up near the top of the frame? I recognized your prints."

"I am generally careful about things like that," snapped Hadley. "Well?"

"Nothing else on the glass. And all the woodwork of that window, frame and sill, is high-gloss varnish that'd take a glove-smudge as clear as a print. There's nothing, not even a smudge. If anybody went out there, he must have stood back and dived out head first without touching anything."

"That's enough, thanks," said Hadley. "Wait downstairs. Get after that back garden, Betts. . . . No, wait, Mr. Mills. Preston will fetch Mr. Pettis, if he's still there. I should like to speak to you."

"It would seem," said Mills, rather shrilly, when the other two had gone, "that we return to doubts about my own story. I assure you I am telling the truth. Here is where I sat. See for yourself."

Hadley opened the door. Ahead of them the high, sombre hallway ran thirty feet to the door opposite—a door brilliantly illuminated by the glow from under the archway.

"I don't suppose there's any possibility of a mistake?" muttered the superintendent. 'That he really didn't go in, or something like that? A lot of funny business might go on in a shuffle at the doorway; I've heard of its being done. I don't suppose the woman was up to any funny business, dressing up in a mask herself, or— No, you saw them together, and anyway. . . . *Hell!*"

"There was absolutely none of what you describe as funny business," said Mills. Even in his perspiring earnestness he handled the last two words with distaste. "I saw all three of them clearly and wide apart. Madame Dumont was in front of the door, yes; but towards the right. The tall man was towards the left, and Dr. Grimaud separating them. The tall man really did go in; he closed the door behind him; and he did not come out.

It is not as though the occurrence took place in half-light. There was no possibility of ever mistaking that man's gigantic stature."

"I don't see how we can doubt it, Hadley," said Dr. Fell, after a pause. "We've got to eliminate the door also." He wheeled round. "What do you know about this man Drayman?"

Mills' eyes narrowed. His sing-song voice had a guarded quality.

"It is true, sir, that he offers a subject for intelligent curiosity. Hurrum! But I know very little. He has been here some years, I am informed; in any event, before I arrived. He was forced to give up his academic work because he had gone almost blind. He is still almost blind, in spite of treatment, although you would not deduce this from the—er—aspect of his eyes. He appealed to Dr. Grimaud for help."

"Had he some sort of claim on Dr. Grimaud?"

The secretary frowned. "I cannot say. I have heard it mentioned that Dr. Grimaud knew him at Paris, where he studied. That is the only bit of information I have, except one remark which Dr. Grimaud made when he had, let us say, imbibed a convivial glass." A superior kind of smile curved round Mills' mouth without opening it; his eyes narrowed, and gleamed in drowsy satire. "Hum! He stated that Mr. Drayman had once saved his life, and described him as the best damned good fellow in the world. Of course, under the circumstances . . ."

Mills had a jerky trick of putting one foot before the other, rocking, and tapping the toe of one shoe with the heel of the other. With his jerky movements, tiny figure, and big shock of hair, he was like a caricature of Swinburne. Dr. Fell looked at him curiously. But Dr. Fell only said:

"So? And why don't *you* like him?"

"I neither like nor dislike him. But he does nothing."

"Is that why Miss Grimaud doesn't like him, either?"

"Miss Grimaud does not like him?" said Mills, opening his eyes and then narrowing them. "Yes, I had fancied that. I watched, but I could not be certain."

"H'mf. And why is he so interested in Guy Fawkes night?"

"Guy Fa— Ah!" Mills broke off in his surprise, and uttered a flat bleat of laughter. "I see! I did not follow. You see, he is very fond of children. He had two children of his own, who were killed—by the falling of a roof, I believe, some years ago. It was one of those foolish, petty tragedies which we shall eliminate when we build the bigger, greater, more spacious world of the future." At this point in the recital Dr. Fell's face was murderous, but Mills went on: "His wife did not survive long. Then he began to lose his sight. . . . He likes to help the children in all their games, and has himself a somewhat childish mind in spite of certain mental qualities." The fish lip lifted a little. "His favourite occasion seems to be the Fifth of November, which was the birthday of one of his unfortunate progeny. He saves up throughout the year to buy illuminations and trappings, and builds a Guy for a procession to—" A sharp knocking at the door was followed by the appearance of Sergeant Preston.

"There's nobody downstairs, sir," he reported. "That gentleman you wanted to see must have left. . . . A chap from the nursing-home just brought this over for you."

He handed over an envelope and a square cardboard box like a jeweller's box. Hadley ripped open the letter, glanced down it, and swore.

"He's gone," snapped Hadley, "and not a word. . . . Here, read this!"

Rampole looked over Dr. Fell's shoulder as the latter read.

For Superintendent Hadley:

Poor Grimaud died at 11:30. I am sending you the bullet. It's a thirty-eight, as I thought. I tried to get in touch with your police surgeon, but he was out on another case, and so I am sending it to you.

He was conscious just before the end. He said certain things which can be attested by two of my nurses and myself; but he might have been wandering and I should be careful of them. I knew him pretty well, but I certainly never knew he had a brother.

First he said he wished to tell me about it; then he spoke exactly as follows:

"It was my brother who did it. I never thought he would shoot. God knows how he got out of that room. One second he was there, and the next he wasn't. Get a pencil and paper, quick! I want to tell you who my brother is, so that you won't think I'm raving."

His shouting brought in the final hemorrhage, and he died without saying anything else. I am holding the body subject to your orders. If there is any help I can give, let me know.

E. H. PETERSON, M. D.

They all looked at each other. The puzzle stood rounded and complete; the facts stood confirmed and the witnesses vindicated; but the terror of the hollow man remained. After a pause the superintendent spoke in a heavy voice. "'God knows,'" repeated Hadley, "'how he got out of that room.'"

2nd
COFFIN

THE PROBLEM OF
CAGLIOSTRO STREET

9
THE BREAKING GRAVE

Dr. Fell walked over aimlessly, sighed, and settled himself down in the largest chair. "Brother Henri—" he rumbled. "H'mf, yes. I was afraid we should get back to Brother Henri."

"Damn Brother Henri," said Hadley in a flat voice. "We're going after Brother Pierre first. He knows! Why haven't I had any message from that constable? Where's the man who was to pick him up at that theatre? Have the whole blasted lot of them gone to sleep and—"

"We mustn't get the wind up about this thing," interposed the other, as Hadley began to stamp and declaim rather wildly. "That's exactly what Brother Henri would want us to do. Now that we've got Grimaud's last statement, we've at least got one clue. . . ."

"To what?"

"To the words he spoke to *us*, the ones we couldn't make any sense of. The unfortunate point is that they may not help us now that we can hazard a theory as to what they mean. With this new evidence, I'm afraid we were listening to Grimaud running up a blind alley. He wasn't telling us anything; he was only trying to ask us a question."

"What's all this?"

"Don't you see that's exactly what he must have been doing? Last statement: 'God knows how he got out of that room. One second he was there and the next he wasn't.' Now let's try to sort out the words from that invaluable notebook of yours. You and friend Ted have slightly different versions; but we'll begin with the words on which you both agree and which we must assume to be correct. Put aside the first puzzlers—I think we can now feel safe in saying that the words were 'Horváth' and 'salt-mine.' Put aside also the terms on which you do not agree. What words are found in both lists?"

Hadley snapped his fingers. "I begin to— Yes! The words are, 'He couldn't use rope. Roof. Snow. Fox. Too much light.' Well, then! If we try to make a composite statement; fit together the words and the sense of both statements; we have his meaning as something like this: 'God knows how he got out. He couldn't use a rope, either up on the roof or down in the snow. One second he was there, and the next he wasn't. There was too much light for me to miss any move he made—' Stop a bit, though! What about. . . ."

"And now," said Dr. Fell, with a disgusted grunt, "you can begin to fit in the differences. Ted heard, 'not suicide.' That goes into the picture as an assurance to accord with the other expressions. 'This isn't suicide; I didn't kill myself.' You heard, 'Got gun'; which isn't difficult to tie up with the sentence out of the other statement, 'I never thought he would shoot.' BAH! All the clues whirl straight round in a circle and become questions. It's the first case I ever heard of in which the murdered man was just as inquisitive as everybody else."

"But what about the word 'fox'? That doesn't fit anywhere."

Dr. Fell regarded him with a sour twinkle in his eye.

"Oh, yes, it does. It's the easiest part of all—though it may be the trickiest, and we mustn't jump to conclusions about applying it. It's a matter of how words strike the ear when they're not spelled out. If I'm using the word-association test (that damned thing) on various people, and I suddenly whisper, 'Fox!' to a horseman, he will probably answer, 'Hounds!' But if I use the same word on a historian, he is likely to yell . . . quick! What?"

"Guy," said Hadley, and swore. After a lurid interval he demanded: "Do you mean that we come back to some babbling about a Guy Fawkes mask, or the resemblance to a Guy Fawkes mask?"

"Well, everybody else has been doing a tall amount of babbling about it," the doctor pointed out, scratching his forehead. "And I'm not surprised it struck the eye of somebody who saw it at somewhat closer quarters. Does that tell you anything?"

"It tells me to have a little talk with Mr. Drayman," said the superintendent, grimly. He strode towards the door, and was startled to find the bony face of Mills poked out in eager listening against the thick glasses.

"Steady, Hadley," Dr. Fell interposed as the superintendent gave indications of an explosion. "It's a queer thing about you: you can be steady as the Guards when riddles are flying, but you never seem able to keep your shirt on when we get within sight of the truth. Let our young friend stop. He should hear all this, if only to hear the end of it." He chuckled. "Does that make you suspicious of Drayman? Pfaa! On the contrary, it should be just the opposite. Remember, we haven't quite finished putting the pieces in our jig-saw. There's one last bit we haven't accounted for, and it was a bit you heard yourself. That pink mask suggested

Drayman to Grimaud, just as he seems to have been suggested to several others. But Grimaud knew whose face was behind the mask. Therefore we have a fairly sensible explanation of those final words you noted down, *'Don't blame poor—'* He seems to have had a great liking for Drayman, you know." After a silence, Dr. Fell turned to Mills, "Now go and fetch him up here, son."

When the door had closed, Hadley sat down wearily and took from his breast pocket the frayed cigar he had not yet lighted. Then he ran a finger round under his collar with that malevolent, broken-necked expression which people have when worry makes them think the collar is too tight.

"More trick marksmanship, eh?" he suggested. "More deductive tight-rope work, and the daring young man on the—um!" He stared at the floor, and then grunted with annoyance. "I must be losing my grip! It's no good getting fantastic notions like the one I just had. Have you got any concrete suggestions?"

"Yes. Later, if you'll permit it, I am going to apply Gross's test."

"Apply what?"

"Gross's test. Don't you remember? We were arguing about it tonight. I'm going to collect very carefully all the mass of burnt and half-burnt paper in that fireplace, to see whether Gross's test will bring out the writing. Be quiet, will you?" he roared, as Hadley made scornful noises. "I don't say all of it, or even half of it, will come out. But I should get a line here and there to give me a hint about what was more important to Grimaud than saving his own life. Purph! Hah! Yes."

"And how do you work this trick?"

"You'll see. Mind, I don't say that thoroughly burnt paper will come out satisfactorily. But there'll be something, especially in the charred parts sandwiched in and only scorched black, that *will* come out. . . . Aside from that, I haven't a suggestion, unless we ask—yes, what is it?"

Sergeant Betts, not quite so plastered with snow this time, made his report woodenly. He looked out the door behind him before he closed it.

"I've been all over that back garden, sir. And the two adjoining ones, and the tops of all the walls. There's no footprint or any kind of mark. . . . But I believe we've caught a fish, Preston and I. As I was coming back through the house, down the stairs comes running a tallish old bloke, plunging away with his hand on the banister rail. He ran over to a clothes closet, and banged about as though he wasn't familiar with the place, until he got on his overcoat and hat, and then made for the door. He says his name's Drayman and that he lives here, but we thought—"

"I think you'll find that his sight isn't any too good," said Dr. Fell. "Send him in."

The man who entered was, in his own way, an impressive figure. His long, quiet face was hollowed at the temples; his grey hair grew far back on the skull, giving him a great height of narrow and wrinkled forehead. His bright blue eyes, which did not seem at all dimmed despite the wrinkles round them, looked gentle and puzzled. He had a hooked nose, and deep furrows running down to a kindly, uncertain mouth; and his trick of wrinkling the forehead, so that one eyebrow was slightly raised, made him look more uncertain still. Despite his stoop he was still tall; despite his bony frailty he was still powerful. He looked like a military man gone senile, a well-brushed man gone slovenly. There was nothing of humour in the face, but a great deal of muddled and apologetic good-nature. He wore a dark overcoat buttoned up to the chin. Standing in the doorway, peering hard at them from under tangled eyebrows, he held a bowler hat pressed against his chest, and hesitated.

"I am sorry, gentlemen. I am honestly very sorry," he said. His deep voice had a curious quality as though the man were unused to speech. "I know I should have come to see you before going over there. But young Mr. Mangan woke me up to tell me what had happened. I felt I had to go over and see Grimaud, to see whether there might be anything I could do—"

Rampole had a feeling that he was still dull-witted and uncertain from sleep or sleeping-drugs; that the bright stare of his eyes might have been so much glass. He moved over, and one hand found the back of a chair. But he did not sit down until Hadley asked him to do so.

"Mr. Mangan told me—" he said, "Dr. Grimaud—"

"Dr. Grimaud is dead," said Hadley.

Drayman remained sitting as bolt upright as his stoop would allow, his hands folded across his hat. There was a heavy silence in the room, while Drayman shut his eyes and opened them again. Then he seemed to stare a long way off, and to breathe with heavy, whistling sluggishness.

"God rest his soul," Drayman said, very quietly. "Charles Grimaud was a good friend."

"Do you know how he died?"

"Yes. Mr. Mangan told me."

Hadley studied him. "Then you will understand that to tell everything, *everything* you might happen to know, will be the only way to help us catch the murderer of your friend?"

"I— Yes, of course."

"Be very certain of that, Mr. Drayman! More certain than you are. We wish to know something of his past life. You knew him well. Where did you first know him?"

The other's long face looked muddled; an illusion as though the features had got out of line. "In Paris. He took his doctorate at the university in 1905, the same year I . . . the same year I knew him." Facts seemed to elude Drayman; he shaded his eyes with his hand, and his voice had a querulous note like a man asking where somebody has hidden his collar studs. "Grimaud was very brilliant. He obtained an associate professorship at Dijon the year afterwards. But a relative died, or something of the sort, and left him well provided for. He—he gave up his work and came to England shortly afterwards. Or so I understand. I did not see him until years afterwards. Was that what you wished to know?"

"Did you ever know him before 1905?"

"No."

Hadley leaned forward. "Where did you save his life?" he asked, sharply.

"Save his life? I don't understand."

"Ever visit Hungary, Mr. Drayman?"

"I—I have travelled on the Continent, and I may have been in Hungary. But that was years ago, when I was young. I don't remember."

And now it was Hadley's turn to pull the trigger in trick marksmanship.

"You saved his life," he stated, "near the prison of Siebenturmen, in the Carpathian Mountains, when he was escaping. *Didn't you?*"

The other sat upright, his bony hands clenched across the bowler. Rampole had a feeling that there was more dogged strength in him now than there had been for a dozen years.

"Did I?" he said.

"There's no use going on with this. We know everything—

even to dates, now that you've supplied them. Károly Horváth, as a free man, wrote the date in a book in 1898. With full academic preparation behind, it would have taken him four years at least to get his doctorate at Paris. We can narrow down the time of his conviction and escape to three years. With that information," said Hadley, coolly, "I can cable to Bucharest and get the full details within twelve hours. You had better tell the truth, you see. I want to know all you know of Károly Horváth—and his two brothers. One of those two brothers killed him. Finally, I'll remind you that withholding information of this kind is a serious offence. Well?"

Drayman remained for a little time with his hand shading his eyes, his foot tapping the carpet. Then he looked up. They were startled to see that, though his puckered eyes kept their blue glassiness, the man was gently smiling.

"A serious offence," he repeated, and nodded. "Is it, indeed? Now, frankly, sir, I don't give a damn for your threats. There are very few things which can move or anger or terrify a man who can see you only in outline, as he sees a poached egg on his plate. Nearly all the fears of the world (and its ambitions, too) are caused by shapes—eyes and gestures and figures. Young people can't understand this, but I had hoped you would. You see, I am not precisely blind. I can see faces and the morning sky, and all those objects which the poets insist blind men should rave about. But I cannot *read*, and the faces I cared most to see have been for eight years blinder than mine. Wait until your whole life is built on those two things, and you will learn that not much can move you when they go." He nodded again, staring across the room. His forehead wrinkled. "Sir, I am perfectly willing to give you any information you wish, if it will help Charles Grimaud. But I don't see the sense of raking up old scandal."

"Not even to find the brother who killed him?"

Drayman made a slight gesture, frowning. "Look here, if it will help you, I can honestly tell you to forget such an idea. I don't know how you learned it. He did have two brothers. And they were imprisoned." He smiled again. "There was nothing terrible about it. They were imprisoned for a political offence. I imagine half the young fire-eaters of the time must have been concerned in it. . . . Forget the two brothers. They have both been dead a good many years."

It was so quiet in the room that Rampole heard the last collapsing rattle of the fire and the wheezing breaths of Dr. Fell. Hadley glanced at Dr. Fell, whose eyes were closed. Then Hadley regarded Drayman as impassively as though the latter's sight had been sharp.

"How do you know that?"

"Grimaud told me," said the other, accentuating the name. "Besides, all the newspapers from Budapest to Brasso were shouting about it at the time. You can easily verify all this." He spoke simply. "They died of bubonic plague."

Hadley was suave. "If, of course, you could prove this beyond any doubt . . ."

"You promise that there would be no old scandal raked up?" (That bright blue stare was difficult to meet. Drayman twisted and untwisted his bony hands.) "If I tell you exactly, and you receive the proof, will you let the dead rest?"

"It depends on your information."

"Very well. I will tell you what I saw myself." He reflected—rather uneasily, Rampole thought. "It was in its own way a horrible business. Grimaud and I never spoke of it afterwards. That was agreed. But I don't intend to lie to you and say I've forgotten it—any detail of it."

He was silent for so long a time, tapping his fingers at his temple, that even the patient Hadley was about to prompt him. Then he went on:

"Excuse me, gentlemen. I was trying to remember the exact date, so that you can verify everything. The best I can do is to say it was in August or September of nineteen hundred . . . or was it nineteen one? Anyhow, it occurs to me that I might begin, with perfect truth, exactly in the style of the contemporary French romances. I might begin, 'Towards dusk of a cool September day in the year 19— a solitary horseman might have been seen hurrying along a road,' and what a devil of a road!—'in a rugged valley below the southeastern Carpathians.' Then I should launch into a description of the wild scenery and so on. I was the horseman; it was coming on to rain, and I was trying to reach Tradj before dark."

He smiled. Hadley stirred in some impatience, though Dr. Fell opened his eyes; and Drayman was quick to take it up.

"I must insist on that sort of novelesque atmosphere, because it fitted into my mood and explains so much. I was at the romantic Byronic age, fired with ideas of political liberty. I rode horseback instead of walking because I thought I cut a good figure; I even took pleasure in carrying a pistol against (mythical) brigands, and a rosary as a charm against ghosts. But if there weren't either ghosts or brigands, there should have been. I know that I several times got the wind up about both. There was a sort of fairy-tale wildness and darkness about those cold forests and gorges. Even about the cultivated parts there was something queer. Transylvania, you see, is shadowed in on three sides by mountains. It startles an English eye to see a rye-field or a vineyard going straight up the side of a steep hill; the red-and-yellow costumes, the garlicky inns, and even, in the bleaker parts, hills made of pure salt.

"Anyhow, there I was going along a snaky road in the bleakest part, with a storm blowing up and no inn for miles. People saw the devil lurking behind every hedge in a way that gave me the creeps, but I had a worse cause for the creeps. Plague had broken out after a hot summer, and was over the whole area like a cloud of gnats, even in the chilly weather. In the last village I passed through—I've forgotten its name—they told me it was raging at the salt-mines in the mountains ahead. But I was hoping to meet an English friend of mine, also a tourist, at Tradj. Also I wanted a look at the prison, which got its name after seven white hills, like a low range of mountains, just behind. So I said I meant to go on.

"I knew I must be getting near the prison, for I could see the white hills ahead. But, just as it was getting too dark to see at all, and the wind seemed to be tearing the trees to pieces, I came down into a hollow past the three graves. They had been freshly dug, for there were still footmarks round them; but no living person was in sight."

Hadley broke across the queer atmosphere which that dreaming voice was beginning to create.

"A place," he said, "just like the one in the painting Dr. Grimaud bought from Mr. Burnaby."

"I—I don't know," answered Drayman, evidently startled. "Is it? I didn't notice."

"Didn't notice? Didn't you see the picture?"

"Not very well. Just a general outline—trees, ordinary landscape—"

"And three headstones . . . ?"

"I don't know where Burnaby got his inspiration," the other said, dully, and rubbed his forehead. "God knows *I* never told him. It's probably a coincidence; there were no headstones over these graves. They wouldn't have bothered. There were simply three crosses made of sticks.

"But I was telling you. I sat there on my horse, looking at those graves, and with a not very pleasant feeling. They looked wild enough, with the greenish-black landscape around and the white hills beyond. But it wasn't that. If they were prison graves, I wondered why they had been dug so far away. The next thing I knew my horse reared and nearly threw me. I slewed round against a tree; and, when I looked back, I saw what was wrong with the horse. The mound of one grave was upheaving and slid-ing. There was a cracking noise; something began to twist and wriggle; and a dark-coloured thing came groping up out of the mound. It was only a hand moving the fingers—but I don't think I have ever seen anything more horrible."

10
THE BLOOD ON THE COAT

"By that time," Drayman went on, "there was something wrong with me as well. I didn't dare dismount, for fear the horse would bolt; and I was ashamed to bolt, myself. I thought of vampires and all the legends of hell coming up out of the twilight. Frankly, the thing scared me silly. I remember battering round on that horse like a teetotum, trying to curb it with one hand while I got out my revolver. When I looked back again, the thing had climbed clear out of the grave and was coming towards me.

"That, gentlemen, was how I met one of my best friends. The man reached down and seized a spade, which somebody who dug the grave must have left there and forgotten. And still he came on. I yelled in English, 'What do you want?'—because I was so fuddled that I couldn't remember a word in any other language. The man stopped. After a second he answered in English, but with an outlandish accent. 'Help,' he said, 'help, milord; don't be afraid,' or something of the sort, and threw down the spade. The horse was quieter, but I wasn't. The man was not tall, but very powerful; his face was dark and swollen, with little scaly spots which gave it a pinkish look in the twilight. And down came the rain while he was still standing there waving his arms.

"He stood in the rain, crying out to me. I won't try to reproduce it, but he said something like, 'Look, milord, I am not dead of plague like those two poor devils,' and pointed at the graves. 'I am not infected at all. See how the rain washes it off. It is my own blood which I have pricked out of my skin.' He even stuck out his tongue to show how it was blackened with soot, and the rain made it clean. It was as mad a sight as the figure and the place. Then he went on to say that he was not a criminal, but a political offender, and was making his escape from the prison."

Drayman's forehead wrinkled. He smiled again.

"Help him? Naturally I did. I was fired by the idea. He explained things to me while we laid plans. He was one of three brothers, students at the University of Klausenburg, who had been arrested in an insurrection for an independent Transylvania under the protection of Austria; as it was before 1860. The three of them were in the same cell, and two had died of the pestilence. With the help of the prison doctor, also a convict, he had faked the same symptoms—and died. It wasn't likely that anybody would go very close to test the doctor's judgment; the whole prison was mad with fear. Even the people who buried those three would keep their heads turned away when they threw the bodies into pine coffins and nailed on the lids. They would bury the bodies at some distance from the prison. Most of all, they would do a quick job of nailing the lids. The doctor had smuggled in a pair of nail-cutters, which my resurrected friend showed me. A powerful man, if he kept his nerve and didn't use up too much air after he had been buried, could force up the lids with his head enough to wedge the nail-cutters into the loose space. Afterwards a powerful man could dig up through loose ground.

"Very well. When he found I was a student at Paris, conversation became easy. His mother had been French, and he spoke the language perfectly. We decided that he had better make for France, where he could set up a new identity without suspicion. He had a little money hidden away, and there was a girl in his native town who—"

Drayman stopped abruptly, like one who remembers that he has gone too far. Hadley merely nodded.

"I think we know who the girl was," he said. "For the moment, we can leave 'Madame Dumont' out of this. What then?"

"She could be trusted to bring the money and follow him to Paris. It wasn't likely that there would be a hue and cry—in fact, there wasn't any. He passed as dead; even if Grimaud was frightened enough to tear away from that neighbourhood before he would even shave or put on a suit of my clothes. We excited no suspicion. There were no passports in those days, and he posed on the way out of Hungary as the English friend of mine I had been expecting to meet at Tradj. Once into France . . . you know all the rest. Now, gentlemen!" Drayman drew a curiously shuddering breath, stiffened, and faced them with his hard blank eyes. "You can verify everything I have said—"

"What about that cracking sound?" interjected Dr. Fell, in an argumentative tone.

The question was so quiet, and yet so startling, that Hadley whirled round. Even Drayman's gaze groped towards him. Dr. Fell's red face was screwed up absently, and he wheezed as he poked at the carpet with his stick.

"I think it's very important," he announced to the fire, as though somebody had contradicted him. "Very important indeed. H'mf. Ha. Look here, Mr. Drayman, I've got only two questions to ask you. You heard a cracking sound—of the lid wrenching on the coffin, hey? Yes. Then that would mean it was a fairly shallow grave Grimaud climbed out of?"

"Quite shallow, yes, or he might never have got out."

"Second question. That prison, now . . . was it a well or badly managed place?"

Drayman was puzzled, but his jaw set grimly. "I do not know, sir. But I do know it was under fire at that time from a number of officials. I think they were bitter against the prison authorities for letting the disease get started—it interfered with the usefulness of the workmen at the mines. By the way, the dead men's names were published; I saw them. And I ask you again, what's the good of raking up old scandals? It can't help you. You can see that it's not any particular discredit to Grimaud, but—"

"Yes, that's the point," rumbled Dr. Fell, peering at him curiously. "That's the thing I want to emphasize. It's not discreditable at all. Is it anything to make a man bury all traces of his past life?"

"—but it might become a discredit to Ernestine Dumont," said Drayman, raising his voice on a fiercer note. "Can't you see what I'm implying? What about Grimaud's daughter? And all this digging into the mess rests on some wild guess that one or both of his brothers might be alive. They're dead, and the dead don't get out of their graves. May I ask where you got such a notion as that one of Grimaud's brothers killed him?"

"From Grimaud himself," said Hadley.

For a second Rampole thought Drayman had not understood. Then the man shakily got up from his chair, as though he could not breathe. He fumbled to open his coat, felt at his throat, and sat down again. Only the glassy look of his eyes did not alter.

"Are you lying to me?" he asked—and it was with a shaky, querulous, childish tone coming through his gravity. "Why do you lie to me?"

"It happens to be the truth. Read this!"

Very quickly he thrust out the note from Dr. Peterson. Drayman made a movement to take it; then he drew back and shook his head.

"It would tell me nothing, sir. I—I— You mean he said something before he . . . ?"

"He said that the murderer was his brother."

"Did he say anything else?" asked Drayman, hesitating. Hadley let the man's imagination work, and did not reply. Presently Drayman went on: "But I tell you it's fantastic! Are you implying that this mountebank who threatened him, this fellow he had never seen before in his life, was one of his brothers? I suppose you are. I still don't understand. From the first moment I learned he had been stabbed . . ."

"*Stabbed?*"

"Yes. As I say, I—"

"He was shot," said Hadley. "What gave you the idea that he had been stabbed?"

Drayman lifted his shoulders. A wry, sardonic, rather despairing expression crept over his wrinkled face.

"I seem to be a very bad witness, gentlemen," he said in an even tone. "I persist with the best intentions, in telling you things you don't believe. Possibly I jumped to conclusions. Mr. Mangan said that Grimaud had been attacked and was dying; that the murderer had disappeared after slashing that painting to pieces. So I assumed—" He rubbed the bridge of his nose. "Was there anything else you wished to ask me?"

"How did you spend the evening?"

"I was asleep. I— You see, there are pains. Here, behind the eyeballs. I had them so badly at dinner that instead of going out (I was to go to a concert at the Albert Hall), I took a sleeping-tablet and lay down. Unfortunately, I don't remember anything from about half-past seven to the time Mr. Mangan woke me."

Hadley was studying his open overcoat, keeping himself very quiet, but with a dangerous expression like a man about to pounce.

"I see. Did you undress when you went to bed, Mr. Drayman?"

"I beg your— Undress? No. I took off my shoes, that's all. Why?"

"Did you leave your room at any time?"

"No."

"Then how did you get that blood on your jacket? . . . Yes, that's it. Get up! Don't run away, now. Stand where you are. Now take off your overcoat."

Rampole saw it when Drayman, standing uncertainly beside his chair and pulling off the overcoat, moved his hand across his own chest with the motions of a man groping on a floor. He was wearing a light gray suit, against which the stain splashed vividly. It was a darkish smear running from the side of the coat down across the right pocket. Drayman's fingers found it and stopped. The fingers rubbed it, then brushed together.

"It can't be blood," he muttered, with the same querulous noise rising in his voice. "I don't know what it is, but it can't be blood, I tell you!"

"We shall have to see about that. Take off the coat, please. I'm afraid I must ask you to leave it with us. Is there anything in the pockets you want to take out?"

"But—"

"Where did you get that stain?"

"I don't know. I swear to God I don't know, and I can't imagine. It isn't blood. What makes you think it is?"

"Give me the coat, please. Good!" He watched sharply while Drayman with unsteady fingers removed from the pockets a few coppers, a concert ticket, a handkerchief, a paper of Woodbine cigarettes, and a box of matches. Then Hadley took the coat and spread it across his knees. "Do you have any objection to your room being searched?— It's only fair to tell you I have no authority to do it, if you refuse."

"No objection at all," said the other, dully. He was rubbing his forehead. "If you'd only tell me how it happened, Inspector! I don't know. I've tried to do the right thing . . . yes. The right thing. . . . I didn't have anything to do with this business." He stopped, and smiled with such sardonic bitterness that Rampole felt more puzzled than suspicious. "Am I under arrest? I have no objection to that, either, you know."

Now, there was something wrong here: and yet not wrong in the proper way. Rampole saw that Hadley shared his own irrational doubts. Here was a man who had made several erratic misstatements. He had told a lurid tale which might or might not be true, but which had a vaguely theatrical, pasteboard flimsiness about it. Finally, there was blood on his coat. And yet, for a reason he could not determine, Rampole was inclined to believe his story—or, at least, the man's own belief in his story. It might have been his complete (apparent) lack of shrewdness; his utter simplicity. There he stood, looking taller, more shrunken and bony in his shirt sleeves, the blue shirt itself faded to a dingy white, the sleeves tucked up on corded arms, his tie askew and the overcoat trailing from one hand. And he was smiling.

Hadley swore under his breath. "Betts!" he called, "Betts!

Preston!" and tapped his heel impatiently on the floor until they answered. "Betts, get this coat to the pathologist for analysis of this stain. See it? Report in the morning. That's all for tonight. Preston, go down with Mr. Drayman and have a look round his room. You have a good idea what to look for; also keep an eye out for something in the mask line. I'll join you in a moment. . . . Think it over, Mr. Drayman. I'm going to ask you to come down to the Yard in the morning. That's all."

Drayman paid no attention. He blundered out in his batlike way, shaking his head and trailing the overcoat behind him. He even plucked Preston by the sleeve. "Where could I have got that blood?" he asked, eagerly. "It's a queer thing, you know, but where could I have got that blood?"

"Dunno, sir," said Preston. "Mind that doorpost!"

Presently the bleak room was quiet. Hadley shook his head slowly.

"It's got me, Fell," he admitted. "I don't know whether I'm coming or going. What do you make of the fellow? He seems gentle and pliable and easy enough; but you can keep pounding him like a punching-bag, and at the end of it he's still swinging gently in the same old place. He doesn't seem to care a rap *what* you think of him. Or what you do to him, for that matter. Maybe that's why the young people don't like him."

"H'm, yes. When I gather up those papers from the fireplace," grunted Dr. Fell, "I'm going home to think. Because what I think now . . ."

"Yes?"

"Is plain horrible."

With a gust of energy Dr. Fell surged up out of the chair, jammed his shovel-hat down over his eyes, and flourished his stick.

"I don't want to go jumping at theories. You'll have to cable for the real truth. Ha! Yes. But it's the story about the three coffins I don't believe—although Drayman may believe it, God knows! Unless our whole theory is blown to blazes, we've got to assume that the two Horváth brothers aren't dead. Hey?"

"The question being . . ."

"What happened to them. Harrumph, yes. What I think might have happened is based on the assumption that Drayman believes he's telling the truth. First point! I don't believe for a second that those brothers were sent to prison for a political offense. Grimaud, with his 'little money saved,' escapes from prison. He lies low for five years or more, and then suddenly 'inherits' a substantial fortune, under an entirely different name, from somebody we haven't heard of. But he slides out of France to enjoy it without comment. Second point, supporting! Where's the dangerous secret in Grimaud's life, if all this is true? Most people would consider that Monte Cristo escape as merely exciting and romantic; and, as for his offense, it would sound to English ears about as hideous and blasting an infamy as pinching a Belisha beacon or pasting a policeman in the eye on boat-race night. Dammit, Hadley, it won't do!"

"You mean—?"

"I mean," said Dr. Fell in a very quiet voice, "Grimaud was alive when he was nailed up in his coffin. Suppose the other two were alive, too? Suppose all three 'deaths' were faked exactly as Grimaud's was faked? Suppose there were two living people in those other coffins when Grimaud climbed out of his? But they couldn't come out . . . because he had the nail-cutters and didn't choose to use 'em. It wasn't likely that there would be more than one pair of cutters. Grimaud had 'em, because he was the strongest. Once he got out, it would have been easy for him to let the others out, as they had arranged. But he prudently decided to let them lie buried, because then there would be nobody to share the money that all three had stolen. A brilliant crime, you see. A brilliant crime."

Nobody spoke. Hadley muttered something under his breath; his face was incredulous and rather wild as he got up.

"Oh, I know it's a black business!" rumbled Dr. Fell; "a black, unholy business that would turn a man's dreams sick if he'd done it. But it's the only thing that will explain this unholy case, and why a man *would* be hounded if those brothers ever climbed up out of their graves. . . . Why was Grimaud so desperately anxious to rush Drayman away from that spot without getting rid of his convict garb as soon as he could? Why would he run the risk of being seen from the road, when a hideaway near a plague grave would be the last place any native would venture? Well, those graves were very shallow. If, as time went on, the brothers found themselves choking to death . . . and still nobody had come to let them out . . . they might begin to shriek and batter and pound in their coffins. It was just possible Drayman might have seen the loose earth trembling or heard the last scream from inside."

Hadley got out a handkerchief and mopped his face.

"Would any swine—" he said in an incredulous voice, which trailed away. "No. We're running off the rails, Fell. It's all imagination. It can't be! Besides, in that case they wouldn't have climbed up out of their graves. They'd be dead."

"Would they?" said Dr. Fell, vacantly. "You're forgetting the spade."

"What spade?"

"The spade that some poor devil in his fear or hurry left behind when he'd dug the grave. Prisons, even the worst prisons, don't permit *that* sort of negligence. They would send back after it. Man, I can see that business in every detail, even if I haven't one shred of proof to support it! Think of every word that crazy Pierre Fley said to Grimaud at the Warwick Tavern, and see if it doesn't fit. . . . Back come a couple of armed, hard-headed warders looking for that discarded spade. They see or hear what Grimaud was afraid Drayman would see or hear. They either tumble to the trick or else they act in common humanity. The coffins are smashed open; the two brothers are rolled out, fainting and bloody, but alive."

"And no hue and cry after Grimaud? Why, they'd have torn Hungary apart looking for the man who had escaped and—"

"H'mf, yes. I thought of that too, and asked about it. The prison authorities would have done just that . . . if they weren't being so bitterly attacked that their heads were in danger at the time. What do you think the attackers would have said if it became known that, through carelessness, they allowed a thing like that to happen? Much better to keep quiet about it, hey? Much better to shove those two brothers into close confinement and keep quiet about the third."

"It's all theory," said Hadley, after a pause. "But, if it's true, I could come close to believing in evil spirits. God knows Grimaud got exactly what he deserved. And we've got to go on trying to find his murderer just the same. If that's the whole story—"

"Of course it's not the whole story!" said Dr. Fell. "It's not the whole story even if it's true, and that's the worst part. You talk of evil spirits. I tell you that in some way I can't fathom there's a worse evil spirit than Grimaud; and that's X, that's the hollow man, that's brother Henri." He pointed out with his stick. "Why? Why does Pierre Fley admit he fears him? It would be reasonable for Grimaud to fear his enemy; but why does Fley

even fear his brother and his ally against the common antag-
onist? Why is a skilled illusionist afraid of illusion, unless this
gentle brother Henri is as rattlebrained as a criminal lunatic and
as clever as Satan?"

Hadley put his notebook in his pocket and buttoned up his
coat.

"*You* go home if you like," he said. "We've finished here. But
I'm going after Fley. Whoever the other brother is, Fley knows.
And he's going to tell, I can promise you that. I'll have a look
round Drayman's room, but I don't anticipate much. Fley is the
key to this cipher, and he's going to lead us to the murderer.
Ready?"

They did not learn it until the next morning; but Fley, as a
matter of fact, was already dead. He had been shot down with
the same pistol that killed Grimaud. And the murderer was invisible before the eyes of witnesses, and still he had left no footprint in the snow.

11
THE MURDER BY MAGIC

When Dr. Fell hammered on the door at nine o'clock next morning, both his guests were in a drowsy state. Rampole had got very little sleep the night before. When he and the doctor returned at half-past one, Dorothy had been hopping with eagerness to hear all the details, and her husband was not at all unwilling to tell them. They equipped themselves with cigarettes and beer, and retired to their room, where Dorothy piled a heap of sofa pillows on the floor like Sherlock Holmes, and sat there with a glass of beer and a sinister expression of wisdom while her husband stalked about the room, declaiming. Her views were vigorous but hazy. She rather liked the descriptions of Mme Dumont and Drayman, but took a violent dislike to Rosette Grimaud. Even when Rampole quoted Rosette's remarks to the debating society, a motto of which they both approved, she was not mollified.

"All the same, you mark my words," said Dorothy, pointing her cigarette at him wisely, "that funny-faced blonde is mixed up in it somehow. She's a wrong un, old boy. I mean she wants ber-lud. Bah! I'll bet she wouldn't even make a good—um—courtesan, to use her own terms. And if I had ever treated you the way she treats Boyd Mangan, and you hadn't landed me a sock under the jaw, I'd never have spoken to either of us again . . . if you see my meaning?"

"Let's omit the personal," said Rampole. "Besides, what's she done to Mangan? Nothing that I can see. And you don't serious-ly think she would kill her father, even if she hadn't been locked in the front room?"

"N-no, because I don't see how she could have put on that fancy costume and fooled Mrs. Dumont," said Dorothy, with an expression of great profundity in her bright dark eyes. "But I'll tell you how it is, Mrs. Dumont and Drayman are both inno-cent. As for Mills—well, Mills does sound rather a prig, but then your view is highly coloured because you don't like science or the Vision of the Future. And you'll admit he does sound as though he's telling the truth?"

"Yes."

She smoked reflectively. "'M. I'm getting tremendous ideas. The people I'm most suspicious of, and the ones against whom it'd be easiest to make out a case, are the two you haven't seen— Pettis and Burnaby."

"*What?*"

"Like this. The objection to Pettis is that he's too small, isn't it? I should have thought Dr. Fell's erudition would have got it like a shot. I was thinking of a story. . . . I can't remember where I've read it, but it comes in one shape or another into several me-diaeval tales. J'you remember? There's always an enormous figure in armour, with its vizor down, who rides in a tournament and smacks everybody flat. Then along comes ye mightiest knight to joust against it. Down he rides with a bang, hits the tall cham-pion's helmet squarely in the middle of the vizor, and to every-

THE THREE COFFINS · 125

body's horror knocks the head clean off. Then up pipes a voice
from inside the shell, and they discover it belongs to a handsome
young lad who's not tall enough to fill up the suit of armour. . . ."

Rampole looked at her. "Beloved," said he, with dignity, "this
is pure drivelling. This is beyond all question the looniest idea
which . . . Look here, are you seriously trying to tell me Pettis
might walk about with a dummy head and shoulders rigged up
on him?"

"You're too conservative," she said, wrinkling her nose. "*I*
think it's a jolly-good idea. And do you want confirmation?
Right! Didn't Mills himself comment on the shiny look about
the back of the head, and say it looked as though the whole head
were made of papier-mâché? What have you got to say to that?"

"I say it's a nightmare. Haven't you any more practical idea?"

"Yes!" said Dorothy, wriggling. She had obviously just been
struck with the inspiration, but she passed it off as an old one.
"It's about the impossible situation. *Why* didn't the murderer want to leave any footprints? You're all going after the most
horribly complicated reasons. And, anyway, they generally end
in your thinking that the murderer just wants to have some fun
with the police. Rats, darling! What's the only real reason, the
first reason anybody would think of outside a murder case, why
a man mightn't want to leave any footprints? Why, because the
footprints would be so distinctive that they'd lead straight to
him! Because he had a deformity or something which would
hang him if he left a footprint. . . ."

"And—?"

"And, you tell me," she said, "this chap Burnaby has a club
foot."

When, towards daylight, Rampole at last fell asleep, he was
haunted by images in which Burnaby's club foot seemed even

more sinister than the man who wore a dummy head. It was all nonsense; but it was a disturbing kind of nonsense to mingle in a dream with the puzzle of the three graves.

He struggled out of bed when Dr. Fell knocked at the door towards nine o'clock on Sunday morning; he shaved and dressed hastily, and stumbled down through a silent house. It was an unearthly hour for Dr. Fell (or anybody else) to be stirring, and Rampole knew some fresh devilry had broken overnight. The hallways were chilly; even the great library, where a roaring fire had been lighted, had that unreal look which all things assume when you get up at daybreak to catch a train. Breakfast—for three—was set out in the embrasure of the bay window overlooking the terrace. It was a leaden day, the sky already moving with snow. Dr. Fell, fully dressed, sat at the table with his head in his hands and stared at a newspaper.

"Brother Henri—" he rumbled, and struck the paper. "Oh yes. He's at it again. Hadley just phoned with more details, and he'll be here any minute. Look at this for a starter. If we thought we'd got a hard problem on our hands last night—oh, Bacchus, look at *this* one! I'm like Drayman—I can't believe it. It's crowded Grimaud's murder clean off the front page. Fortunately, they haven't spotted the connection between 'em, or else Hadley's given 'em the word to keep off. Here!"

Rampole, as coffee was poured out for him, saw the headlines. "MAGICIAN MURDERED BY MAGIC!" said one, which must have given great pleasure to the writer. "RIDDLE OF CAGLIOSTRO STREET." "'THE SECOND BULLET IS FOR YOU!'"

"Cagliostro Street?" the American repeated. "Where in the name of sanity is Cagliostro Street? I thought I'd heard of some funny street names, but this one—"

"You'd never hear of it ordinarily," grunted Dr. Fell. "It's one of those streets hidden behind streets, that you only stumble on by accident when you're looking for a short-cut, and you're startled to find a whole community lost in the middle of London. . . . Anyway, Cagliostro Street is not more than three minutes' walk from Grimaud's house. It's a little cul-de-sac behind Guilford Street, on the other side of Russell Square. So far as I remember, it has a lot of tradesmen's shops overflowing from Lamb's Conduit Street, and the rest lodging-houses. . . . Brother Henri left Grimaud's place after the shooting, walked over there, hung about for a little time, and then completed his work."

Rampole ran his eye down the story:

The body of the man found murdered last night in Cagliostro Street, W. C. 1, has been identified as that of Pierre Fley, a French conjuror and illusionist. Although he had been performing for some months at a music-hall in Commercial Road, E.C., he took lodgings two weeks ago in Cagliostro Street. About half-past ten last night, he was found shot to death under circumstances which seem to indicate that a magician was murdered by magic. Nothing was seen and no trace left—three witnesses testify—although they all distinctly heard a voice say, "*The second bullet is for you.*"

Cagliostro Street is two hundred yards long, and ends in a blank brick wall. There are a few shops at the beginning of the street, closed at that time, although a few night lights were burning, and the pavements were swept in front of them. But, beginning some twenty yards on, there was unbroken snow on the pavement and the street.

Mr. Jesse Short and Mr. R. G. Blackwin, Birmingham visitors to London, were on their way to visit a friend with lodgings near the end of the street. They were walking on the right-hand pavement, and had their backs to the mouth of the street. Mr. Blackwin, who was turning round to make sure of the numbers on the doors, noticed a man walking some distance behind them. This man was walking slowly and rather nervously, looking round him as though he expected to see some one near. He was walking in the middle of the street. But the light was dim, and, aside from seeing that he was tall and wore a slouch-hat, neither Mr. Short nor Mr. Blackwin noticed anything else. At the same time, P. C. Henry Withers—whose beat was along Lamb's Conduit Street—reached the entrance to Cagliostro Street. He saw the man walking in the snow, but glanced back again without noticing him. And in the space of three or four seconds the thing happened.

Mr. Short and Mr. Blackwin heard behind them a cry that was nearer a scream. They then heard some one distinctly say the words, "The second bullet is for you," and a laugh followed by a muffled pistol-shot. As they whirled round, the man behind staggered, screamed again, and pitched forward on his face.

The street, they could see, was absolutely empty from end to end. Moreover, the man was walking in the middle of it, and both state that there were no footprints in the snow but his own. This is confirmed by P. C. Withers, who came running from the mouth of the street. In the light from a jeweller's window, they could see the victim lying face downward, his arms spread out, and blood jetting from a bullet-hole under his left shoulder blade. The weapon—a long-barrelled .38 Colt revolver, of a pattern thirty years out of date—had been thrown away some ten feet behind.

Despite the words they had all heard, and the gun lying at some distance, the witnesses thought because of the empty street that he must have shot himself. They saw that the man was still breathing, and carried him to the office of Dr. M. R. Jenkins near the end of the street, while the constable made certain there were no footprints anywhere. The victim, however, died, without speaking, not long afterwards.

Then occurred the most startling disclosures. The man's overcoat round the wound was burnt and singed black, showing that the weapon must have been pressed against his back or held only a few inches away. But Dr. Jenkins gave it as his opinion—later confirmed by the police—that suicide was not possible. No man, he stated, could have held any pistol in such a way as to shoot himself through the back at that angle, and more especially with the long-barrelled weapon which was used. It was murder, but an incredible murder. If the man had been shot from some distance away, from a window or door, the absence of a murderer and even the absence of footprints would mean nothing. But he was shot by some one who stood beside him, spoke to him, and vanished.

No papers or marks of identification could be found in the man's clothes, and nobody seemed to know him. After some delay he was sent to the mortuary—

"But what about the officer Hadley sent round to pick him up?" Rampole asked. "Couldn't he identify the man?"

"He did identify him, later," growled Dr. Fell. "But the whole hullabaloo was over by the time he got there. He ran into the policeman, Hadley says, when Withers was still making inquiries from door to door. Then he put two and two together. Meantime, the man Hadley had sent to the music-hall also in quest of Fley had phoned through that Fley wasn't there. Fley had coolly told the theatre manager he had no intention of doing his turn that night, and walked out with some sort of cryptic remark. . . . Well, to identify the body at the mortuary they got hold of Fley's landlord in Cagliostro Street. And, to make sure it was the same person, they asked for somebody from the music-hall to come along. An Irishman with an Italian name, who was also on the bill but couldn't do his turn that night because of some sort of injury, volunteered. Harrumph, yes. It was Fley, and he's dead, and we're in a hell of a mess. Bah!"

"And this story," cried Rampole, "is actually true?"

He was answered by Hadley, whose ring at the bell was belligerent. Hadley stamped in, carrying his briefcase like a tomahawk, and released some of his grievances before he would even touch bacon and eggs.

"It's true, right enough," he said, grimly, stamping his heels before the fire. "I let the papers splash it out so we could broadcast an appeal for information from anybody who knew Pierre Fley or his —— —— —— brother Henri. By God! Fell, I'm losing my mind! That damned nickname of yours sticks in my head, and I can't get rid of it. I find myself referring to brother Henri as though I knew that was his real name. I find myself getting imaginary pictures of brother Henri. At least we soon ought to know what his real name is. I've cabled to Bucharest. Brother Henri! Brother Henri! We've picked up his trail again, and lost it again. Bro—"

"For Lord's sake go easy!" urged Dr. Fell, puffing uneasily. "Don't rave; it's bad enough now. I suppose you've been at it nearly all night? And got some more information? H'mf, yes. Now sit down and console the inner man. Then we can approach in—humph—a philosophic spirit, hey?"

Hadley said he wanted nothing to eat. But, after he had finished two helpings, drunk several cups of coffee, and lighted a cigar, he mellowed into a more normal mood.

"Now, then! Let's begin," he said, squaring himself determinedly as he took papers from the briefcase, "by checking over this newspaper account point by point—as well as what it doesn't say. Hum! First, as to these chaps Blackwin and Short. They're reliable; besides, it's certain neither of them is brother Henri. We wired Birmingham, and found they've been well known in their district all their lives. They're prosperous, sound people who wouldn't go off the handle as witnesses in a thing like this. The constable, Withers, is a thoroughly reliable man; in fact, he's painstaking to the extent of a vice. If those people say they didn't see anybody, they may have been deceived, but at least they were telling the truth as they knew it."

"Deceived . . . how?"

"*I don't know,*" growled Hadley, drawing a deep breath and shaking his head grimly, "except that they must have been. I had a brief look at the street, although I didn't go through Fley's room. It's no Piccadilly Circus for illumination, but at least it's not dark enough for any man in his five wits to be mistaken about what he saw. Shadows—I don't know! As to footprints, if Withers swears there weren't any, I'll take his word for it. And there we are."

Dr. Fell only grunted, and Hadley went on:

"Now, about the weapon. Fley was shot with a bullet from

that Colt .38, and so was Grimaud. There were two exploded cartridge-cases in the magazine, only two bullets, and bro—and the murderer scored with each. The modern revolver, you see, ejects its shells like an automatic; but this gun is so old that we haven't a ghost of a chance of being able to trace it. It's in good working order, it fires modern steel-jacket ammunition, but somebody has kept it hidden away for years."

"He didn't forget anything, Harry didn't. Well. Did you trace Fley's movements?"

"Yes. He was going to call on Henri."

Dr. Fell's eyes snapped open. *"Eh?* Look here, you mean you've got a lead about—"

"It's the only lead we have got. And," said Hadley, with bitter satisfaction, "if it doesn't produce results within a couple of hours I'll eat that briefcase. You remember, I told you over the phone that Fley had refused to perform and walked out of the theatre last night? Yes. My plainclothes officer got the story both from the theatre-manager, fellow named Isaacstein, and from an acrobat named O'Rourke, who was friendlier with Fley than anybody else and identified the body later.

"Saturday, naturally, is the big night down Limehouse way. The theatre runs continuous variety from one in the afternoon until eleven at night. Business was booming in the evening, and Fley's first night turn was to begin at eight-fifteen. About five minutes before then, O'Rourke—who had broken his wrist and couldn't go on that night—sneaked down into the cellar for a smoke. They have a coal furnace for hot-water pipes there."

Hadley unfolded a closely written sheet.

"Here is what O'Rourke said, just as Somers took it down and O'Rourke later initialled.

"The minute I got through the asbestos door and downstairs, I heard a noise like somebody smashing up kin-
dling-wood. Then I did get a jump. The furnace door was
open, and there was old Loony with a hatchet in his hand,
busting hell out of the few properties he owned and shov-
ing them all in the fire. I said, 'For cat's sake, Loony, what
are you doing?' He said, in that queer way of his, 'I am de-
stroying my equipment, Signor Pagliacci.' (I use the name
of Pagliacci the Great, you understand, but then he always
talked like that, so help me!) Well, he said, 'My work is
finished; I shall not need them any longer'—and, zingo! in
went his faked ropes and the hollow bamboo rods for his
cabinet. I said, 'Loony, great goddelmighty, pull yourself
together.' I said, 'You go on in a few minutes, and you're
not even dressed.' He said: 'Didn't I tell you? I am going
to see my brother. He will do something that will settle an
old affair for both of us.'

"Well, he walked over to the stairs and then turned
around sharp. Loony's got a face like a white horse, Lord
pity me for saying it, and it had a queer creepy look with
the fire from the furnace shining on it. He said, 'In case
anything happens to me after he has done the business,
you will find my brother in the same street where I myself
live. That is not where he really resides, but he has taken
a room there.' Just then down comes old Isaacstein, looking for him. He couldn't believe his ears when he heard
Loony refuse to go on. There was a row. Isaacstein bawled,
'You know what'll happen if you don't go on?' And Loony
says, as pleasant as a three-card man, 'Yes, I know what will
happen.' Then he lifts his hat very courteously, and says,

'Good night, gentlemen. I am going back to my grave.'
And up the stairs this lunatic walks without another word."

Hadley folded up the sheet and replaced it in his briefcase.

"Yes, he was a good showman," said Dr. Fell, struggling to light his pipe. "It seems a pity brother Henri had to . . . what then?"

"Now, it may or may not mean anything to track Henri down in Cagliostro Street, but we're sure to get his temporary hideout," Hadley went on. "The question occurred to me, where was Fley *going* when he was shot? Where was he walking to? Not to his own room. He lived at number 2B, at the beginning of the street, and he was going in the other direction. When he was shot he was a little over halfway down, between number 18 on his right and number 21 on his left—but in the middle of the street, of course. That's a good trail, and I've sent Somers out on it. He's to turn out every house past the middle, looking for *any* new or suspicious or otherwise noticeable lodger. Landladies being what they are, we shall probably get dozens, but that doesn't matter."

Dr. Fell, who was slouched as far down in the big chair as the bulk of his weight would allow, ruffled his hair.

"Yes, but I shouldn't concentrate too much on any end of the street. Rip 'em all up, say I. You see, suppose Fley was running from somebody, trying to get away from somebody, when he was shot?"

"Running away into a blind alley?"

"It's *wrong!* I tell you it's all wrong!" roared the doctor, hoisting himself up in the chair. "Not merely because I can't see anywhere a chink or glimmer of reason (which I freely admit), but because the simplicity of the thing is so maddening. It's no matter of hocus-pocus within four walls. There's a street. There's a man walking along it in the snow. Scream, whispered words, bang! Witnesses turn, and murderer gone. Where? Did the pistol come flying through the air like a thrown knife, explode against Fley's back, and spin away?"

"Rubbish!"

"I know it's rubbish. But I still ask the question," nodded Dr. Fell. He let his eye-glasses drop and pressed his hands over his eyes. "I say, how does this new development affect the Russell Square group? I mean, considering that everybody is official-ly under suspicion, can't we eliminate a few of those? Even if they were telling us lies at Grimaud's house, they still weren't out hurling Colt revolvers in the middle of Cagliostro Street."

The superintendent's face was ugly with sarcasm. "Now there's another bit of luck for us, kindly notice. I forgot that! We could eliminate one or two—if the Cagliostro Street business had oc-curred a little later, or even a little earlier. It didn't. Fley was shot at just ten-twenty-five. In other words, about fifteen minutes after Grimaud. Brother Henri took no chances. He anticipated exactly what we would do: send out a man to pick up Fley as soon as the alarm was given. Only brother Henri (or somebody) anticipated us in both ways. He was there with his little vanish-ing-trick."

"'Or somebody'?" repeated Dr. Fell. "Your mental processes are interesting. Why 'or somebody'?"

"That's what I'm getting at—the unfortunate, unobserved fifteen minutes just after Grimaud's murder. I'm learning new wrinkles in crime, Fell. If you want to commit a couple of shrewd murders, don't commit one and then hang about waiting for the dramatic moment to pull off the other. Hit once—and then hit again instantly, while the watchers are still so muddled by the first that nobody, including the police, can definitely remember who was where at a given time. Can we?"

"Now, now," growled Dr. Fell, to conceal the fact that he couldn't. "It ought to be easy to work out a time-table. Let's see. We arrived at Grimaud's . . . when?"

Hadley was jotting on a slip of paper. "Just as Mangan jumped out the window, which couldn't have been more than two minutes after the shot. Say ten-twelve. We ran upstairs, found the door locked, got the pliers, and opened the door. Say three minutes more."

"Isn't that allowing a small margin of time?" Rampole interposed. "It seemed to me we were doing a good deal of tearing around."

"People often think so. In fact," said Hadley, "I thought so myself until I handled that Kynaston knifing case (remember, Fell?), where a damned clever killer depended for his alibi on the tendency of witnesses always to *over*-estimate time. That's because we think in minutes rather than seconds. Try it yourself. Put a watch on the table, shut your eyes, and look again when you think a minute is up. You'll probably look thirty seconds too soon. No, say three minutes here!" He scowled. "Mangan phoned, and the ambulance was round very quickly. Did you notice the address of that nursing-home, Fell?"

"No. I leave these sordid details to you," said Dr. Fell, with dignity. "Somebody said it was just round the corner, I remember. Humph. Ha."

"In Guilford Street, next to the Children's Hospital. In fact," said Hadley, "backed up against Cagliostro Street so closely that the back garden must be in line. . . . Well, say five minutes to get the ambulance to Russell Square. That's ten-twenty. And what about the next five minutes, the time just before the second murder, and the equally important five or ten or fifteen minutes afterwards? Rosette Grimaud, alone, rode over in the ambulance with her father, and didn't return for some time. Mangan, alone, was downstairs doing some telephoning for me, and didn't come upstairs until Rosette returned. I don't seriously consider either of 'em, but take it all for the sake of argument. Drayman? Nobody saw Drayman all this time and for a long while afterwards. As to Mills and the Dumont woman—h'm. Well, yes; I'm afraid it does clear them. Mills was talking to us all the earlier part of the time, until at least ten-thirty anyhow, and Madame Dumont joined him very shortly; they both stayed with us for a while. That tears it."

Dr. Fell chuckled.

"In fact," he said, reflectively, "we know exactly what we did before, no more and no less. The only people it clears are the ones we were sure were innocent, and who had to be telling the truth if we made any sanity of the story. Hadley, it's the cussedness of things in general which makes me raise my hat. By the way, did you get anything last night out of searching Drayman's room? And what about that blood?"

"Oh, it's human blood, right enough, but there was nothing in Drayman's room that gave a clue to it—or to anything else. There were several of those pasteboard masks, yes. But they were all elaborate affairs with whiskers and goggle eyes: more the sort of thing that would appeal to a kid. Nothing, anyway, in the—the plain pink style. There was a lot of stuff for kids' amateur theatricals, some old sparklers and pinwheels and the like, and a toy theatre. . . ."

"Penny plain and twopence coloured," said Dr. Fell, with a wheeze of reminiscent pleasure. "Gone forever the glory of childhood. Wow! The grandeur of a toy theatre! In my innocent childhood days, Hadley, when I came trailing clouds of glory to the view (a thesis, by the way, which might have been open to considerable debate on the part of my parents); in my childhood days, I say, I owned a toy theatre with sixteen changes of scenery. Half of 'em, I am pleased to say, were jail scenes. Why does the young imagination run so strongly to jail scenes, I wonder? Why—"

"What the hell's the matter with you?" demanded Hadley, staring. "Why the sentimentality?"

"Because I have suddenly got an idea," said Dr. Fell, gently. "And, oh, my sacred hat, what an idea!" He remained blinking at Hadley. "What about Drayman? Are you going to arrest him?"

"No. In the first place, I don't see how he could have done it, and I couldn't even get a warrant. In the second place—"

"You don't believe he's guilty?"

"H'm," grunted Hadley, with an innate caution about doubting anybody's innocence. "I don't say that, but I think he's likely to be less culpable than anybody else. Anyhow, we've got to get a move on! Cagliostro Street first, then to interview several people. Finally—"

They heard the door-bell ring, and a sleepy maidservant tumbled down to answer it.

"There's a gentleman downstairs, sir," said Vida, poking her head into the room, "who says he wants to see either you or the superintendent. A Mr. Anthony Pettis, sir."

12
THE PICTURE

DR. FELL, rumbling and chuckling and spilling ashes from his pipe like the Spirit of the Volcano, surged up to greet the visitor with a cordiality which seemed to put Mr. Anthony Pettis much more at his ease. Mr. Pettis bowed slightly to each of them.

"You must excuse me, gentlemen, for intruding so early," he said. "But I had to get it off my mind, and couldn't feel easy until I did. I understand you were—um—looking for me last night. And I had an unpleasant night of it, I can tell you." He smiled. "My one criminal adventure was when I forgot to renew a dog license, and my guilty conscience was all over me. Every time I went out with that confounded dog I thought every policeman in London was eyeing me in a sinister way. I began to slink. So in this case I thought I'd better hunt you out. They gave me this address at Scotland Yard."

Dr. Fell was already stripping off his guest's overcoat, with a gesture that nearly upset Mr. Pettis, and hurling him into a chair. Mr. Pettis grinned. He was a small, neat, starched man with a shiny bald head and a startlingly booming voice. He had prominent eyes, looking more shrewd with a wrinkle of concentration between them, a humorous mouth and a square cleft chin. It was a bony face—imaginative, ascetic, rather nervous. When he spoke he had a trick of sitting forward in his chair, clasping his hands, and frowning at the floor.

"It's a bad business about Grimaud," he said, and hesitated. "Naturally I'll follow the formula of saying I wish to do everything I can to help. In this case it happens to be true." He smiled again. "Er—do you want me sitting with my face to the light, or what? Outside novels, this is my first experience with the police."

"Nonsense," said Dr. Fell, introducing everybody. "I've been wanting to meet you for some time; we've written a few things on the same lines. What'll you drink? Whisky? Brandy and soda?"

"It's rather early," said Pettis, doubtfully. "Still, if you insist—thanks! I'm very familiar with your book on the supernatural in English fiction, Doctor; you're a great deal more popular than I shall ever be. And it's sound." He frowned. "It's very sound. But I don't entirely agree with you (or Dr. James) that a ghost in a story should always be malignant. . . ."

"Of course it should always be malignant. The more malignant," thundered Dr. Fell, screwing his own face up into a tolerably hideous leer, "then the better. I want no sighing of gentle airs round *my* couch. I want no sweet whispers o'er Eden. I want blood!" He looked at Pettis in a way which seemed to give the latter an uncomfortable idea that it was his blood. "Harrumph. Ha. I will give you rules, sir. The ghost should be malignant. It should never speak. It should never be transparent, but solid. It should never hold the stage for long, but appear in brief vivid flashes like the poking of a face round a corner. It should never appear in too much light. It should have an old, an academic or ecclesiastical background; a flavour of cloisters or Latin manuscripts. There is an unfortunate tendency nowadays to sneer at old libraries or ancient ruins; to say that the really horrible phantom would appear in a confectioner's shop or at a lemonade stand. This is what they call applying the 'modern test.' Very well; apply the test of real life. Now, people in real life honestly *have* been frightened out of their five wits in old ruins or churchyards. Nobody would deny that. But, until somebody in actual life really does scream out and faint at the sight of something at a lemonade stand (other, of course, than that beverage itself), then there is nothing to be said for this theory except that it is rubbish."

"Some people would say," observed Pettis, cocking one eyebrow, "that the old ruins were rubbish. Don't you believe that good ghost stories can be written nowadays?"

"Of course they can be written nowadays, and there are more brilliant people to write 'em . . . if they would. The point is, they are afraid of the thing called Melodrama. So, if they can't eliminate the melodrama, they try to hide it by writing in such an oblique, upside-down way that nobody under heaven can understand what they are talking about. Instead of saying flat out what the character saw or heard, they try to give Impressions. It's as though a butler, in announcing guests at a ball, were to throw open the drawing-room doors and cry: 'Flicker of a top-hat, vacantly seen, or is it my complex fixed on the umbrella stand faintly gleaming?' Now, his employer might not find this satisfactory. He might want to know who in blazes was calling on him. Terror ceases to be terror if it has to be worked out like an algebra problem. It may be deplorable if a man is told a joke on Saturday night and suddenly bursts out laughing in church next morning. But it is much more deplorable if a man reads a terrifying ghost story on Saturday night, and two weeks later suddenly snaps his fingers and realizes that he ought to have been scared. Sir, I say now—"

For some time an irritated superintendent of the C.I.D. had been fuming and clearing his throat in the background. Now Hadley settled matters by slamming his fist down on the table.

"Easy on, will you?" he demanded. "We don't want to hear any lecture now. And it's Mr. Pettis who wants to do the talking. So—" When he saw Dr. Fell's puffings subside into a grin, he went on, smoothly, "As a matter of fact, it is a Saturday night I want to talk about; last night."

"And about a ghost?" Pettis inquired, whimsically. Dr. Fell's outburst had put him entirely at his ease. "The ghost who called on poor Grimaud?"

"Yes. . . . First, just as a matter of form, I must ask you to give an account of your movements last night. Especially between, say, nine-thirty and ten-thirty?"

Pettis put down his glass. His face had grown troubled again. 'Then you mean, Mr. Hadley—after all, I *am* under suspicion?"

"The ghost said he was you. Didn't you know that?"

"Said he was. . . . Good God, no!" cried Pettis, springing up like a bald-headed jack-in-the-box. "Said he was me? I mean—er—said he was—hang the grammar! I want to know what you're talking about? What do you mean?" He sat down quietly and stared as Hadley explained. But he fussed with his cuffs, fussed with his tie, and several times nearly interrupted.

"Therefore, if you'll disprove it by giving an account of your movements last night . . ." Hadley took out his notebook.

"Nobody told me about this last night. I was at Grimaud's after he was shot, but nobody told me," said Pettis, troubled. "As for last night, I went to the theatre: to His Majesty's Theatre."

"You can establish that, of course."

Pettis frowned. "I don't know. I sincerely hope so. I can tell you about the play, although I don't suppose that's much good. Oh yes; and I think I've still got my ticket stub somewhere, or my program. But you'll want to know if I met anybody I knew. Eh? No, I'm afraid not—unless I could find somebody who remembered me. I went alone. You see, every one of the few friends I have runs in a set groove. We know exactly where he is at most times, especially Saturday evenings, and we don't try to change the orbit." There was a wry twinkle in his eye. "It's—it's a kind of respectable Bohemianism, not to say stodgy Bohemianism."

"That," said Hadley, "would interest the murderer. What are these orbits?"

"Grimaud always works . . . excuse me; I can't get used to the idea that he's dead . . . always works until eleven. Afterwards you could disturb him as much as you liked; he's a night owl; but not before. Burnaby always plays poker at his club. Mangan, who's a sort of acolyte, is with Grimaud's daughter. He's with her most evenings, for that matter. I go to the theatre or the films, but not always. I'm the exception."

"I see. And after the theatre last night? What time did you get out?"

"Near enough to eleven or a little past. I was restless. I thought I might drop in on Grimaud and have a drink with him. And—well, you know what happened. Mills told me. I asked to see you, or whoever was in charge. After I had waited downstairs for a long time, without anybody paying any attention to me,"—he spoke rather snappishly—"I went across to the nursing-home to see how Grimaud was getting on. I got there just as he died. Now, Mr. Hadley, I know this is a terrible business, but I will swear to you—"

"Why did you ask to see me?"

"I was at the public house when this man Fley uttered his threat, and I thought I might be of some help. Of course I supposed at the time it was Fley who had shot him; but this morning I see in the paper—"

"Just a minute! Before we go on to that, I understand that whoever imitated you used all your tricks of address, and so on, correctly? Good! Then who in your circle (or out of it) would you suspect of being able to do that?"

"Or wanting to do it," the other said, sharply.

He sat back, being careful about the knife-crease of his trousers. His nervousness was clearly giving way before the twistings of a dry, curious, insatiable brain; an abstract problem intrigued him. Putting his fingertips together, he stared out of the long windows.

"Don't think I'm trying to evade your question, Mr. Hadley," he said, with an abrupt little cough. "Frankly, I can't think of anybody. But this puzzle bothers me apart from the danger, in a way, to myself. If you think my ideas suffer from too much subtlety, or from too much plain damned nonsense, I'll put it up to Dr. Fell. Let's suppose, for the sake of argument, that I am the murderer."

He looked mockingly at Hadley, who had straightened up.

"Hold on! I am not the murderer, but let's suppose it. I go to kill Grimaud in some outlandish disguise (which, by the way, I *would* rather commit a murder than be seen wearing). Hum! I indulge in all the rest of the tomfoolery. Is it likely that, after all these things, I would blatantly sing out my real name to those young people?"

He paused, tapping his fingers.

"That's the first view, the short-sighted view. But the very shrewd investigator would answer: 'Yes, a clever murderer might do just that. It would be the most effective way of bamboo-zling all the people who had jumped to the first conclusion. He changed his voice a very little, just enough so that people would remember it afterwards. He spoke as Pettis because he wanted people to think it *wasn't* Pettis.' Had you thought of that?"

"Oh yes," said Dr. Fell, beaming broadly. "It was the first thing I did think of."

Pettis nodded. "Then you will have thought of the answer to that, which clears me either way. If I were to do a thing like that, it isn't my voice I should have altered slightly. If the hearers accepted it to begin with, they might not later have the doubts I wanted them to have. *But*," he said, pointing, "what I should have done was to make one slip in my speech. I should have said something unusual, something wrong and obviously not like myself, which later they would have remembered. And this the visitor didn't do. His imitation was too thorough, which seems to excuse me. Whether you take the forthright view or the subtle one, I can plead not guilty either because I'm not a fool or because I am."

Hadley laughed. His amused gaze travelled from Pettis to Dr. Fell, and he could keep his worried expression no longer.

"You two are birds of a feather," he said. "I like these gyrations. But I'll tell you from practical experience, Mr. Pettis, that a criminal who tried anything like that would find himself in the soup. The police wouldn't stop to consider whether he was a fool or whether he wasn't. The police would take the forthright view—and hang him."

"As you would hang me," said Pettis, "if you could find contributory evidence?"

"Exactly."

"Well—er—that's frank, anyhow," said Pettis, though he

seemed acutely uneasy and startled at the reply. "Er—shall I go on? You've rather taken the wind out of my sails."

"Go on, certainly," urged the superintendent, with an affable gesture. "We can get ideas even from a clever man. What else have you to suggest?"

Whether or not that was a deliberate sting, it had a result nobody had expected. Pettis smiled, but his eyes had a fixed quality and his face seemed to become more bony.

"Yes, I think you can," he agreed. "Even ideas you should have had yourselves. Let me take one instance. You—or somebody——got himself quoted at some length in all the papers this morning, about Grimaud's murder. You showed how the murderer was careful to ensure unbroken snow for his vanishing-trick, whatever it was. He could be sure that it would snow last night, lay all his plans accordingly, and gamble on waiting until the snow stopped for the working of his scheme. In any event, he could reasonably depend on there being some snow. Is that correct?"

"I said something of the sort, yes. What of it?"

"Then I think you should have remembered," Pettis answered, evenly, "that the weather forecast said he could do nothing of the kind. Yesterday's weather forecast announced that there would be no snow at all."

"Oh, Bacchus!" boomed Dr. Fell, and brought his fist down on the table after a pause in which he blinked at Pettis. "Well done! I never thought of it. Hadley, this changes things altogether! This—"

Pettis relaxed. He took out a cigarette-case and opened it. "Of course, there is an objection. I mean, you can make the obvious retort that the murderer knew it was bound to snow because the weather forecast said it wouldn't. But in that case *you'd* be the one who took subtlety to the edge of comedy. I can't follow it so far. Fact is, I think the weather forecast comes in for as many untrue jeers as the telephone service. It dropped a brick in this instance, yes . . . but that doesn't matter. Don't you believe me? Look up last night's papers and see."

Hadley swore, and then grinned.

"Sorry," he said. "I didn't mean to touch you on the raw, but I'm glad I did. Yes, it does seem to alter matters. Blast it, if a man intended to commit a crime that depended on snow, he'd certainly treat the forecast with some sort of consideration." Hadley drummed on the table. "Never mind; we'll come back to that. I seriously ask for ideas now."

"That's all, I'm afraid. Criminology is more in Burnaby's line than in mine. I only happened to notice," Pettis admitted, with a jeering look at his own clothes, "so as to decide whether I ought to wear overshoes. Habit! . . . As to the person who imitated my voice, why try to implicate *me?* I'm a harmless enough old codger, I assure you. I don't fit into the rôle of gigantic nemesis. The only reason I can think of is that I'm the only one of the group who has no definite orbit on Saturday night and might not be able to prove an alibi. But as to who could have done it . . . Any good mimic could have pulled it off; still, who knew just how I addressed those people?"

"What about the circle at the Warwick Tavern? There were others besides the ones we've heard about, weren't there?"

"Oh yes. There were two other irregulars. But I can't see either as a candidate. There's old Mornington, who has had a post at the Museum for over fifty years; he's got a cracked tenor that would never pass for me. There's Swayle, but I believe he was speaking on the wireless last night, about ant life or something, and should have an alibi. . . ."

"Speaking at what time?"

"Nine forty-five or thereabouts, I believe, although I wouldn't swear to it. Besides, neither of them ever visited Grimaud's house.—And casual drifters at the pub? Well, some may have listened or sat down at the back of the room, though nobody ever joined the conversation. I suppose that's your best lead, even if it's a very thin one." Pettis took out a cigarette and closed the case with a snap. "Yes. We'd better *decide* it was an unknown quantity, or we shall be in all kinds of quicksand, eh? Burnaby and I were Grimaud's only close friends. But I didn't do it, and Burnaby was playing cards."

Hadley looked at him. "I suppose Mr. Burnaby really was playing cards?"

"I don't know," the other admitted, with flat candour. "But I'll give you odds he was, all the same. Burnaby's no fool. And a man would have to be rather an outstanding fathead to commit a murder on the one night when his absence from a certain group would be certain to be noticed."

Clearly this impressed the superintendent more than anything Pettis had yet said. He continued to drum on the table, scowling. Dr. Fell was occupied with some obscure, cross-eyed meditation of his own. Pettis looked curiously from one to the other of them.

"If I have given you food for thought, gentlemen—?" he suggested, and Hadley became brisk.

"Yes, yes! No end! Now, about Burnaby: you know he painted the picture which Dr. Grimaud bought to defend himself?"

"To defend himself? How? From what?"

"We don't know. I was hoping you might be able to explain it." Hadley studied him. "The taste for making cryptic remarks seems to run in his family. Do you know anything about his family, by the way?"

Pettis was evidently puzzled. "Well, Rosette is a very charming girl. Er—though I shouldn't say she had a taste for making cryptic remarks. Quite the contrary. She's a little too modern for my taste." His forehead wrinkled. "I never knew Grimaud's wife; she's been dead some years. But I still don't see—"

"Never mind. What do you think of Drayman?"

Pettis chuckled. "Old Hubert Drayman is the most unsuspicious man I ever met. So unsuspicious that some people think it hides a deep and devilish cunning. Excuse me, but have you got him on the carpet? If you have, I should forget it."

"We'll go back to Burnaby, then. Do you know how he came to paint that picture, or when he did it, or anything about it?"

"I think he did it a year or two ago. I remember it particularly, because it was the biggest canvas at his studio; he used it as a screen or a partition, turned up endways, whenever he needed one. I asked him once what it was intended to represent. He said, 'An imaginative conception of something I never saw.' It had some French name, *Dans l'Ombre des Montagnes du Sel*, or something of the sort." He stopped tapping the still unlighted cigarette on the case. His curious, restless brain was probing again. "Hullo! Now that I remember it, Burnaby said, 'Don't you like it? It gave Grimaud a hell of a turn when he saw it.'"

"Why?"

"I paid no attention. I naturally supposed it was some joke or piece of bragging; he laughed when he said it, and Burnaby's like that. But the thing had been lying about the studio, collecting dust, for such a long time that I was surprised when Grimaud came charging in on Friday morning and asked for it."

Hadley leaned forward sharply. "You were there then?"

"At the studio? Yes. I'd dropped in early for some reason or other—I forget what. Grimaud came stumping in . . ."

"Upset?"

"Yes. N-no. Say excited." Pettis reflected, studying Hadley covertly. "Grimaud said, with that machine-gun snap of his, 'Burnaby, where's your salt-mountain picture? I want it. What's your price?' Burnaby looked at him in a queer way. He came hobbling over and pointed to the picture and said, 'The thing's yours, man, if you want it; take it.' Grimaud said, 'No, I have a use for it and I insist on buying it.' Well, when Burnaby named some fool price like ten shillings, Grimaud quite solemnly got out a cheque-book and wrote a cheque for ten shillings. He would say nothing except that he had a place on the wall where it ought to go, in his study. That's all. He took the picture downstairs, and I got him a cab to take it away in. . . ."

"Was it wrapped up?" asked Dr. Fell, sharply; so sharply that Pettis jumped a little.

Dr. Fell had been showing more interest, not to say fierce concentration, in this recital than in anything Pettis had yet said. The doctor was bending forward with his hands clasped over his stick, and Pettis regarded him curiously.

"I wonder why you ask that?" he said. "It's what I was just going to mention—the fuss Grimaud made about wrapping it. He asked for paper, and Burnaby said, 'Where do you think I'd get a sheet of paper big enough to go round that? Why be ashamed of it? Take it as it is.' But Grimaud insisted on going downstairs and getting yards of brown paper off one of those rolls in somebody's shop. It seemed to annoy Burnaby a good deal."

"You don't know whether Grimaud went straight home with it?"

"No . . . I think he was going to have it framed, but I'm not sure."

Dr. Fell sat back with a grunt and let the subject go without more questions, in spite of Pettis's hints. Although Hadley kept on questioning for some time, nothing of importance was elicited so far as Rampole could see. On the personal side Pettis spoke guardedly; but there was, he said, little to conceal. There had been no friction in Grimaud's household, and none in the immediate circle except an antagonism between Mangan and Burnaby. Burnaby, although nearly thirty years older, had a strong interest in Rosette Grimaud, at once lazy and jealous. Dr. Grimaud had said nothing about this; if anything, he encouraged it, although so far as Pettis could observe he made no objection to Mangan.

"But I think you'll find, gentlemen," concluded Pettis, as he rose to go when Big Ben was striking ten, "that all these are side issues. It would be difficult to associate the *crime passionel* with any of our group. As to the financial side of affairs, I can't tell you much, either. Grimaud was fairly well-to-do, I should think. His solicitors, I happen to know, are Tennant and Williams of Gray's Inn. . . . By the way, I wonder if you'd all have lunch with me on a dreary Sunday? I'm just at the other side of Russell Square, you know; I've had a suite of rooms at the Imperial for fifteen years. You're investigating in that neighbourhood, and it might be handy; besides, if Dr. Fell feels inclined to discuss ghost stories—?"

He smiled. The doctor cut in to accept before Hadley could refuse, and Pettis left with a much more jaunty air than he had worn at his entrance. Afterwards they all looked at each other.

"Well?" growled Hadley. "Straightforward enough, it seemed to me. Of course we'll check it up. The point, the impressive point, is: why should *any* of them commit a crime on the one night when absence would be bound to be noticed? We'll go after this chap Burnaby, but he sounds out of it, too, if only for that reason. . . ."

"And the weather forecast said it wouldn't snow," said Dr. Fell, with a kind of obstinacy. "Hadley, that shoots everything to blazes! It turns the whole case upside down somehow, but I don't see . . . Cagliostro Street! Let's go on to Cagliostro Street. Anywhere is better than this darkness."

Fuming, he stumped over after his cloak and shovel-hat.

13
THE SECRET FLAT

LONDON, ON the morning of a grey winter Sunday, was deserted to the point of ghostliness along miles of streets. And Cagliostro Street, into which Hadley's car presently turned, looked as though it would never wake up.

Cagliostro Street, as Dr. Fell had said, contained a thin dingy overflow of both shops and rooming-houses. It was a backwater of Lamb's Conduit Street—which itself is a long and narrow thoroughfare, a shopping centre of its own, stretching north to the barrack-windowed quiet of Guilford Street, and south to the main artery of traffic along Theobald's Road. Towards the Guilford Street end on the west side, the entrance to Cagliostro Street is tucked between a stationer's and a butcher's. It looks so much like an alley that you would miss it altogether if you were not watching for the sign. Past these two buildings, it suddenly widens to an unexpected breadth, and runs straight for two hundred yards to a blank brick wall at the end.

This eerie feeling of streets in hiding, or whole rows of houses created by illusory magic to trick you, had never deserted Rampole in his prowlings through London. It was like wondering whether, if you walked out your own front door, you might not find the whole street mysteriously changed overnight, and strange faces grinning out of houses you had never seen before. He stood with Hadley and Dr. Fell at the entrance, staring down. The overflow of shops stretched only a little way on either side. They were all shuttered, or had their windows covered with a folding steel fretwork, with an air of defying customers as a fort would defy attackers. Even the gilt signs had an air of defiance. The windows were at all stages of cleanliness, from the bright gloss of a jeweller's farthest down on the right, to the grey murkiness of a tobacconist's nearest on the right: a tobacconist's that seemed to have dried up worse than ancient tobacco, shrunk together, and hidden itself behind news placards headlining news you never remembered having heard of. Beyond there were two rows of flat three-story houses in dark red brick, with window-frames in white or yellow, and drawn curtains of which a few (on the ground floor) showed a sportive bit of lace. They had darkened to the same hue with soot; they looked like one house except where iron railings went to the front doors from the lone line of area rails; they sprouted with hopeful signs announcing furnished rooms. Over them the chimney-pots stood up dark against a heavy grey sky. The snow had melted to patches of grey slush, despite a sharp wind that was swooping through the entrance and chasing a discarded newspaper with flaps and rustlings round a lamp-post.

"Cheerful," grunted Dr. Fell. He lumbered forward, and there were echoes of his footsteps. "Now, let's get this all straight before we attract attention. Show me where Fley was when he was hit. Stop a bit! Where did he live, by the way?"

Hadley pointed at the tobacconist's near which they were standing.

"Up over that place; just at the beginning of the street, as I told you. We'll go up presently—although Somers has been there, and says there's nothing at all. Now, come along and get roughly the middle point of the street . . ." He went ahead, pacing off a yard at a stride. "The swept pavements and the marked street ended somewhere about here; say, more or less, a hundred and fifty feet. Then unmarked snow. A good distance beyond that, nearer to another hundred and fifty . . . *here.*"

He stopped and turned round slowly.

"Halfway up, centre of the roadway. You can see how broad the road is; walking there, he was a good thirty feet from any house on *either* side. If he'd been walking on the pavement, we might have constructed some wild theory of a person leaning out of a window or an areaway, with the gun fastened to the end of a pole or something, and—"

"Nonsense!"

"All right, nonsense; but what else can we think?" demanded Hadley, with some violence, and made a broad gesture with his briefcase. "As you said, yourself, here's the street; it's plain, simple, and impossible! I know there was no hanky-panky like that, but what *was* there? Also, the witnesses didn't see anything; and, if there had been anything, they must have seen it. Look here! Stay where you are, now, and keep facing the same direction." He paced again to a point some distance farther on, and turned after inspecting the numbers. Then he moved over to the right-hand pavement. "Here's where Blackwin and Short were when they heard the scream. You're walking along there in the middle of the street. I'm ahead of you. I whirl around—so. How far am I from you now?"

Rampole, who had drawn off from both of them, saw Dr. Fell standing big and alone in the middle of an empty rectangle.

"Shorter distance this time. Those two chaps," said the doctor, pushing back his shovel-hat, "were not much more than thirty feet ahead! Hadley, this is even rummier than I thought. He was in the middle of a snow desert. Yet they whirl round when they hear the shot . . . h'm . . . h'mf. . . . ."

"Exactly. Next, as to lights. You're taking the part of Fley. On your right—a little distance ahead, and just beyond the door of number 18—you see a street lamp. A little distance behind, also on the right, you see that jeweller's window? Right. There was a light burning in that; not a bright one, but still it was there. Now, can you explain to me how two people, standing where I'm standing now, could possibly be mistaken about whether they saw anybody near Fley?"

His voice rose, and the street gave it a satiric echo. The discarded newspaper, caught again by an eddy of the wind, scuttled along with a sudden rush; and the wind tore with a hollow roar among chimney-pots as though it blew through a tunnel. Dr. Fell's black cloak flapped about him, and the ribbon on his eye-glasses danced wildly.

"Jeweller's—" he repeated, and stared. "Jeweller's! And a light in it. . . . Was there anybody there?"

"No. Withers thought of that and went to see. It was a show-light. The wire fretwork was stretched across both the window and the door; just as it is now. Nobody could have got in or out of there. Besides, it's much too far away from Fley."

Dr. Fell craned his neck round, and then went over to look owlishly into the protected window. Inside were displayed velvet trays of cheap rings and watches, an array of candlesticks, and in the middle a big round-hooded German clock with moving eyes in its sun of a face, which began to tinkle eleven. Dr. Fell stared at the moving eyes, which had an unpleasant effect of seeming to watch with idiot amusement the place where a man had been killed. It lent a touch of the horrible to Cagliostro Street. Then Dr. Fell stumped back to the middle of the street.

"But that," he said—obstinately, as though he were continuing an argument—"that is on the right-hand side of the street. And Fley was shot through the back from the *left* side. If we assume, as apparently we must assume, that the attacker approached from the left . . . or at least the flying pistol travelled over from the left . . . I don't know! Even granting that the murderer could walk on snow without leaving a footprint, can we at least decide where he came from?"

"He came from here," said a voice.

The rising of the wind seem to whirl the words about them, as though they came from empty air. For one second in that gusty half-light Rampole experienced a worse shock than he had known even in the days of the Chatterham Prison case. He had a mad vision of flying things, and of hearing words from an invisible man exactly as the two witnesses had heard the hollow murderer whisper the night before. For one second, then, something took him by the throat—before he turned and, with a drop of anticlimax, saw the explanation. A thick-set young man with a reddish face and a bowler pulled down on his for head (which gave him a somewhat sinister air) was coming down the steps from the open door of number 18. The young man grinned broadly as he saluted Hadley.

"He came from here, sir. I'm Somers, sir. You remember, you asked me to find out where the dead one, the Frenchie, was going when he was killed? And to find out what landlady had any sort of rum lodger that might be the man we're looking for? . . .

Well, I've found out about the rum lodger, and it oughtn't to be difficult to find him. He came from *here*. Excuse my interrupting you."

Hadley, trying not to show that the interruption had been unpleasantly startling, growled a pleased word. His eyes travelled up to the doorway, where another figure stood hesitating. Somers followed the glance.

"Oh no, sir. That's not the lodger," he said, and grinned again. "That's Mr. O'Rourke; chap from the music-hall, you know, who identified the Frenchie last night. He's been giving me a bit of help this morning."

The figure detached itself from the gloom and came down the steps. He looked thin despite his heavy overcoat; thin and powerful, with the quick smooth steps carried on the ball of the foot which mark the trapeze or high-wire man. He was affable, easy, and bent slightly backwards as he spoke, like a man who wants room for his gestures. In looks he was rather swarthily reminiscent of the Italian: an effect that was heightened by a luxuriant black moustache with waxed ends, which curled under his hooked nose. Beneath this a large curved pipe hung from one corner of his mouth, and he was puffing with evident enjoyment. His wrinkled eyes had a humorous blue gleam; and he pushed back an elaborate fawn-coloured hat as he introduced himself. This was the Irishman with the Italian pseudonym; he spoke like an American, and in point of fact was, he explained, a Canadian.

"O'Rourke's the name, yes," he said. "John L. Sullivan O'Rourke. Does anybody know what my middle name is? You know, the name of the—" He squared back and took a hard right-hander at the empty air—"the greatest of 'em all? *I* don't. My old man didn't, when he named me. *L.* is all I know. I hope you don't mind my butting in. You see, I knew old Loony—" He paused, grinned, and twisted his moustache. "I see, gents! You're all looking at this soup-strainer of mine. Everybody does. It's on account of that goddam song. You know. The management thought it'd be a good idea if I got myself up like the fellow in the song. Oh, it's real! Look"—he pulled—"nothing phony about it, see? But I was telling you, excuse my butting in. I'm damn sorry for old Loony. . . ." His face clouded.

"That's all right," said Hadley. "Thanks for all the help as it is. It saves me seeing you at the theatre—"

"I'm not working, anyway," said O'Rourke, gloomily. He thrust his left hand out of a long overcoat sleeve. The wrist was wound into a cast and bandaged. "If I'd had any sense I'd have followed Loony last night. But here! Don't let me interrupt. . . ."

"Yes. If you'll come along, sir," Somers interposed, grimly, "I've got something pretty important to show you. *As* well as tell you. The landlady's downstairs getting dressed up, and she'll tell you about the lodger. There's no doubt he's the man you want. But first I'd like you to see his rooms."

"What's in his rooms?"

"Well, sir, there's blood, for one thing," replied Somers. "And also a very queer sort of rope. . . ." He assumed an expression of satisfaction as he saw Hadley's face. "You'll be interested in that rope, and in other things. The fellow's a burglar—at least a crook of some sort, by the look of his outfit. He's put a special lock on the door, so that Miss Hake (that's the landlady) couldn't get in. But I used one of my keys—there's nothing illegal about that, sir; the fellow's evidently cleared out. Miss Hake says he's had the rooms for some time, but he's only used them one or two times since . . ."

"Come *on*," said Hadley.

Somers, closing the door behind, led them into a gloomy hall-way and up three flights of stairs. The house was narrow, and had on each floor one furnished flat which ran the whole depth from back to front. The door of the top floor—close up near a ladder which led to the roof—stood open, its extra lock gleaming above the ordinary keyhole. Somers took them into a darkish passage with three doors.

"In here first, sir," he said, indicating the first on the left. "It's the bathroom. I had to put a shilling in the electric meter to get any light—now!"

He pressed a switch. The bathroom was a dingy convert-ed box-room, with glazed paper on the wall in imitation of tile, worn oilcloth on the floor, a top-heavy geyser-bath whose tank had gone to rust, and a wavy mirror hung over a washstand with bowl and pitcher on the floor.

"Effort made to clean the place up, you see, sir." Somers went on. "But you'll still see reddish traces in the bath where the water was poured out. That was where he washed his hands. And over behind this clothes-hamper, now—"

With dramatic satisfaction he swung the hamper to one side, reached into the dust behind, and produced a still-damp face-cloth with sodden patches that had turned to dull pink.

"—he sponged his clothes with that," said Somers, nodding.

"Well done," said Hadley, softly. He juggled the facecloth, glanced at Dr. Fell, smiled, and put down the find. "The other rooms, now. I'm curious about that rope."

Somebody's personality permeated those rooms like the sick-ly yellow of the electric lights; like the chilly chemical smell which was not quite obliterated by the strong tobacco O'Rourke smoked. It was a den in more senses than one. Heavy curtains were drawn across the windows in a fairly large front room. Under a powerful light on a broad table lay an assortment of little steel or wire tools with rounded heads and curved ends, (Hadley said, "Lockpicks, eh?" and whistled), an assortment of detached locks, and a sheaf of notes. There was a powerful microscope, a box fitted with glass slides, a bench of chemicals on which six labelled test-tubes were arranged in a rack, a wall of books, and in one corner a small iron safe at the sight of which Hadley uttered an exclamation.

"If he's a burglar," said the superintendent, "he's the most modern and scientific burglar I've seen in a long time. I didn't know this trick was known in England. You've been dipping into this, Fell. Recognize it?"

"There's a big hole cut right out of the iron in the top, sir," put in Somers. "If he used a blow-pipe, it's the neatest acetylene-cutting job I ever saw. He—"

"He didn't use a blow-pipe," said Hadley. "It's neater and easier than that. This is the Krupp preparation. I'm not strong on chemistry, but I think this is powdered aluminum and ferrous oxide. You mix the powder on top of the safe, you add—what is it?—powdered magnesium, and set a match to it. It doesn't explode. It simply generates a heat of several thousand degrees and melts a hole straight through the metal. . . . See that metal tube on the table? We have one at the Black Museum. It's a detectascope, or what they call a fish-eye lens, with a refraction over half a sphere like the eye of a fish. You can put it to a hole in the wall and see everything that's going on in the next room. What do you think of this, Fell?"

"Yes, yes," said the doctor, with a vacant stare as though all this were of no importance; "I hope you see what it suggests. The mystery, the— But where's that rope? I'm very much interested in that rope."

"Other room, sir. Back room," said Somers. "It's got up in rather grand style, like an Eastern . . . you know."

Presumably he meant divan; or even harem. There was a spurious Turkish floridity and mysteriousness about the rich-coloured couches and hangings; the tassels, gimcracks, and weapon-groups; yet your eye was almost startled into belief by finding such things in such a place. Hadley flung back the curtains. Bloomsbury intruded with winter daylight, making sickly the illusion. They looked out on the backs of the houses along Guilford Street, on paved yards below, and an alley winding up towards the back of the Children's Hospital. But Hadley did not consider that for long. He pounced on the coil of rope that lay across a divan.

It was thin but very strong, knotted at intervals of two feet apart; an ordinary rope except for the curious device hooked to one end. This looked like a black rubber cup, something larger than a coffee-cup, of great toughness and with a grip edge like a car tire.

"Wow!" said Dr. Fell. "Look here, is that—?"

Hadley nodded. "I've heard of them, but I never saw one before and I didn't believe they existed. See here! It's an air-suction cup. You've probably seen the same sort of thing in a child's toy. A spring toy-pistol fires at a smooth card a little rod with a miniature suction-cup in soft rubber on the end. It strikes the card, and the suction of the air holds it."

"You mean," said Rampole, "that a burglar could force that thing against the side of a wall, and its pressure would hold him on the rope?"

Hadley hesitated. "That's how they *say* it works. Of course, I don't—"

"But how would he get it loose again? That is, would he just walk away and leave it hanging there?"

"He'd need a confederate, naturally. If you pressed the edges of this thing at the bottom, they would let the air in and destroy the grip. Even so, I don't see how the devil it could have been used for—"

O'Rourke, who had been eyeing the rope in a bothered way, cleared his throat. He took the pipe out of his mouth and cleared his throat again for attention.

"Look, gents," he said in his hoarse, confidential voice. "I don't want to butt in, but I think that's all bunk."

Hadley swung round. "How so? Do you know anything about it?"

"I'll make you a little bet," nodded the other, and poked at the air with his pipe-stem for emphasis, "that this thing belonged to Loony Fley. Give it to me for a second and I'll see. Mind, I don't *swear* it belonged to Loony. There are plenty of queer things in this joint. But—"

He took the rope, and ran his fingers gently along it until he reached the middle. Then he winked and nodded with satisfaction. He twirled his fingers, and then suddenly held his hands apart with the air of a conjuror. The rope came in two pieces.

"Uh-huh. Yes. I thought it was one of Loony's trick ropes. See this? The rope's tapped. It's fitted with a screw in one side and a thread in the other, and you can twist it together just like a screw in wood. You can't see the joint; you can examine the rope all you like, and yet it won't come apart under any pressure. Get the idea? Members of the audience tie the illusionist, or whatdyecallum—tie him up tight in his cabinet. This joint of the rope goes across his hands. The watchers outside can hold the ends of the rope tight to make sure he don't try to get out of it. See? But he unscrews the thing with his teeth, holds the rope taut with his knees, and all kinds of hell start to pop inside the cabinet. Wonder! Mystification! Greatest show on earth!" said O'Rourke, hoarsely. He regarded them amiably, put the pipe back in his mouth, and inhaled deeply. "Yes. That was one of Loony's ropes, I'll bet anything."

"I don't doubt that," said Hadley. "But what about the suction-cup?"

Again O'Rourke bent slightly backwards to give room for his gestures.

"We-el, Loony was as secretive as they make 'em, of course. But I haven't been around with magic acts and the rest of that stuff without keeping my eyes peeled. . . . Wait a minute; don't get me wrong! Loony had tricks that were good, and I mean good. This was just routine stuff that everybody knew about. Well. He was working on one. . . . You've heard of the Indian rope trick, haven't you? Fakir throws a rope up in the air; it stands upright; boy climbs up it—whoosh! he disappears. Eh?"

A cloud of smoke whirled up and vanished before his broad gesture.

"I've also heard," said Dr. Fell, blinking at him, "that nobody has ever yet seen it performed."

"Sure! Exactly! That's just it," O'Rourke returned, with a sort of pounce. "That's why Loony was trying to dope out a means of doing it. God knows whether he did. I think that suction-cup was to catch the rope somewhere when it was thrown up. But don't ask me how."

"And somebody was to climb up," said Hadley, in a heavy voice; "climb up, and disappear?"

"We-el, a kid—!" O'Rourke brushed the idea away. "But I'll

tell you this much: that thing you've got won't support a full-grown man's weight. Look, gents! I'd try it for you, and swing out the window, only I don't want to break my goddam neck; and besides, my wrist is out of kilter."

"I think we've got enough evidence just the same," said Hadley. "You say this fellow's bolted, Somers? Any description of him?"

Somers nodded with great satisfaction.

"We shouldn't have any difficulty in pulling him in, sir. He goes under the name of 'Jerome Burnaby,' which is probably a fake; but he's got a pretty distinctive appearance—and he has a club foot."

14
THE CLUE OF THE CHURCH BELLS

THE NEXT sound was the vast, dust-shaking noise of Dr. Fell's mirth. The doctor did not only chuckle; he roared. Sitting down on a red-and-yellow divan, which sagged and creaked alarmingly, he chortled away and pounded his stick on the floor.

"Stung!" said Dr. Fell. "Stung, me bonny boys! Heh-heh-heh. Bang goes the ghost. Bang goes the evidence. Oh, my eye!"

"What do you mean, stung?" demanded Hadley. "I don't see anything funny in getting our man dead to rights. Doesn't this pretty well convince you that Burnaby's guilty?"

"It convinces me absolutely that he's innocent," said Dr. Fell. He got out a red bandana and wiped his eyes as the amusement subsided. "I was afraid we should find just this sort of thing when we saw the other room. It was a little too good to be true. Burnaby is the Sphinx without a secret; the criminal without a crime—or at least this particular sort of crime."

"If you would mind explaining . . . ?"

"Not at all," said the doctor, affably. "Hadley, take a look around and tell me what this whole place reminds you of. Did you ever know of any burglar, any criminal at all, who ever had his secret hideaway arranged with such atmospheric effect, with such romantic setting? With the lockpicks arranged on the table, the brooding microscope, the sinister chemicals and so on? The real burglar, the real criminal of any kind, takes care to have his haunt looking a little more respectable than a churchwarden's. This display doesn't even remind me of somebody playing at being a burglar. But if you'll think for a second you'll see what it does remind you of, out of a hundred stories and films. I know that," the doctor explained, "because I'm so fond of the atmosphere, even the theatrical atmosphere, myself. . . . It sounds like somebody playing detective."

Hadley stopped, rubbing his chin thoughtfully. He peered round.

"When you were a kid," pursued Dr. Fell, with relish, "didn't you ever wish for a secret passage in your house?—and pretend that some hole in the attic *was* a secret passage, and go crawling through it with a candle, and nearly burn the place down? Didn't you ever play the Great Detective, and wish for a secret lair in some secret street, where you could pursue your deadly studies under an assumed name? Didn't somebody say Burnaby was a fierce amateur criminologist? Maybe he's writing a book. Anyhow, he has the time and the money to do, in rather a sophisticated way, just what a lot of other grown-up children have wished to do. He's created an *alter ego*. He's done it on the quiet, because his circle would have roared with laughter if they had known. Relentlessly the bloodhounds of Scotland Yard have tracked down his deadly secret; and his deadly secret is a joke."

"But, sir—!" protested Somers, in a kind of yelp.

"Stop a bit," said Hadley, meditatively, and gestured him to silence. The superintendent again examined the place with a half-angry doubt. "I admit there's an unconvincing look about the place, yes. I admit it has a movie-ish appearance. But what about that blood and this rope? This rope is Fley's, remember. And the blood . . ."

Dr. Fell nodded.

"H'mf, yes. Don't misunderstand. I don't say these rooms mightn't play a part in the business; I'm only warning you not to believe too much in Burnaby's evil double life."

"We'll soon find out about that. And," growled Hadley, "if the fellow's a murderer I don't care how innocent his double life as a burglar may be. Somers!"

"Sir?"

"Go over to Mr. Jerome Burnaby's flat—yes, I know you don't understand, but I mean his other flat. I've got the address. H'm. 13A Bloomsbury Square, second floor. Got it? Bring him here; use any pretext you like, but see that he comes. Don't answer any questions about this place, or ask any. Got that? And when you go downstairs, see if you can hurry up that landlady."

He stalked about the room, kicking at the edges of the furniture, as a bewildered and crestfallen Somers hurried out. O'Rourke, who had sat down and was regarding them with amiable interest, waved his pipe.

"Well, gents," he said, "I like to see the bloodhounds on the trail, at that. I don't know who this Burnaby is, but he seems to be somebody you already know. Is there anything you'd like to ask *me?* I told what I knew about Loony to Sergeant, or whatever he is, Somers. But if there's anything else . . . ?"

Hadley drew a deep breath and set his shoulder back to work again. He went through the papers in his briefcase.

"This is your statement—right?" The superintendent read it briefly. "Have you anything to add to that? I mean, are you positive he said his brother had taken lodgings in this street?"

"That's what he said, yes, sir. He said he'd seen him hanging around here."

Hadley glanced up sharply. "That's not the same thing, is it? Which did he say?"

O'Rourke seemed to think this a quibble. He shifted. "Oh, well, he said that just afterwards. He said, 'He's got a room there; I've seen him hanging around.' Or something. That's the honest truth, now!"

"But not very definite, is it?" demanded Hadley. "Think again!"

"Well hell's bells, I *am* thinking!" protested O'Rourke in an aggrieved tone. "Take it easy. Somebody reels off a lot of stuff like that; and then afterwards they ask you questions about it and seem to think you're lying if you can't repeat every word. Sorry, partner, but that's the best I can do."

"What do you know about this brother of his? Since you've known Fley, what has he told you?"

"Not a thing! Not one word! I don't want you to get the wrong idea. When I say I knew Loony better than most people, that don't mean I know anything about him. Nobody did. If you ever saw him, you'd know he was the last person you could get confidential with over a few drinks, and tell about yourself. It would be like treating Dracula to a couple of beers. Wait a minute!—I mean somebody who looked like Dracula, that's all. Loony was a pretty good sport in his own way."

Hadley reflected, and then decided on a course.

"The biggest problem we have now—you'll have guessed that—is an impossible situation. I suppose you've seen the newspapers?"

"Yes." O'Rourke's eyes narrowed. "Why ask me about that?"

"Some sort of illusion, or stage trick, must have been used to kill both those men. You say you've known magicians and escape artists. Can you think of any trick that would explain how it was done?"

O'Rourke laughed, showing gleaming teeth under the elaborate moustache. The wrinkles of amusement deepened round his eyes.

"Oh, well! That's different! That's a lot different. Look, I'll tell you straight. When I offered to swing out the window on that rope, I noticed you. I was afraid you were getting ideas. Get me? I mean about me." He chuckled. "Forget it! It'd take a miracle man to work any stunt like that with a rope, even if he had a rope and could walk without leaving any tracks. But as for the other business . . ." Frowningly O'Rourke brushed up his moustache with the stem of his pipe. He stared across the room. "It's this way. I'm no authority. I don't know very much about it, and what I do know I generally keep mum about. Kind of"—he gestured—"kind of professional etiquette, if you get me. Also, for things like escapes from locked boxes, and disappearances and the rest of it . . . well, I've given up even talking about 'em."

"Why?"

"Because," said O'Rourke, with great emphasis, "most people are so damned disappointed when they know the secret. Either, in the first place, the thing is so smart and simple—so simple it's funny—that they won't believe they could have been fooled by it. They'll say, 'Oh, hell! don't tell us that stuff! I'd have seen it in a second.' Or, in the second place, it's a trick worked with a confederate. That disappoints 'em even more. They say, 'Oh, well, if you're going to have somebody to help—!' as though anything was possible then."

He smoked reflectively.

"It's a funny thing about people. They go to see an illusion; you tell 'em it's an illusion; they pay their money to see an illusion. And yet for some funny reason they get sore because it isn't *real* magic. When they hear an explanation of how somebody got out of a locked box or a roped sack that they've examined, they get sore because it *was* a trick. They say it's farfetched when they know how they were deceived. Now, it takes BRAINS, I'm telling you, to work out one of those simple tricks. And, to be a good escape-artist, a man's got to be cool, strong, experienced and quick as greased lightning. But they never think of the cleverness it takes just to fool 'em under their noses. I think they'd like the secret of an escape to be some unholy business like real magic; something that nobody on God's earth could ever do. Now, no man who ever lived can make himself as thin as a postcard and slide out through a crack. No man ever crawled out through a keyhole, or pushed himself through a piece of wood. Want me to give you an example?"

"Go on," said Hadley, who was looking at him curiously.

"All right. Take the second sort first! Take the roped and sealed sack trick: one way of doing it."* O'Rourke was enjoying himself. "Out comes the performer—in the middle of a group of people, if you want him to—with a light sack made out of black muslin or sateen, and big enough for him to stand up in. He gets inside. His assistant draws it up, holds the sack about six inches below the mouth, and ties it round tightly with a long handkerchief. Then the people watching can add more knots if they want to, and seal his knots and theirs with wax, and stamp 'em with signets . . . anything at all. Bang! Up goes a screen round the performer. Thirty seconds later out he walks, with the knots still tied and sealed and stamped, and the sack over his arm. Heigh-ho!"

"Well?"

---

* See the admirable and startling book by Mr. J. C. Cannell.

O'Rourke grinned, made the usual play with his moustache (he could not seem to leave off twisting it), and rolled on the divan.

"Now, gents, here's where you take a poke at me. There's dublicate sacks, exactly alike. One of 'em the performer's got all folded up and stuck inside his vest. When he gets into the sack, and he's moving and jerking it around, and the assistant is pulling it up over his head—why, out comes the duplicate. The mouth of the other black sack is pushed up through the mouth of the first; six inches or so; it *looks* like the mouth of the first. The assistant grabs it round, and what he honest-to-God ties is the mouth of the duplicate sack, with such a thin edge of the real one included so that you can't see the joining. Bang! On go the knots and seals. When the performer gets behind his screen, all he does is shove loose the tied sack, drop the one he's standing in, stick the loose sack under his vest, and walk out holding the duplicate sack roped and sealed. Get it? See? It's simple, it's easy, and yet people go nuts trying to figure out how it was done. But when they hear how it *was* done, they say, 'Oh, well, with a confederate—!'" He gestured.

Hadley was interested in spite of his professional manner, and Dr. Fell was listening with a childlike gaping.

"Yes, I know," said the superintendent, as though urging an argument, "but the man we're after, the man who committed these two murders, couldn't have had a confederate! Besides, that's not a vanishing-trick. . . ."

"All right," said O'Rourke, and pushed his hat to one side of his head. "I'll give you an example of a whopping-big vanishing-trick. This is a stage illusion, mind. All very fancy. But you can work it in an outdoor theatre, if you want to, where there's no trapdoors, no wires from the flies, no props or funny business at all. Just a stretch of ground. Out rides the illusionist, in a grand blue uniform, on a grand white horse. Out come his gang of attendants, in white uniforms, with the usual hoop-la like a circus. They go round in a circle once, and then two attendants whisk up a great big fan which—just for a moment, see?—hides the man on the horse. Down comes the fan, which is tossed out in the audience to show it's O.K.; but the man on the horse has vanished. He's vanished straight from the middle of a ten-acre field. Heigh-ho!"

"And how do you get out of that one?" demanded Dr. Fell.

"Easy! The man's never left the field. But you don't see him. You don't see him because that grand blue uniform is made of paper—*over* a real white one. As soon as the fan goes up, he tears off the blue one and stuffs it under the white. He jumps down off the horse, and just joins in the gang of white-uniformed attendants. Point is, nobody ever takes the trouble to *count* them attendants beforehand, and they all exit without anybody ever seeing. That's the basis of most tricks. You're looking at something you don't see, or you'll swear you've seen something that's not there. Hey presto! Bang! Greatest show on earth!"

The stuffy, gaudily coloured room was quiet. Wind rattled at the windows. Distantly there was a noise of church bells, and the honking of a taxi that passed and died. Hadley shook his notebook.

"We're getting off the track," he said. "It's clever enough, yes; but how does it apply to this problem?"

"It don't," admitted O'Rourke, who seemed convulsed by a noiseless mirth. "I'm telling you—well, because you asked. And to show you what you're up against. I'm giving you the straight dope, Mr. Superintendent: I don't want to discourage you, but if you're up against a smart illusionist, you haven't got the chance of a snowball in hell; you haven't got the chance of *that*." He snapped his fingers. "They're trained to it. It's their business. And there ain't a prison on earth that can hold 'em."

Hadley's jaw tightened. "We'll see about that when the time comes. What bothers me, and what's been bothering me for some time, is why Fley sent his brother to do the killing. Fley was the illusionist. Fley would have been the man to do it. But he didn't. Was his brother in the same line?"

"Dunno. At least, I never saw his name billed anywhere. But—"

Dr. Fell interrupted. With a heavy wheeze, he lumbered up from the couch and spoke sharply.

"Clear the decks for action, Hadley. We're going to have visitors in about two minutes. Look out there!—but keep back from the window."

He was pointing with his stick. Below them, where the alley curved out between the blank windows of houses, two figures shouldered against the wind. They had turned in from Guilford Street; and, fortunately had their heads down. One Rampole recognized as that of Rosette Grimaud. The other was a tall man whose shoulder lunged and swung as he walked with the aid of a cane; a man whose leg had a crooked twist and whose right boot was of abnormal thickness.

"Get the lights out in those other rooms," said Hadley, swiftly. He turned to O'Rourke. "I'll ask you a big favour. Get downstairs as quickly as you can; stop that landlady from coming up and saying anything; keep her there until you hear from me. Pull the door shut after you!"

He was already out into the narrow passage, snapping off the lights. Dr. Fell looked mildly harassed.

"Look here, you don't mean we're going to hide and overhear terrible secrets, do you?" he demanded. "I've not got what Mills would call the anatomical structure for such tomfoolery. Besides, they'll spot us in a second. This place is full of smoke—O'Rourke's shag."

Hadley muttered profanities. He drew the curtains so that only a pencil of light slanted into the room.

"Can't be helped; we've got to chance it. We'll sit here quietly. If they've got anything on their minds, they may blurt it out as soon as they get inside the flat and the door is shut. People do. What do you think of O'Rourke, by the way?"

"I think," stated Dr. Fell, with energy, "that O'Rourke is the most stimulating, enlightening, and suggestive witness we have heard so far in this nightmare. He has saved my intellectual self-respect. He is, in fact, almost as enlightening as the church bells."

Hadley, who was peering through the crack between the curtains, turned his head round. The line of light across his eyes showed a certain wildness.

"Church bells? What church bells?"

"Any church bells," said Dr. Fell's voice out of the gloom. "I tell you that to me in my heathen blindness the thought of those bells has brought light and balm. It may save me from making an awful mistake. . . . Yes, I'm quite sane." The ferrule of a stick rapped the floor and his voice became tense. "Light, Hadley! Light at last, and glorious messages in the belfry."

"Are you sure it's not something else in the belfry? Yes? Then for God's sake will you stop this mystification and tell me what you mean? I suppose the church bells tell you how the vanishing-trick was worked?"

"Oh no," said Dr. Fell. "Unfortunately not. They only tell me the name of the murderer."

There was a palpable stillness in the room, a physical heaviness, as of breath restrained to bursting. Dr. Fell spoke in a blank, almost an incredulous voice which carried conviction in its mere incredulity. Downstairs a back door closed. Faintly through the quiet house they heard footsteps on the staircase. One set of footsteps was sharp, light, and impatient. The other had a drag and then a heavy stamp; there was the noise of a cane knocking the banisters. The noises grew louder, but no word was spoken. A key scraped into the lock of the outer door, which opened and closed again with a click of the spring-lock. There was another click as the light in the hallway was snapped on. Then—evidently when they could see each other—the two burst out as though they had been the ones who held in breath to suffocation.

"So you've lost the key I gave you," a man's thin, harsh, quiet voice spoke. It was mocking and yet repressed. "And you say you didn't come here last night, after all?"

"Not last night," said Rosette Grimaud's voice, which had a flat and yet furious tone; "not last night or any other night." She laughed. "I never had any intention of coming at all. You frightened me a little. Well, what of it? And now that I *am* here, I don't think so much of your hideout. Did you have a pleasant time waiting last night?"

There was a movement as though she had stepped forward, and been restrained. The man's voice rose.

"Now, you little devil," said the man, with equal quietness, "I'm going to tell you something for the good of your soul. I wasn't here. I had no intention of coming. If you think all you have to do is crack the whip to send people through hoops—well, I wasn't here, do you see? You can go through the hoops yourself. I wasn't here."

"That's a lie, Jerome," said Rosette, calmly.

"You think so, eh? Why?"

Two figures appeared against the light of the partly opened door. Hadley reached out and drew back the curtains with a rattle of rings.

"We also would like to know the answer to that, Mr. Burnaby," he said.

The flood of murky daylight in their faces caught them off-guard; so much off-guard that expressions were hollowed out as though snapped by a camera. Rosette Grimaud cried out, making a movement of her raised arm as though she would dodge under it, but the flash of the previous look had been bitter, watchful, dangerously triumphant. Jerome Burnaby stood motionless, his chest rising and falling. Silhouetted against the sickly electric light behind, and wearing an old-fashioned broad-brimmed black hat, he bore a curious resemblance to the lean Sandeman figure in the advertisement. But he was more than a silhouette. He had a strong, furrowed face, that ordinarily might have been bluff and amiable like his gestures; an underhung jaw, and eyes which seemed to have lost their colour with anger. Taking off his hat, he tossed it on a divan with a swash-buckling air that struck Rampole as rather theatrical. His wiry brown hair, patched with grey round the temples, stood up as though released from pressure like a jack-in-the-box.

"Well?" he said with a sort of thin, bluff jocularity, and took a lurching step forward, on the club foot. "Is this a hold-up, or what? Three to one, I see. I happen to have a sword-stick, though—"

"It won't be needed, Jerome," said the girl. "They're the police."

Burnaby stopped; stopped and rubbed his mouth with a big hand. He seemed nervous, though he went on with ironical jocularity. "Oh! The police, eh? I'm honoured. Breaking and entering, I see."

"You are the tenant of this flat," said Hadley, returning an equal suavity, "not the owner or landlord of the house. If suspicious behaviour is seen. . . . I don't know about suspicious, Mr. Burnaby, but I think your friends would be amused at these— Oriental surroundings. Wouldn't they?"

That smile, that tone of voice, struck through to a raw place. Burnaby's face became a muddy colour.

"Damn you," he said, and half raised the cane, "what do you want here?"

"First of all, before we forget it, about what you were saying when you came in here . . ."

"You overheard it, eh?"

"Yes. It's unfortunate," said Hadley, composedly, "that we couldn't have overheard more. Miss Grimaud said that you were in this flat last night. Were you?"

"I was not."

"You were not. . . . Was he, Miss Grimaud?"

Her colour had come back; come back strongly, for she was angry with a quiet, smiling poise. She spoke in a breathless way, and her long hazel eyes had that fixity, that luminous strained expression, of one who determines to show no emotion. She was pressing her gloves between the fingers, and in the jerkiness of her breathing there was less anger than fear.

"Since you overheard it," she answered, after a speculative pause while she glanced from one to the other, "it's no good my denying it, is there? I don't see why you're interested. It can't have

anything to do with—my father's death. That's certain. Whatever else Jerome is," she showed her teeth in an unsteady smile,
"he's not a murderer. But since for some reason you *are* interested, I've a good mind to have the whole thing thrashed out now.
Some version of this, I can see, is going to get back to Boyd. It
might as well be the true one. . . . I'll begin by saying, yes, Jerome
was in this flat last night."

"How do you know that, Miss Grimaud? Were you here?"

"No. But I saw a light in this room at half-past ten."

15
THE LIGHTED WINDOW

BURNABY, STILL rubbing his chin, looked down at her in dull blankness. Rampole could have sworn that the man was genuinely startled; so startled that he could not quite understand her words, and peered at her as though he had never seen her before. Then he spoke in a quiet, common-sense tone which contrasted with his earlier one.

"I say, Rosette," he observed, "be careful now. Are you sure you know what you're talking about?"

"Yes. Quite sure."

Hadley cut in briskly. "At half-past ten? How did you happen to see this light, Miss Grimaud, when you were at your own home with us?"

"Oh no, I wasn't—if you remember. Not at that time. I was at the nursing-home, with the doctor in the room where my father was dying. I don't know whether you know it, but the back of the nursing-home faces the back of this house. I happened to be near a window, and I noticed. There was a light in this room; and, I think, the bathroom, too, though I'm not positive of that . . ."

"How do you know the rooms," said Hadley, sharply, "if you've never been here before?"

"I took jolly good care to observe when we came in just now," she answered, with a serene and imperturbable smile which somehow reminded Rampole of Mills. "I *didn't* know the rooms last night; I only knew he had this flat, and where the windows were. The curtains weren't quite drawn. That's how I came to notice the light."

Burnaby was still contemplating her with the same heavy curiosity.

"Just a moment, Mr.—Inspector—er—!" He humped his shoulder. "Are you sure you couldn't have been mistaken about the rooms, Rosette?"

"Positive, my dear. This is the house on the left hand side at the corner of the alley, and you have the top floor."

"And you say you saw *me?*"

"No, I say I saw a light. But you and I are the only ones who know about this flat. And, since you'd invited me here, and said you would be here . . ."

"By God!" said Burnaby, "I'm curious to see how far you'll go." He hobbled over, with a trick of pulling down the corner of his mouth each time he lunged on the cane; he sat down heavily in a chair, and continued to study her out of his pale eyes. That upstanding hair gave him somehow a queerly alert look. "Please go on! You interest me. Yes. I'm curious to see how far you have the nerve to go."

"Are you really," said Rosette, in a flat voice. She whirled round; but her resolution seemed to crack and she succeeded in looking only miserable to the point of tears. "I wish I knew myself! I—I wish I knew about *you!* . . . I said we'd have this out," she appealed to Hadley, "but now I don't know whether I want to have it out. If I could decide about him, whether he's really sympathetic, and just a nice bluff old—old—"

"Don't say friend of the family," snapped Burnaby. "For Lord's sake don't say friend of the family. Personally, I wish I could decide about you. I wish I could decide whether you think you're telling the truth, or whether you're (excuse me for forgetting my chivalry for a moment!) a lying little vixen."

She went on steadily: "—or whether he's a sort of polite blackmailer. Oh, not for money!" she blazed again. "Vixen? Yes. Bitch if you like. I admit it. I've been both—but why? Because you've poisoned everything with all the hints you've dropped . . . if I could be sure they were hints and not just my imagination; if I could even be sure you were an honest blackmailer! . . ."

Hadley intervened. "Hints about what?"

"Oh, about my father's past life, if you must know." She clenched her hands. "About my birth, for one thing, and whether we mightn't add another nice term to bitch. But that's not important. That doesn't bother me at all. It's this business about some horrible thing—about my father—I don't know! Maybe they're not even hints. But . . . I've got it in my head somehow that old Drayman is a blackmailer. . . . Then, last night, Jerome asked me to come over here—why, why? I thought: well, is it because that's the night Boyd always sees me, and it will tickle Jerome's vanity no end to choose just that night? But I don't and I didn't—please understand me!—want to think Jerome was trying a little blackmail himself. I do like him; I can't help it; and that's what makes it so awful . . ."

"We might clear it up, then," said Hadley. "Were you 'hinting,' Mr. Burnaby?"

There was a long silence while Burnaby examined his hands. Something in the posture of his bent head, in his slow heavy breathing, as though he were bewilderedly trying to make up his mind, kept Hadley from prompting him until he raised his head.

"I never thought—" he said. "Hinting. Yes. Yes, in strict accuracy, I suppose I was. But never intentionally, I'll swear. I never thought—" He stared at Rosette. "Those things slip out. Maybe you mean only what you think *is* a subtle question. . . ." He puffed out his breath in a sort of despairing hiss, and shrugged his shoulders. "To me it was an interesting deductive game, that's all. I didn't even think of it as prying. I swear I never thought anybody noticed, let alone taking it to heart. Rosette, if that's the only reason for your interest in me—thinking I was a blackmailer, and afraid of me—then I'm sorry I learned. Or am I?" He looked down at his hands again, opened and shut them, and then looked slowly round the room. "Take a look at this place, gentlemen. The front room especially . . . but you'll have seen that. Then you know the answer. The Great Detective. The poor ass with the deformed foot, dreaming."

For a second Hadley hesitated.

"And did the Great Detective find out anything about Dr. Grimaud's past?"

"No. . . . If I had, do you think I'd be apt to tell you?"

"We'll see if we can't persuade you. Do you know that there are bloodstains in that bathroom of yours, where Miss Grimaud says she saw a light last night? Do you know that Pierre Fley was murdered outside your door not long before half-past ten?"

Rosette Grimaud cried out, and Burnaby jerked up his head.

"Fley mur . . . Bloodstains! No! Where? Man, what do you mean?"

"Fley had a room in this street. We think he was coming here when he died. Anyhow, he was shot in the street outside here by the same man who killed Dr. Grimaud. Can you prove who you are, Mr. Burnaby? Can you prove, for instance, that you are not actually Dr. Grimaud's and Fley's brother?"

The other stared at him. He hoisted himself up shakily from the chair.

"Good God! man, are you mad?" he asked, in a quiet voice. "Brother! Now I see! . . . No, I'm not his brother. Do you think if I were his brother I should be interested in . . ." He checked himself, glanced at Rosette, and his expression became rather wild. "Certainly I can prove it. I ought to have a birth certificate somewhere. I—I can produce people who've known me all my life. Brother!"

Hadley reached round to the divan and held up the coil of rope.

"What about this rope? Is it a part of your Great Detective scheme, too?"

"That thing? No. What is it? I never saw it before. Brother!"

Rampole glanced at Rosette Grimaud, and saw that she was crying. She stood motionless, her hands at her sides and her face set; but the tears brimmed over her eyes.

"And can you prove," Hadley continued, "that you were not in this flat last night?"

Burnaby drew a deep breath. Relief lightened his heavy face.

"Yes, fortunately I can. I was at my club last night from eight o'clock—or thereabouts; maybe a little earlier—until past eleven. Dozens of people will tell you that. If you want me to be specific, ask the three I played poker with the whole of that time. Do you want an alibi? Right! There's as strong an alibi as you're ever likely to get. I wasn't here. I didn't leave any bloodstains, wherever the devil you say you found some: I didn't kill Fley, or Grimaud, or anybody else." His heavy jaw came out. "Now, then, what do you think of *that?*"

The superintendent swung his batteries so quickly that Burn-aby had hardly finished speaking before Hadley had turned to Rosette.

"You still insist that you saw a light here at half-past ten?"

"Yes! . . . But, Jerome, truly, I never meant—!"

"Even though, when my man arrived here this morning, the electric meter was cut off and the lights would not work?"

"I . . . Yes, it's still true! But what I wanted to say—"

"Let's suppose Mr. Burnaby is telling the truth about last night. You say he invited you here. Is it likely that he invited you here when he intended to be at his club?"

Burnaby lurched forward and put a hand on Hadley's arm. "Steady! Let's get this straightened out, Inspector. That's what I did. It was a swine's trick, but—I did it. Look here, have I *got* to explain?"

"Now, now, now!" struck in the quiet, rumbling, deprecating tones of Dr. Fell. He took out the red bandana and blew his nose with a loud honking noise, to attract attention. Then he blinked at them, mildly disturbed. "Hadley, we're confused enough as it is. Let me put in a soothing word. Mr. Burnaby did that, as he expressed it himself, to make her jump through a hoop. Hurrum! Excuse my bluntness, ma'am, but then it's all right because that particular leopard wouldn't jump, eh?— About the question of the light not working, that's not nearly so ominous as it sounds. It's a shilling meter, d'ye see. Somebody was here. Somebody left the lights burning, possibly all night. Well, the meter used up a bob's worth of electricity, and then the lights went out. We don't know which way the switches were turned, because Somers got here first. Blast it, Hadley, we've got ample proof that there *was* somebody here last night. The question is, who?" He looked at the others. "H'm. You two say that nobody else knew of this place. But—assuming your story to be straight, Mr. Burnaby; and you'd be a first-class fathead to lie about a thing so easily checked up as that story—then somebody else must have known of it."

"I can only tell you I wasn't likely to speak of it," insisted Burnaby, rubbing his chin. "Unless somebody noticed me coming here . . . unless . . ."

"Unless, in other words, I told somebody about it?" Rosette flared again. Her sharp teeth bit at her under lip. "But I didn't. I—I don't know why I didn't"—she seemed fiercely puzzled—"but I never mentioned it to anybody. There!"

"But you have a key to the place?" asked Dr. Fell.

"I had a key to the place. I lost it."

"When?"

"Oh, how should I know? I never noticed." She had folded her arms and was walking round the room with excited little movements of her head. "I kept it in my bag, and I only noticed this morning, when we were coming over here, that it was gone. But one thing I insist on knowing." She stopped, facing Burnaby. "I—I don't know whether I'm fond of you or whether I hate you. If it was only a nasty little fondness for detective work, if that's all it really was and you didn't mean anything, then speak up. What do you know about my father? Tell me! *I* don't mind. They're the police, and they'll find out anyway. Now, now, don't act! I hate your acting. Tell me. What's this about brothers?"

"That's good advice, Mr. Burnaby. You painted a picture," said Hadley, "that I was going to ask about next. What did you know about Dr. Grimaud?"

Burnaby, leaning back against the window with an unconsciously swaggering gesture, shrugged his shoulders. His pale grey eyes, with their pin-point black pupils, shifted and gleamed sardonically.

He said: "Rosette, if I had ever known, if I had ever suspected, that my detective efforts were being interpreted as . . . Very well! I'll tell you in a few words what I'd have told you long ago, if I had known it worried you at all. Your father was once imprisoned at the salt-mines in Hungary, and he escaped. Not very terrible, is it?"

"In prison! What for?"

"For trying to start a revolution, I was told. . . . My own guess is for theft. You see, I'm being frank."

Hadley cut in quickly. "Where did you learn that? From Drayman?"

"So Drayman knows, does he?" Burnaby stiffened, and his eyes narrowed. "Yes, I rather thought he did. Ah! Yes. That was another thing I tried to find out, and it seems to have been construed into . . . And, come to think of it, what do *you* fellows know about it, anyhow?" Then he burst out. "Look here, I'm no busybody! I'd better tell you if only to prove it. I was dragged into the thing; Grimaud wouldn't let me alone. You talk about that picture. The picture was the cause rather than the effect. It was all accident—though I had a bad time persuading Grimaud of that. It was all on account of a damned magic-lantern lecture."

"A what?"

"Fact! A magic-lantern lecture. I ducked into the thing to get out of the rain one night; it was out in North London somewhere, a parish hall, about eighteen months ago." Wryly Burnaby twiddled his thumbs. For the first time there was an honest and homely expression on his face. "I'd like to make a romantic story out of this. But you asked for the truth. Right! Chap was lecturing on Hungary: lantern-slides and plenty of ghostly atmosphere to thrill the church-goers. But it caught my imagination; by George, it did!" His eyes gleamed. "There was one slide—something like what I painted. Nothing effective about it; but the story that went with it, about the three lonely graves in an unhallowed place, gave me a good idea for a nightmare. The lecturer inferred that they were vampires' graves, you see? I came home and worked like fury on the idea. Well, I frankly told everybody it was an imaginative conception of something I never saw. But for some reason nobody believed me. Then Grimaud saw it . . ."

"Mr. Pettis told us," Hadley remarked, woodenly, "that it gave him a turn. Or that you said it did."

"Gave him a turn? I should say it did! He hunched his head down into his shoulders and stood as quiet as a mummy, looking at it. I took it as a tribute. And then, in my sinister innocence," said Burnaby, with a kind of leer, "out I came with the remark, 'You'll notice how the earth is cracking on one grave. He's just getting out.' My mind was still running on vampires, of course. But he didn't know that. For a second I thought he was coming at me with a palette knife."

It was a straightforward story Burnaby told. Grimaud, he said, had questioned him about that picture; questioned, watched, questioned again, until even a less imaginative man would have been suspicious. The uneasy tension of being always under surveillance had set him to solve the puzzle in ordinary self-defence. A few pieces of handwriting in books in Grimaud's library; the shield of arms over the mantelpiece; a casual word dropped . . . Burnaby looked at Rosette with a grim smile. Then, he continued, about three months before the murder Grimaud had collared him and, under an oath of secrecy, told him the truth. The "truth" was exactly the story Drayman had told Hadley and Dr. Fell last night: the plague, the two dead brothers, the escape.

During this time Rosette had been staring out of the window with an incredulous, half-witted blankness which ended in something like a tearfulness of relief.

"And that's *all?*" she cried, breathing hard. "That's all there is to it? That's what I've been worrying about all this time?"

"That's all, my dear," Burnaby answered, folding his arms. "I told you it wasn't very terrible. But I didn't want to tell it to the police. Now, however, that you've insisted . . ."

"Be careful, Hadley," grunted Dr. Fell in a low voice, and knocked against the superintendent's arm. He cleared his throat. "Harrumph! Yes. We have some reason to believe the story, too, Miss Grimaud."

Hadley took a new line. "Supposing all this to be true, Mr. Burnaby: you were at the Warwick Tavern the night Fley came in first?"

"Yes."

"Well, then? Knowing what you did, didn't you connect him with that business in the past? Especially after his remarks about the three coffins?"

Burnaby hesitated, and then gestured. "Frankly, yes. I walked home with Grimaud on that night—the Wednesday night. I didn't say anything, but I thought he was going to tell me something. We sat down on either side of the fire in his study, and he took an extra large whisky, a thing he seldom does. I noticed he seemed to be looking very hard at the fireplace. . . ."

"By the way," Dr. Fell put in, with such casualness that Rampole jumped, "where did he keep his private and personal papers? Do you know?"

The other darted a sharp glance at him.

"Mills would be better able to tell you that than I," he returned. (Something veiled, something guarded, some cloud of dust here?) "He may have had a safe. So far as I know, he kept them in a locked drawer at the side of that big desk."

"Go on."

"For a long time neither of us said anything. There was one of those uncomfortable strains when each person wants to introduce a subject, but wonders whether the other is thinking about it, too. Well, I took the plunge, and said, 'Who was it?' He made one of those noises of his like a dog just before it barks, and shifted round in the chair. Finally he said: 'I don't know. It's been a long time. It may have been the doctor; it looked like the doctor.'"

"Doctor? You mean the one who certified him as dead of plague at the prison?" asked Hadley. Rosette Grimaud shivered, and suddenly sat down with her face in her hands. Burnaby grew uncomfortable.

"Yes. Look here, must I go on with this? . . . All right, all right! 'Back for a little blackmail,' he said. You know the look of the stoutish opera stars, who sing Mephistopheles in 'Faust'? He looked just like that when he turned round towards me, with his hands on the arms of the chair, and his elbows hooked as though he were going to get up. Face reddish with the firelight, clipped beard, raised eyebrows—everything. I said, 'Yes, but actually what can he do?' You see, I was trying to draw him out. I thought it must be more serious than a political offence or it wouldn't carry any weight after so long. He said, 'Oh, *he* won't do anything. He never had the nerve. *He* won't do anything.'

"Now," snapped Burnaby, looking round, "you asked for everything, and here it is. I don't mind. Everybody knows it. Grimaud said, with that barking directness of his, 'You want to marry Rosette, don't you?' I admitted it. He said, 'Very well; you shall,' and began nodding and drumming on the arm of the chair. I laughed and said . . . Well! I said something about Rosette's having preference in another direction. He said: 'Bah! the young one! I'll fix that.'"

Rosette was looking at him with a hard, luminous, inscrutable stare, her eyes nearly closed. She spoke in a tone too puzzling to identify. She said:

"So you had it all arranged, did you?"

"O Lord, don't fly off the handle! You know better than that. I was asked what happened, and here it is. The last thing he said was that, whatever happened to him, I was to keep my mouth shut about what I knew—"

"Which you didn't . . ."

"At your express orders, no." He turned back to the others. "Well, gentlemen, that's all I can tell you. When he came hurrying in on Friday morning to get that picture, I was a good deal puzzled. But I had been told to keep out of it entirely, and I did."

Hadley, who had been writing in his notebook, went on without speaking until he came to the end of the page. Then he looked at Rosette, who was sitting back on the divan with a pillow under her elbow. Under the fur coat she wore a dark dress, but her head was bare as usual; so that the heavy blonde hair and square face seemed to fit with the gaudy red-and-yellow divan. She turned her hand outward from the wrist, shakily.

"I know. You're going to ask me what *I* think of all this. About my father . . . and all." She stared at the ceiling. "I don't know. It takes such a load off my mind, it's so much too good to be true, that I'm afraid somebody's not telling the truth. Why, I'd have admired the old boy for a thing like that! It's—it's awful and terrible, and I'm glad he had so much of the devil in him! Of course if it was because he was a thief"—she smiled in some pleasure at the idea—"you can't blame him for keeping it quiet, can you?"

"That was not what I was going to ask," said Hadley, who seemed a good deal taken aback by this frankly broad-minded attitude. "I do want to know why, if you always refused to come over here with Mr. Burnaby, you suddenly decided on coming this morning?"

"To have it out with him, of course. And I—I wanted to get drunk or something. Then things were so unpleasant, you see, when we found that coat with the blood on it hanging in the closet. . . ."

She stopped as she saw faces change, and jerked back a little.

"When you found *what?*" said Hadley, in the midst of a heavy silence.

"The coat with blood inside it, all stained down the inside of the front," she answered, with something of a gulp. "I—er—I didn't mention it, did I? Well, you didn't give me any chance! The minute we walked in here, you leaped out at us like . . . like . . . Yes, that's it! The coat was hanging up in the coat-closet in the hall. Jerome found it when he was hanging up his own."

"Whose coat?"

"Nobody's! That's the odd part! I never saw it before. It wouldn't have fitted anybody at our house. It was too big for father—and it's a flashy tweed overcoat of the kind he'd have shuddered at, anyway; it would have swallowed Stuart Mills, and yet it isn't quite big enough for old Drayman. It's a new coat. It looks as though it had never been worn before . . ."

"*I see,*" said Dr. Fell, and puffed out his cheeks.

"You see what?" snapped Hadley. "This is a fine state of affairs now! You told Pettis you wanted blood. Well, you're getting blood—too infernally much blood!—and all in the wrong places. What's on your mind now?"

"I see," replied Dr. Fell, pointing with his stick, "where Drayman got the blood on him last night."

"You mean he wore the coat?"

"No, no! Think back. Remember what your sergeant said. He said that Drayman, half-blind, came blundering and rushing downstairs; blundered round in the clothes-closet getting his hat and coat. Hadley, he brushed close up against that coat when the blood was fresh. And it's no wonder he couldn't understand afterwards how it got there. Doesn't that clear up a good deal?"

"No, I'm damned if it does! It clears up one point by substituting another twice as bad. An extra coat! Come along. We're going over there at once. If you will go with us, Miss Grimaud, and you, Mr. . . . ."

Dr. Fell shook his head. "You go along, Hadley. There's something I must see now. Something that changes the whole twist of the case; something that has become the most vitally important thing in it."

"What?"

"Pierre Fley's lodgings," said Dr. Fell, and shouldered out with his cape whirling behind him.

3rd
COFFIN

THE PROBLEM OF
SEVEN TOWERS

16

THE CHAMELEON OVERCOAT

BETWEEN THAT discovery and the time they were to meet Pettis for lunch, Dr. Fell's spirits sank to a depth of gloom Rampole would not have believed possible, and which he certainly could not understand.

To begin with, the doctor refused to go straight back to Russell Square with Hadley, although he insisted Hadley should go. He said the essential clue must be at Fley's room. He said he would keep Rampole behind for some "dirty work of a strenuous pattern." Finally, he swore at himself with such heart-felt violence that even Hadley, sometimes sharing the views he expressed, was moved to remonstrate.

"But what do you expect to find there?" insisted Hadley. "Somers has already been through the place!"

"I don't expect anything. I can only say I hope," grumbled the doctor, "to find certain traces of brother Henri. His trademark, so to speak. His whiskers. His . . . oh, my hat, brother Henri, damn you!"

Hadley said that they could forego the Soliloquy in a Spanish Cloister, and could not understand why his friend's rage at the elusive Henri seemed to have grown to the status of a mania. There appeared nothing fresh to inspire it. Besides, the doctor, before leaving Burnaby's lodging-house, held up everybody for some time with a searching examination of Miss Hake, the landlady. O'Rourke had been gallantly keeping her downstairs with reminiscences of his trouping days; but both of them were tall talkers, and it is to be doubted whether he reminisced any more than Miss Hake did.

The questioning of Miss Hake, Dr. Fell admitted, was not productive. Miss Hake was a faded, agreeable spinster with good intentions but somewhat wandering wits, and a tendency to confuse erratic lodgers with burglars or murderers. When she was at last persuaded out of her belief that Burnaby was a burglar, she could give little information. She had not been at home last night. She had been at the moving pictures from eight o'clock until eleven, and at a friend's house in Gray's Inn Road until nearly midnight. She could not tell who might have used Burnaby's room; she had not even known of the murder until that morning. As to her other lodgers, there were three: an American student and his wife on the ground floor, and a veterinary surgeon on the floor above. All three had been out on the night before.

Somers, who had returned from his futile errand to Bloomsbury Square, was put to work on this lead; Hadley set out for Grimaud's house with Rosette and Burnaby, and Dr. Fell, who was doggedly intent on tackling another communicative landlady, found instead an uncommunicative landlord.

The premises over and under the tobacconist's shop at number 2 looked as flimsy as one of those half-houses which stand out from the side of the stage in a musical comedy. But they were bleak, dark-painted, and filled with the mustiness of the shop

THE THREE COFFINS · 199

itself. Energy at a clanking bell at last brought James Dolberman, tobacconist and news agent, materializing slowly from the
shadows at the back of his shop. He was a small, tight-lipped
old man with large knuckles and a black muslin coat that shone
like armour in a cave of fly-blown novelettes and mummified
peppermints. His view of the whole matter was that it was no
business of his.

Staring past them at the shop window, as though he were
waiting for some one to come and give him an excuse to leave
off talking, he bit off a few grudging answers. Yes, he had a
lodger; yes, it was a man named Fley—a foreigner. Fley occupied a bed-sitting-room on the top floor. He had been there
two weeks, paying in advance. No, the landlord didn't know
anything about him, and didn't want to, except that he gave no
trouble. He had a habit of talking to himself in a foreign language, that was all. The landlord didn't know anything about
him, because he hardly ever saw him. There were no other
lodgers; he (James Dolberman) wasn't carrying hot water upstairs for anybody. Why did Fley choose the top floor? How
should he know? They had better ask Fley.

Didn't he know Fley was dead? Yes, he did; there had been a
policeman here asking fool questions already, and taking him to
identify the body. But it wasn't any business of his. What about
the shooting at twenty-five minutes past ten last night? James
Dolberman looked as though he might say something, but
snapped his jaws shut and stared even harder at the window. He
had been belowstairs in his kitchen with the radio on; he knew
nothing about it, and wouldn't have come out to see if he had.

Had Fley ever had any visitors? No. Were there ever any
suspicious-looking strangers, any people associated with Fley,
hereabouts?

This had an unexpected result: the landlord's jaws still moved in a somnambulistic way, but he grew almost voluble. Yes, there was something the police ought to see to, instead of wasting taxpayer's money! He had seen somebody dodging round this place, watching it, once even speaking to Fley and then darting up the street. Nasty-looking customer. Criminal most likely! He didn't like people who dodged. No, he couldn't give any description of him—that was the police's business. Besides, it was always at night.

"But isn't there anything," said Dr. Fell, who was nearly at the limit of his affability and was wiping his face with the bandana, "you can give as description? Any clothes, anything of that sort? Hey?"

"He might," Dolberman conceded, after a tight-lipped struggle with the window, "he *might* have been wearing a kind of fancy overcoat, or the like. Of a light yellow tweed; with red spots in it, maybe. That's your business. You wish to go upstairs? Here is the key. The door is outside."

As they were stamping up a dark and narrow stairway, through a house surprisingly solid despite its flimsy appearance, Rampole fumed.

"You're right, sir," he said, "in saying that the whole case has been turned upside down. It has been—on a matter of overcoats—and it makes less sense than anything else. We've been looking for the sinister figure in the long black overcoat. And now along comes another figure in a bloodstained tweed coat that you can at least call gay in colour. Which is which, and does the whole business turn on a matter of overcoats?"

Dr. Fell puffed as he hauled himself up. "Well, I wasn't thinking of that," he said, doubtfully, "when I said that the case had been turned upside down—or perhaps I should say wrong way round. But in a way it may depend on overcoats. H'm. The Man with Two Overcoats. Yes, I think it's the same murderer, even if he doesn't happen to to be sartorially consistent."

"You said you had an idea as to who the murderer might be?"

"I know who he is!" roared Dr. Fell. "And do you know why I feel an urge to kick myself? Not only because he's been right under my nose all the time, but *because he's been practically telling me the truth the whole time,* and yet I've never had the sense to see it. He's been so truthful that it hurts me to think of how I disbelieved him and thought he was innocent!"

"But the vanishing-trick?"

"No, I don't know how it was done. Here we are."

There was only one room on the top floor, to which a grimy skylight admitted a faint glow on the landing. The room had a door of plain boards painted green; it stood ajar, and opened on a low cave of a room whose window had evidently not been opened in some time. After fumbling round in the gloom, Dr. Fell found a gas-mantle in a tipsy globe. The ragged light showed a neat, but very grimy, room with blue cabbages on the wall-paper and a white iron bed. On the bureau lay a folded note under a bottle of ink. Only one touch remained of Pierre Fley's weird and twisted brain: it was as though they saw Fley himself, in his rusty evening clothes and top-hat, standing by the bureau for a performance. Over the mirror hung framed an old-fashioned motto in curly script of gilt and black and red. The spidery scrollwork read, *"Vengeance is Mine, Saith the Lord; I Will Repay."* But it was hung upside down.

Wheezing in the quiet, Dr. Fell lumbered over to the bureau and picked up the folded note. The handwriting was flowery, Rampole saw, and the short message had almost the air of a proclamation.

James Dolberman, Esq.

I am leaving you my few belongings, such as they are, in lieu of a week's notice. I shall not need them again. I am going back to my grave.

PIERRE FLEY.

"Why," said Rampole, "this insistent harping on 'I am going back to my grave'? It sounds as though it ought to have a meaning, even if it doesn't. . . . I suppose there really was such a person as Fley? He existed; he wasn't somebody else pretending to be Fley, or the like?"

Dr. Fell did not answer that. He was at the beginning of a mood of gloom which sank lower and lower as he inspected the tattered grey carpet on the floor.

"Not a trace," he groaned. "Not a trace or a bus ticket or anything. Serene and unswept and traceless. His possessions? No, I don't want to see his possessions. I suppose Somers had a look through those. Come on; we'll go back and join Hadley."

They walked to Russell Square through a gloom of mind as well as overcast sky. As they went up the steps, Hadley saw them through the drawing-room window and came to open the front door. Making sure the drawing-room door was closed—there was a mutter of voices beyond—Hadley faced them in the dimness of the ornate hallway. Behind him the devil mask on the suit of Japanese armour gave a fair caricature of his face.

"More trouble, I perceive," said Dr. Fell, almost genially. "Well, out with it. I have nothing to report. I was afraid my expedition would be a failure, but I have no consolation merely from being a good prophet. What's up?"

"That overcoat—" Hadley stopped. He was in such a state that wrath could go no farther; he touched the other side, and ended with a sour grin. "Come in and listen to it, Fell. Maybe it'll make sense to you. If Mangan is lying, I don't see any good reason why he could be lying. But that overcoat . . . we've got it right enough. A new coat, brand new. Nothing in the pockets, not even the usual grit and fluff and tobacco ash that you get when you've worn a coat a little while. But first we were faced with the problem of two overcoats. Now we have what you would proba-bly call the Mystery of the Chameleon Overcoat. . . ."

"What's the matter with the overcoat?"

"It's changed colour," said Hadley.

Dr. Fell blinked. He examined the superintendent with an air of refreshed interest. "I don't imagine by any chance," he said, "that this business has turned your brain, has it? Changed colour, hey? Are you about to tell me that the overcoat is now a bright emerald green?"

"I mean it's changed colour since . . . Come on!"

Tension was thick in the air when he threw open the door on a drawing-room furnished in heavy old-fashioned luxury, with bronze groups holding lights, gilt cornices, and curtains stiff with such an overdose of lace that they looked like frozen waterfalls. All the lights were on. Burnaby lounged on a sofa. Rosette was walking about with quick, angry steps. In the cor-ner by the radio stood Ernestine Dumont, her hands on her hips and her lower lip folded across the upper, amused, or sa-tiric, or both. Finally, Boyd Mangan stood with his back to the fire hopping a little and moving from one side to the other as though it burnt him. But it was excitement, or something else, that burnt him.

". . . I know the damn thing fits me!" he was saying, with an air of fierce repetition. "I know it. I admit it. The overcoat fits me, but it's not my coat. In the first place, I always wear a waterproof; it's hanging up in the hall now. In the second place, I could never afford a coat like that; the thing must have cost twenty guineas if it cost a penny. In the third place—"

Hadley figuratively rapped for attention. The entrance of Dr. Fell and Rampole seemed to soothe Mangan.

"Would you mind repeating," said Hadley, "what you've just been telling us?"

Mangan lit a cigarette. The match-flame gleamed in dark eyes that were a little bloodshot. He twitched out the match, inhaled, and expelled smoke with the air of one who is determined to be convicted in a good cause.

"Personally, I don't see why everybody should want to jump all over me," he said. "It may have been another overcoat, although I don't see why anybody should want to strew his wardrobe all over the place. . . . Look here, Ted, I'll put it up to you." He seized Rampole's arm and dragged him over in front of the fire as though he were setting up an exhibit. "When I got here for dinner last night, I went to hang up my coat—my waterproof, mind you—in the clothes-closet in the hall. Generally you don't bother to turn on the light in there. You just grope round and stick your coat on the first convenient hook. I wouldn't have bothered then, but I was carrying a parcel of books I wanted to put on the shelf. So I switched on the light. And I saw an overcoat, an extra coat, hanging by itself over in the far corner. It was about the same size as the yellow tweed one you've got; just the same, I should have said, only it was black."

"An extra coat," repeated Dr. Fell. He drew in his chins and looked curiously at Mangan. "Why do you say an extra coat, my boy? If you see a line of coats in somebody's house, does the idea of an extra one ever enter your head? My experience is that the least noticed things in a house are coats hanging on a peg; you have a vague idea that one of 'em must be your own, but you're not even sure which it is. Eh?"

"I knew the coats people have here, all the same. *And,*" replied Mangan, "I particularly noticed this one, because I thought it must be Burnaby's. They hadn't told me he was here, and I wondered if he was. . . ."

Burnaby had adopted a very bluff, indulgent air towards Mangan. He was not now the thin-skinned figure they had seen sitting on the divan in Cagliostro Street; he was an elder chiding youth with a theatrical wave of his hand.

"Mangan," he said, "is very observant, Dr. Fell. A very observant young man. Ha-ha-ha! Especially where I am concerned."

"Got any objections?" asked Mangan, lowering his voice to a calm note.

". . . But let him tell you the story. Rosette, my dear, may I offer you a cigarette? By the way, I may say that it wasn't my coat."

Mangan's anger grew without his seeming to know exactly why. But he turned back to Dr. Fell. "Anyway, I noticed it. Then, when Burnaby came here this morning and found that coat with the blood inside it . . . well, the light one was hanging in the same place. Of course, the only explanation is that there were two overcoats. But what kind of crazy business is it? I'll swear that coat last night didn't belong to anybody here. You can see

206 · JOHN DICKSON CARR

for yourself that the tweed one doesn't. Did the murderer wear one coat, or both, or neither? Besides, that black coat had a queer look about it—"

"Queer?" interrupted Dr. Fell, so sharply that Mangan turned round. "How do you mean, queer?"

Ernestine Dumont came forward from beside the radio, her flat-heeled shoes creaking a little. She looked more withered this morning; the high cheekbones more accentuated, the nose more flat, the eyes so puffed round the lids that they gave her a hooded, furtive appearance. Yet, despite the gritty look, her black eyes still had their glitter.

"Ah, bah!" she said, and made a sharp, somehow wooden gesture. "What is the reason to go on with all this foolishness? Why do you not ask me? I would know more about such things than he. Would I not?" She looked at Mangan and her forehead wrinkled. "No, no, I think you are trying to tell the truth, you understand. But I think you have mixed it up a little. That is easy, as the Dr. Fell says. . . . The yellow coat was there last night, yes. Early in the evening, before dinner. It was hanging on the hook where he says he saw the black one. I saw it myself."

"But—" cried Mangan.

"Now, now," boomed Dr. Fell, soothingly. "Let's see if we can't straighten this out. If you saw the coat there, ma'am, didn't it strike you as unusual? A little queer, hey, if you knew it didn't belong to anybody here?"

"No, not at all." She nodded towards Mangan. "I did not see him arrive. I supposed it was his."

"Who did let you in, by the way?" Dr. Fell asked Mangan, sleepily.

"Annie. But I hung up my things myself. I'll swear—"

"Better ring the bell and have Annie up, if she's here, Hadley," said Dr. Fell. "This problem of the chameleon overcoat intrigues me. Oh, Bacchus, it intrigues me! Now, ma'am, I'm not saying you're not telling the truth any more than you say it of our friend Mangan. I was telling Ted Rampole a while ago how unfortunately truthful a certain person has been. Hah! Incidentally have you spoken to Annie?"

"Oh yes," Hadley answered, as Rosette Grimaud strode past him and rang a bell. "She tells a straight story. She was out last night, and didn't get back until past twelve. But I haven't asked her about this."

"I don't see what all the fuss is about!" cried Rosette. "What difference does it make? Haven't you better things to do than go fooling about trying to decide whether an overcoat was yellow or black?"

Mangan turned on her. "It makes a lot of difference, and you know it. I wasn't seeing things. No, and I don't think she was, either! But somebody's got to be right. Though I admit Annie probably won't know. God! I don't know anything!"

"Quite right," said Burnaby.

"Go to hell," said Mangan. "Do you mind?"

Hadley strode over between them and spoke quietly but to the point. Burnaby, who looked rather white, sat down on the couch again. The fray and strain of nerves showed raw in that room; everybody seemed eager to be quiet when Annie answered the bell. Annie was a quiet, long-nosed serious-minded girl who showed none of that quality which is called nonsense. She looked capable; she also looked hard-worked. Standing rather bent at the doorway, her cap so precise on her head that it seemed to have been stamped there, she regarded Hadley with level brown eyes. She was a little upset, but not in the least nervous.

"One thing I neglected to ask you about last night—er," said the superintendent, not too easy himself. "Hum! You let Mr. Mangan in, did you?"

"Yes, sir."

"About what time was that?"

"Couldn't say, sir." She seemed puzzled. "Might have been half an hour before dinner. Couldn't say exactly."

"Did you see him hang up hat and coat?"

"*Yes,* sir! He never gives them to me, or of course I'd have—"

"But did you look into the clothes-closet?"

"Oh, I see. . . . Yes, sir, I did! You see, when I'd let him in, I went straight back to the dining-room, but then I discovered I had to go downstairs to the kitchen. So I went back through the front hall. And I noticed he'd gone away and left the light on in the clothes-closet so I went down and turned it out. . . ."

Hadley leaned forward. "Now be careful! You know the light tweed overcoat that was found in that closet this morning? You knew about that, did you? Good! Do you remember the hook it was hanging from?"

"Yes, sir, I do." Her lips closed tightly. "I was in the front hall this morning when Mr. Burnaby found it, and the rest came round. Mr. Mills said we must leave it where it was, with that blood on it and all, because the police . . ."

"Exactly. The question, Annie, is about the colour of that coat. When you looked into that closet last night, was the coat a light brown or a black? Can you remember?"

She stared at him. "Yes, sir, I can re— Light brown or black, sir? Do you mean it? Well, sir, strictly speaking, it wasn't either. *Because there was no coat hanging from that hook at all.*"

A babble of voices crossed and clashed: Mangan furious, Rosette almost hysterically mocking, Burnaby amused. Only Ernestine Dumont remained wearily and contemptuously silent. For a full minute Hadley studied the set, now fighting-earnest face of the witness: Annie had her hands clenched and her neck thrust out. Hadley moved over towards the window, saying nothing in a markedly violent fashion.

Then Dr. Fell chuckled.

"Well, cheer up," he urged. "At least it hasn't turned another colour on us. And I must insist it's a very revealing fact, although I shall be in some danger of having that chair chucked at my head. H'mf. Hah! Yes. Come along, Hadley. Lunch is what we want. Lunch!"

17
THE LOCKED-ROOM LECTURE

THE COFFEE was on the table, the wine-bottles were empty, cigars lighted. Hadley, Pettis, Rampole, and Dr. Fell sat round the glow of a red-shaded table lamp in the vast, dusky dining-room at Pettis's hotel. They had stayed on beyond most, and only a few people remained at other tables in that lazy, replete hour of a winter afternoon when the fire is most comfortable and snowflakes begin to sift past the windows. Under the dark gleam of armour and armorial bearings, Dr. Fell looked more than ever like a feudal baron. He glanced with contempt at the demitasse, which he seemed in danger of swallowing cup and all. He made an expansive, settling gesture with his cigar. He cleared his throat.

"I will now lecture," announced the doctor, with amiable firmness, "on the general mechanics and development of that situation which is known in detective fiction as the 'hermetically sealed chamber.'"

Hadley groaned. "Some other time," he suggested. "We don't want to hear any lecture after this excellent lunch, and especially when there's work to be done. Now, as I was saying a moment ago—"

"I will now lecture," said Dr. Fell, inexorably, "on the general mechanics and development of the situation which is known in detective fiction as the 'hermetically sealed chamber.' Harrumph. All those opposing can skip this chapter. Harrumph. To begin with, gentlemen! Having been improving my mind with sensational fiction for the last forty years, I can say—"

"But, if you're going to analyze impossible situations," interrupted Pettis, "why discuss detective fiction?"

"Because," said the doctor, frankly, "we're in a detective story, and we don't fool the reader by pretending we're not. Let's not invent elaborate excuses to drag in a discussion of detective stories. Let's candidly glory in the noblest pursuits possible to characters in a book.

"But to continue: In discussing 'em, gentlemen, I am not going to start an argument by attempting to lay down rules. I mean to speak solely of personal tastes and preferences. We can tamper with Kipling thus: There are nine and sixty ways to construct a murder maze, and every single one of them is right.' Now, if I said that to me every single one of them was equally interesting, then I should be—to put the matter as civilly as possible—a cock-eyed liar. But that is not the point. When I say that a story about a hermetically sealed chamber is more interesting than anything else in detective fiction, that's merely a prejudice. I like my murders to be frequent, gory, and grotesque. I like some vividness of colour and imagination flashing out of my plot, since I cannot find a story enthralling solely on the grounds that it sounds as though it might really have happened. All these things, I admit, are happy, cheerful, rational prejudices, and entail no criticism of more tepid (or more able) work.

"But this point must be made, because a few people who do not like the slightly lurid insist on treating their preferences as rules. They use, as a stamp of condemnation, the word 'improbable.' And thereby they gull the unwary into their own belief that 'improbable' simply means 'bad.'

"Now, it seems reasonable to point out that the word improbable is the very last which should ever be used to curse detective fiction in any case. A great part of our liking for detective fiction is *based* on a liking for improbability. When A is murdered, and B and C are under strong suspicion, it is improbable that the innocent-looking D can be guilty. But he is. If G has a perfect alibi, sworn to at every point by every other letter in the alphabet, it is improbable that G can have committed the crime. But he has. When the detective picks up a fleck of coal dust at the seashore, it is improbable that such an insignificant thing can have any importance. But it will. In short, you come to a point where the word improbable grows meaningless as a jeer. There can be no such thing as any probability until the end of the story. And then, if you wish the murder to be fastened on an unlikely person (as some of us old fogies do), you can hardly complain because he acted from motives less likely or necessarily less apparent than those of the person first suspected.

"When the cry of 'This-sort-of-thing-wouldn't-happen!' goes up, when you complain about half-faced fiends and hooded phantoms and blond hypnotic sirens, you are merely saying, 'I don't like this sort of story.' That's fair enough. If you do not like it, you are howlingly right to say so. But when you twist this matter of taste into a rule for judging the merit or even the probability of the story, you are merely saying, 'This series of events couldn't happen, because I shouldn't enjoy it if it did.'

"What would seem to be the truth of the matter? We might test it out by taking the hermetically sealed chamber as an example, because this situation has been under a hotter fire than any other on the grounds of being unconvincing.

"Most people, I am delighted to say, are fond of the locked room. But—here's the damned rub—even its friends are often dubious. I cheerfully admit that *I* frequently am. So, for the moment, we'll all side together on the score and see what we can discover. Why are we dubious when we hear the explanation of the locked room? Not in the least because we are incredulous, but simply because in some vague way we are *disappointed*. And from that feeling it is only natural to take an unfair step farther, and call the whole business incredible or impossible or flatly ridiculous.

"Precisely, in short," boomed Dr. Fell, pointing his cigar, "what O'Rourke was telling us today about illusions that are performed *in real life*. Lord! gents, what chance has a story got when we even jeer at real occurrences? The very fact that they do happen, and that the illusionist gets away with it, seems to make the deception worse. When it occurs in a detective story, we call it incredible. When it happens in real life, and we are forced to credit it, we merely call the explanation disappointing. And the secret of both disappointments is the same—we expect too much.

"You see, the effect is so magical that we somehow expect the cause to be magical also. When we see that it isn't wizardry, we call it tomfoolery. Which is hardly fair play. The last thing we should complain about with regard to the murderer is his erratic conduct. The whole test is, *can* the thing be done? If so, the question of whether it *would* be done does not enter into it. A man escapes from a locked room—well? Since apparently he has violated the laws of nature for our entertainment, then heaven knows he is entitled to violate the laws of Probable Behaviour! If a man offers to stand on his head, we can hardly make the stipulation that he must keep his feet on the ground while he does it. Bear that in mind, gents, when you judge. Call the result uninteresting, if you like, or anything else that is a matter of personal taste. But be very careful about making the nonsensical statement that it is improbable or far fetched."

"All right, all right," said Hadley, shifting in his chair. "I don't feel very strongly on the matter myself. But if you insist on lecturing—apparently with some application to this case—?"

"Yes."

"Then why take the hermetically sealed room? You yourself said that Grimaud's murder wasn't our biggest problem. The main puzzle is the business of a man shot in the middle of an empty street. . . ."

"Oh, that?" said Dr. Fell, with such a contemptuous wave of his hand that Hadley stared at him. "That part of it? I knew the explanation of that as soon as I heard the church bells.—Tut, tut, such language! I'm quite serious. It's the escape from the room that bothers me. And, to see if we can't get a lead, I am going to outline roughly some of the various means of committing murders in locked rooms, under separate classifications. This crime belongs under one of them. It's got to! No matter how wide the variation may be, it's *only* a variation of a few central methods.

"H'mf! Ha! Now, here is your box with one door, one window, and solid walls. In discussing ways of escaping when both door and window are sealed, I shall not mention the low (and nowadays very rare) trick of having a secret passage to a locked room.

This so puts a story beyond the pale that a self-respecting author scarcely needs even to mention that there is no such thing. We don't need to discuss minor variations of this outrage: the panel which is only large enough to admit a hand; or the plugged hole in the ceiling through which a knife is dropped, the plug replaced undetectably, and the floor of the attic above sprayed with dust so that no one seems to have walked there. This is only the same foul in miniature. The principal remains the same whether the secret opening is as small as a thimble or as big as a barn door. . . . As to legitimate classification, you might jot some of these down, Mr. Pettis. . . ."

"Right," said Pettis, who was grinning. "Go on."

"First! There is the crime committed in a hermetically sealed room which really is hermetically sealed, and from which no murderer has escaped because no murderer was actually in the room. Explanations:

"1. It is not murder, but a series of coincidences ending in an accident which looks like murder. At an earlier time, before the room was locked, there has been a robbery, an attack, a wound, or a breaking of furniture which suggests a murder struggle. Later the victim is either accidentally killed or stunned in a locked room, and all these incidents are assumed to have taken place at the same time. In this case the means of death is usually a crack on the head—presumably by a bludgeon, but really from some piece of furniture. It may be from the corner of a table or the sharp edge of a chair, but the most popular object is an iron fender. The murderous fender, by the way, has been killing people in a way that looks like murder ever since Sherlock Holmes' adventure with the Crooked Man. The most thoroughly satisfying solution of this type of plot, which includes a murderer, is in Gaston Leroux's *The Mystery of the Yellow Room*—the best detective tale ever written.

"2. It is murder, but the victim is impelled to kill himself or crash into an accidental death. This may be by the effect of a haunted room, by suggestion, or more usually by a gas introduced from outside the room. This gas or poison makes the victim go beserk, smash up the room as though there had been a struggle, and die of a knife-slash inflicted on himself. In other variations he drives the spike of the chandelier through his head, is hanged on a loop of wire, or even strangles himself with his own hands.

"3. It is murder, by a mechanical device already planted in the room, and hidden undetectably in some innocent-looking piece of furniture. It may be a trap set by somebody long dead, and work either automatically or be set anew by the modern killer. It may be some fresh quirk of devilry from present-day science. We have, for instance, the gun-mechanism concealed in the telephone receiver, which fires a bullet into the victim's head as he lifts the receiver. We have the pistol with a string to the trigger, which is pulled by the expansion of water as it freezes. We have the clock that fires a bullet when you wind it; and (clocks being popular) we have the ingenious grandfather clock which sets ringing a hideously clanging bell on its top, so that when you reach up to shut off the din your own touch releases a blade that slashes open your stomach. We have the weight that swings down from the ceiling, and the weight that crashes out on your skull from the high back of a chair. There is the bed that exhales a deadly gas when your body warms it, the poisoned needle that leaves no trace, the—

"You see," said Dr. Fell, stabbing out with his cigar at each point, "when we become involved with these mechanical devices we are rather in the sphere of the general 'impossible situation' than the narrower one of the locked room. It would be possible to go on forever, even on mechanical devices for electrocuting people. A cord in front of a row of pictures is electrified. A chessboard is electrified. Even a glove is electrified. There is death in every article of furniture, including a tea-urn. But these things seem to have no present application, so we go on to:

"4. It is suicide, which is intended to look like murder. A man stabs himself with an icicle; the icicle melts! and, no weapon being found in the locked room, murder is presumed. A man shoots himself with a gun fastened on the end of an elastic—the gun, as he releases it, being carried up out of sight into the chimney. Variations of this trick (not locked-room affairs) have been the pistol with a string attached to a weight, which is whisked over the parapet of a bridge into the water after the shot; and, in the same style, the pistol jerked out of a window into a snowdrift.

"5. It is a murder which derives its problem from illusion and impersonation. Thus: the victim, still thought to be alive, is already lying murdered inside a room, of which the door is under observation. The murderer, either dressed as his victim or mistaken from behind for the victim, hurries in at the door. He whirls round, gets rid of his disguise, and instantly comes out of the room *as himself.* The illusion is that he has merely passed the other man in coming out. In any event, he has an alibi; since, when the body is discovered later, the murder is presumed to have taken place some time after the impersonated 'victim' entered the room.

"6. It is a murder which, although committed by somebody outside the room at the time, nevertheless seems to have been committed by somebody who must have been inside.

"In explaining this," said Dr. Fell, breaking off, "I will classify this type of murder under the general name of the Long-Distance or Icicle Crime, since it is usually a variation of that principle. I've spoken of icicles; you understand what I mean. The door is locked, the window too small to admit a murderer; yet the victim has apparently been stabbed from inside the room and the weapon is missing. Well, the icicle has been fired as a bullet from outside—we will not discuss whether this is practical, any more than we have discussed the mysterious gases previously mentioned—and it melts without a trace. I believe Anna Katherine Green was the first to use this trick in detective fiction, in a novel called *Initials Only.*

"(By the way, she was responsible for starting a number of traditions. In her first detective novel, over fifty years ago, she founded the legend of the murderous secretary killing his employer, and I think present-day statistics would prove that the secretary is still the commonest murderer in fiction. Butlers have long gone out of fashion; the invalid in the wheel-chair is too suspect; and the placid middle-aged spinster has long ago given up homicidal mania in order to become a detective. Doctors, too, are better behaved nowadays, unless, of course, they grow eminent and turn into Mad Scientists. Lawyers, while they remain persistently crooked, are only in some cases actively dangerous. But cycles return! Edgar Allan Poe, eighty years ago, blew the gaff by calling his murderer Goodfellow; and the most popular modern mystery-writer does precisely the same thing by calling his arch-villain Goodman. Meanwhile, those secretaries are still the most dangerous people to have about the house.)

"To continue with regard to the icicle: Its actual use has been attributed to the Medici, and in one of the admirable Fleming Stone stories an epigram of Martial is quoted to show that it had its deadly origin in Rome in the first century A.D. Well, it has been fired, thrown, or shot from a crossbow as in one adventure of Hamilton Cleek (that magnificent character of the *Forty Faces*). Variants of the same theme, a soluble missile, have been rock-salt bullets and even bullets made of frozen blood.

"But it illustrates what I mean in crimes committed inside a room by somebody who was outside. There are other methods. The victim may be stabbed by a thin swordstick blade, passed between the twinings of a summerhouse and withdrawn; or he may be stabbed with a blade so thin that he does not know he is hurt at all, and walks into another room before he suddenly collapses in death. Or he is lured into looking out of a window inaccessible from below; yet from above our old friend ice smashes down on his head, leaving him with a smashed skull but no weapon because the weapon has melted.

"Under this heading (although it might equally well go under · head number 3) we might list murders committed by means of poisonous snakes or insects. Snakes can be concealed not only in chests and safes, but also deftly hidden in flowerpots, books, chandeliers, and walking-sticks. I even remember one cheerful item in which the amber stem of a pipe, grotesquely carven as a scorpion, comes to life a real scorpion as the victim is about to put it into his mouth. But for the greatest long-range murder ever committed in a locked room, gents, I commend you to one of the most brilliant short detective stories in the history of detective fiction. (In fact, it shares the honours for supreme untouchable top-notch excellence with Thomas Burke's, *The Hands of Mr. Ottermole,* Chesterton's, *The Man in the Passage,* and Jacques Futrelle's, *The Problem of Cell 13.*) This is Melville Davisson Post's, *The Doomdorf Mystery*—and the long-range assassin is the sun. The sun strikes through the window of the locked room, makes a burning-glass of a bottle of Doomdorf's own raw white wood-alcohol liquor on the table, and ignites through it the percussion cap of a gun hanging on the wall: so that the breast of the hated one is blown open as he lies in his bed. Then, again, we have . . .

"Steady! Harrumph. Ha. I'd better not meander; I'll round off this classification with the final heading:

"7. This is a murder depending on an effect exactly the reverse of number 5. That is, the victim is presumed to be dead long before he actually is. The victim lies asleep (drugged but unharmed) in a locked room. Knockings on the door fail to rouse him. The murderer starts a foul-play scare; forces the door; gets in ahead and kills by stabbing or throat-cutting, while suggesting to other watchers that they have seen something they have not seen. The honour of inventing this device belongs to Israel Zangwill, and it has since been used in many forms. It has been done (usually by stabbing) on a ship, in a ruined house, in a conservatory, in an attic, and even in the open air—where the victim has first stumbled and stunned himself before the assassin bends over him. So—"

"Steady! Wait a minute!" interposed Hadley, pounding on the table for attention. Dr. Fell, the muscles of whose eloquence were oiling up in a satisfactory way, turned agreeably and beamed on him. Hadley went on: "This may be all very well. You've dealt with all the locked-room situations—"

"All of them?" snorted Dr. Fell, opening his eyes wide. "Of course I haven't. That doesn't even deal comprehensively with the methods under that particular classification; it's only a rough offhand outline; but I'll let it stand. I was going to speak of the other classification: the various means of hocussing doors and windows so that they can be locked on the inside. H'mf! Hah! So, gentlemen, I continue—"

"Not yet you don't," said the superintendent, doggedly. "I'll argue the thing on your own grounds. You say we can get a lead from stating the various ways in which the stunt has been worked. You've stated seven points; but, applied to *this* case, each one must be ruled out according to your own classification-head. You head the whole list, 'No murderer escaped from the room because no murderer was ever actually in it at the time of the crime.' Out goes everything! The one thing we definitely do know, unless we presume Mills and Dumont to be liars, is that the murderer really was in the room! What about that?"

Pettis was sitting forward, his bald head gleaming by the glow of the red-shaded lamp as he bent over an envelope. He was making neat notes with a neat gold pencil. Now he raised his prominent eyes, which seemed more prominent and rather frog-like as he studied Dr. Fell.

"Er—yes," he said, with a short cough. "But that point number 5 is suggestive, I should think! Illusion! What if Mills and Mrs. Dumont really didn't see somebody go in that door; that they were hoaxed somehow or that the whole thing was an illusion like a magic-lantern?"

"Illusion me foot," said Hadley. "Sorry! I thought of that, too. I hammered Mills about it last night, and I had another word or two with him this morning. Whatever else the murderer was, he wasn't an illusion and he did go in that door. He was solid enough to cast a shadow and make the hall vibrate when he walked. He was solid enough to talk and slam a door. You agree with that, Fell?"

The doctor nodded disconsolately. He drew in absent puffs on his dead cigar.

"Oh yes, I agree to that. He was solid enough, and he did go in."

"And even," Hadley pursued, while Pettis summoned the waiter to get more coffee, "granting what we know is untrue. Even granting a magic-lantern shadow did all that, a magic-lantern shadow didn't kill Grimaud. It was a solid pistol in a solid hand. And for the rest of the points, Lord knows Grimaud didn't get shot by a mechanical device. What's more, he didn't shoot himself—and have the gun whisk up the chimney like the one in your example. In the first place, a man can't shoot himself from some feet away. And in the second place, the gun can't whisk up the chimney and sail across the roofs to Cagliostro Street, shoot Fley, and tumble down with its work finished. Blast it, Fell, my conversation is getting like yours! It's too much exposure to your habits of thought. I'm expecting a call from the office any minute, and I want to get back to sanity. What's the matter with you?"

Dr. Fell, his little eyes opened wide, was staring at the lamp, and his fist came down slowly on the table.

"Chimney!" he said. "Chimney! Wow! I wonder if—? Lord! Hadley, what an ass I've been!"

"What about the chimney?" asked the superintendent. "We've proved the murderer couldn't have got out like that: getting up the chimney."

"Yes, of course; but I didn't mean that. I begin to get a glimmer, even if it may be a glimmer of moonshine. I must have another look at that chimney."

Pettis chuckled, tapping the gold pencil on his notes. "Anyhow," he suggested, "you may as well round out this discussion. I agree with the superintendent about one thing. You might do better to outline ways of tampering with doors, windows, or chimneys."

"Chimneys, I regret to say," Dr. Fell pursued, his gusto returning as his abstraction left him, "chimneys, I regret to say, are not favoured as a means of escape in detective fiction—except, of course, for secret passages. There they are supreme. There is the hollow chimney with the secret room behind; the back of the fireplace opening like a curtain; the fireplace that swings out; even the room under the hearthstone. Moreover, all kinds of things can be dropped *down* chimneys, chiefly poisonous things. But the murderer who makes his escape by climbing up is very rare. Besides being next to impossible, it is a much grimier business than monkeying with doors or windows. Of the two chief classifications, doors and windows, the door is by far the more popular, and we may list thus a few means of tampering with it so that it seems to be locked on the inside:

"1. Tampering with the key which is still in the lock. This was the favourite old-fashioned method, but its variations are too well-known nowadays for anybody to use it seriously. The stem of the key can be gripped and turned with pliers from outside; we did this ourselves to *open* the door of Grimaud's study. One practical little mechanism consists of a thin metal bar about two inches long, to which is attached a length of stout string. Before leaving the room, this bar is thrust into the hole at the head of the key, one end under and one end over, so that it acts as a lever; the string is dropped down and run under the door to the outside. The door is closed from outside. You have only to pull on the string, and the lever turns the lock; you then shake or pull out the loose bar by means of the string, and when it drops, draw it under the door to you. There are various applications of this same principle, all entailing the use of string.

"2. Simply removing the hinges of the door without disturbing lock or bolt. This is a neat trick, known to most schoolboys when they want to burgle a locked cupboard; but of course the hinges must be on the outside of the door.

"3. Tampering with the bolt. String again: this time with a mechanism of pins and darning-needles, by which the bolt is shot from the outside by leverage of a pin stuck on the inside of the door, and the string is worked through the keyhole. Philo Vance, to whom my hat is lifted, has shown us this best application of the stunt. There are simpler, but not so effective, variations using one piece of string. A 'tomfool' knot, which a sharp jerk will straighten out, is looped in one end of a long piece of cord. This loop is passed round the knob of the bolt, down, and under the door. The door is then closed, and, by drawing the string along to the left or right, the bolt is shot. A jerk releases the knot from the knob, and the string drawn out. Ellery Queen has shown us still another method, entailing the use of the dead man himself—but a bald statement of this, taken out of its context, would sound so wild as to be unfair to that brilliant gentleman.

"4. Tampering with a falling bar or latch. This usually consists in propping something under the latch, which can be pulled away after the door is closed from the outside, and let the bar drop. The best method by far is by the use of the ever-helpful ice, a cube of which is propped under the latch; and, when it melts, the latch falls. There is one case in which the mere slam of the door suffices to drop the bar inside.

"5. An illusion, simple but effective. The murderer, after committing his crime, has locked the door from the outside and kept the key. It is assumed, however, that the key is still in the lock on the inside. The murderer, who is first to raise a scare and find the body smashes the upper glass panel of the door, puts his hand through with the key concealed in it, and 'finds' the key in the lock inside, by which he opens the door. This device has also been used with the breaking of a panel out of an ordinary wooden door.

"There are miscellaneous methods, such as locking a door from the outside and returning the key to the room by means of string again, but you can see for yourselves that in this case none of them can have any application. We found the door locked on the inside. Well, there are many ways by which it could have

226 · JOHN DICKSON CARR

been done—but it was *not* done, because Mills was watching the door the whole time. This room was only locked in a technical sense. It was watched, and that shoots us all to blazes."

"I don't like to drag in famous platitudes," said Pettis, his forehead wrinkled, "but it would seem plenty sound to say exclude the impossible and whatever remains, however improbable, must be the truth. You've excluded the door; I presume you also exclude the chimney?"

"I do," grunted Dr. Fell.

"Then we come back in a circle to the window, don't we?" demanded Hadley. "You've gone on and on about ways that obviously couldn't have been used. But in this catalogue of sensationalism you've omitted all mention of the only means of exit the murderer *could* have used. . . ."

"Because it wasn't a locked window, don't you see?" cried Dr. Fell. "I can tell you several brands of funny business with windows if they're only locked. It can be traced down from the earliest dummy nail-heads to the latest hocus-pocus with steel shutters. You can smash a window, carefully turn its catch to lock it, and then, when you leave, simply replace the whole pane with a new pane of glass and putty it round; so that the new pane looks like the original and the window is locked inside. But this window wasn't locked or even closed—it was only inaccessible."

"I seem to have read somewhere of human flies . . ." Pettis suggested.

Dr. Fell shook his head. "We won't debate whether a human fly can walk on a sheer smooth wall. Since I've cheerfully accepted so much, I might believe that if the fly had any place to light. That is, he would have to start from somewhere and end somewhere. But he didn't; not on the roof, not on the ground below. . . ." Dr. Fell hammered his fists against his temples. "However, if you want a suggestion or two in that respect, I will tell you—"

He stopped, raising his head. At the end of the quiet, now deserted dining-room a line of windows showed pale light now flickering with snow. A figure had darted in silhouette against them, hesitating, peering from side to side, and then hurrying down towards them. Hadley uttered a muffled exclamation as they saw it was Mangan. Mangan was pale.

"Not something else?" asked Hadley, as coolly as he could. He pushed back his chair. "Not something else about coats changing colour or—"

"No," said Mangan. He stood by the table, drawing his breath in gasps. "But you'd better get over there. Something's happened to Drayman; apoplectic stroke or something like that. No, he's not dead or anything. But he's in a bad way. He was trying to get in touch with you when he had the stroke. . . . He keeps talking wildly about somebody in his room, and fireworks, and chimneys."

18

THE CHIMNEY

AGAIN THERE were three people—three people strained and
with frayed nerves—waiting in the drawing-room. Even Stuart
Mills, who stood with his back to the fireplace, kept clearing his
throat in a way that seemed to drive Rosette half frantic. Ernestine Dumont sat quietly by the fire when Mangan led in Dr. Fell,
Hadley, Pettis, and Rampole. The lights had been turned off;
only the bleakness of the snow-shadowed afternoon penetrated
through heavy lace curtains, and Mills' shadow blocked the tired
gleam of the fire. Burnaby had gone.

"You cannot see him," said the woman, with her eyes fixed on
that shadow. "The doctor is with him now. Things all come at
once. Probably he is mad."

Rosette, her arms folded, had been pacing about with her
own feline grace. She faced the newcomers and spoke with harsh
suddenness.

"I can't stand this, you know. It can go on just so long, and
then— *Have* you any idea of what happened? Do you know
how my father was killed, or who killed him? For God's sake say
something, even if you only accuse me!"

"Suppose you tell us exactly what happened to Mr. Drayman," Hadley said, quietly, "and when it happened. Is he in any grave danger?"

Mme Dumont shrugged. "That is possible. His heart . . . I do not know. He collapsed. He is unconscious now. As to whether he will ever come alive again, that I do not know, either. About what happened to him, we have no idea what caused it. . . ."

Again Mills cleared his throat. His head was in the air, and his fixed smile looked rather ghastly. He said:

"If, sir, you have any idea of—um—foul play, or any suspicion that he was murderously set upon, you may dismiss it. And, strangely enough, you will receive confirmation of it from us in—what shall I say—pairs? I mean that the same people were together this afternoon who were together last night. The Pythoness and I," he bowed gravely towards Ernestine Dumont, "were together upstairs in my little workroom. I am given to understand that Miss Grimaud and our friend Mangan were down here. . . ."

Rosette jerked her head. "You had better hear it from the beginning. Did Boyd tell you about Drayman coming down here first?"

"No, I didn't tell 'em anything," Mangan answered, with some bitterness. "After that business of the overcoat, I wanted somebody to give me a little confirmation." He swung round, the muscles tightening at his temples. "It was about half an hour ago, you see. Rosette and I were here alone. I'd had a row with Burnaby—well, the usual thing. Everybody was yelling and fighting about that overcoat affair, and we'd all separated. Burnaby had gone. I hadn't seen Drayman at all; he'd kept to his room this morning. Anyhow, Drayman walked in here and asked me how he could get in touch with you."

"You mean he had discovered something?"

Rosette sniffed. "Or wanted us to think he had. Very mysterious! He came in with that doddering way of his, and as Boyd says, asked where he could find you. Boyd asked him what was up. . . ."

"Did he act as though he might have—well, found something important?"

"Yes, he did. We both nearly jumped out of our shoes. . . ."

"Why?"

"So would you," said Rosette, coolly, "if you were innocent." She twitched her shoulders, her arms still folded, as though she were cold. "So we said, 'What is it, anyhow?' He doddered a little, and said, 'I've found something missing from my room, and it makes me remember something I'd forgotten about last night.' It was all a lot of nonsense about some subconscious memory, though he wasn't very clear on the point. It came down to some hallucination that, while he was lying down last night after he'd taken the sleeping-powder, somebody had come into his room."

"Before the—crime?"

"Yes."

"Who came into his room?"

"That's it! He either didn't know, or wouldn't say, or else the whole thing was a plain dream. Of course that's probably what it was. I won't suggest," said Rosette, still coolly, "the other alternative. When we asked him, he simply tapped his head, and hedged, and said, 'I really can't say,' in that infuriating way of his. . . . Lord! how I hate these people who won't come out and say what they mean! We both got rather annoyed—"

"Oh, he's all right," said Mangan, whose discomfort appeared to be growing. "Only, damn it all, if I hadn't said what I did . . ."

"Said what?" asked Hadley, quickly.

Mangan hunched his shoulders and looked moodily at the fire. "I said, 'Well, if you've discovered so much, why don't you go up to the scene of the 'orrid murder and see if you can't discover some more?' Yes, I was sore. He took me seriously. He looked at me for a minute and said: 'Yes, I believe I will. I had better make sure.' And with that out he went! It was maybe twenty minutes later that we heard a noise like somebody banging downstairs. . . . You see, we hadn't left the room, although—" He checked himself suddenly.

"You might as well go on and say it," Rosette told him, with an air of surprised indifference. "I don't mind who knows it. I wanted to sneak up after him and watch him. But we didn't. After that twenty minutes, we heard him blundering downstairs. Then, apparently when he'd just got to the last step, we heard a choking sound and a thud—*flap*, like that. Boyd opened the door, and there he was lying doubled up. His face was all congested, and the veins up round the forehead were standing out in a blue colour; horrible business! Of course we sent for the doctor. He hasn't said anything except to rave about 'chimneys' and 'fireworks.'"

Ernestine Dumont still remained stolid, her eyes not moving from the fire. Mills took a little hopping step forward.

"If you will allow me to take up the story," he said, inclining his head, "I think it probable that I can fill the gap. That is, of course, with the Pythoness' permission. . . ."

"Ah, bah!" the woman cried. Her face was in shadow as she looked up, there was about her a rigidity as of whalebone, but Rampole was startled to see that her eyes blazed. "You must always act the fool, must you not? The Pythoness this, the Pythoness that. Very well, I must tell you. I am Pythoness enough to know that you did not like poor Drayman, and that my little

Rosette does not like him, either. God! what do you know of human men or sympathy or . . . Drayman is a good man, even if he may be a little mad. He may be mistaken. He may be full of drugs. But he is a good man at the heart, and if he dies I shall pray for his soul."

"Shall I—er—go on?" observed Mills, imperturbably.

"Yes, you shall go on," the woman mimicked, and was silent.

"The Pythoness and I were in my workroom on the top floor; opposite the study, as you know. And again the door was open. I was shifting some papers, and I noticed Mr. Drayman come up and go into the study . . ."

"Do you know what he did there?" asked Hadley.

"Unfortunately, no. He closed the door. I could not even venture a deduction as to what he might be doing, since I could hear nothing. After some time he came out, in what I can only describe as a panting and unsteady condition—"

"What do you mean by that?"

Mills frowned. "I regret, sir, that it is impossible to be more precise. I can only say that I received an impression as though he had been indulging in violent exercise. This, I have no doubt, caused or hastened the collapse, since there were clear evidences of an apoplectic stroke. If I may correct the Pythoness, it had nothing to do with his heart. Er—I might add something which has not yet been mentioned. When he was picked up after the stroke, I observed that his hands and sleeves were covered with soot."

"The chimney again," Pettis murmured, very softly, and Hadley turned round towards Dr. Fell. It gave Rampole a shock to see that the doctor was no longer in the room. A person of his weight and girth can, as a rule, make small success of an effort to fade mysteriously away; but he was gone, and Rampole thought he knew where.

"Follow him up there," Hadley said quickly to the American. "And see that he doesn't work any of his blasted mystification. Now, Mr. Mills—"

Rampole heard Hadley's questions probing and crackling as he went out into the sombre hall. The house was very quiet; so quiet that, as he mounted the stairs, the sudden shrilling of the telephone bell in the lower hall made him jump a little. Passing Drayman's door upstairs, he heard hoarse breathing inside, and quiet footfalls tiptoeing about the room: through the door he could see the doctor's medicine-case and hat on a chair. No lights burned on the top floor; again such a stillness that he could distinctly hear Annie's voice answering the telephone far below.

The study was dusky. Despite the few snowflakes, some faint lurid light, dull red-and-orange with sunset, glimmered through the window. It made a stormy glow across the room; it kindled the colours of the shield of arms, glittered on the crossed fencing-foils above the fireplace, and made vast and shadowy the white busts on the bookshelves. The shape of Charles Grimaud, half-studious, half-barbaric like the room, seemed to move and chuckle here after Charles Grimaud was dead. That vast blank space in the panelled wall, where the picture was to have hung, faced Rampole in mockery. And, standing motionless in his black cloak before the window, Dr. Fell leaned on his cane and stared out into the sunset.

The creaking of the door did not rouse him. Rampole, his voice seeming to make echoes, said:

"Did you—?"

Dr. Fell blinked round. His breath, when he puffed it out with a sort of weary explosiveness, turned to smoke in the sharp air.

"Eh? Oh! Did I what?"

"Find anything."

"Well, I think I know the truth. I think I know the truth," he answered, with a sort of reflective stubbornness, "and tonight I shall probably be able to prove it. H'mf. Hah. Yes. D'ye see, I've been standing here wondering what to do about it. It's the old problem, son, and it becomes more difficult each year I live: when the sky grows nobler, and the old chair more comfortable, and maybe the human heart—" He brushed his hand across his forehead. "What is justice? I've asked it at the end of nearly every case I ever handled. I see faces rise, and sick souls and bad dreams. . . . No matter. Shall we go downstairs?"

"But what about the fireplace?" insisted Rampole. He went over, peered at it, hammered it, and still he could see nothing out of the way. A little soot had been scattered on the hearth, and there was a crooked streak in the coating of soot on the back of the fireplace. "What's wrong with it? Is there a secret passage, after all?"

"Oh no. There's nothing wrong with it in the way you mean. Nobody got up there. No," he added, as Rampole put his hand into the long opening of the flue and groped round. "I'm afraid you're wasting your time; there's nothing up there to find."

"But," said Rampole, desperately, "if this brother Henri—"

"Yes," said a heavy voice from the doorway, "brother Henri."

The voice was so unlike Hadley's that at the moment they did not recognize it. Hadley stood in the doorway, a sheet of paper crumpled in his hand; his face was in shadow, but there was such a dull quietness in his tones that Rampole recognized something like despair. Closing the door softly behind him, Hadley stood in the darkening and went on calmly:

"It was our own fault, I know, for being hypnotized by a theory. It ran away with us—and now we've got to start the whole case afresh. Fell, when you said this morning that the case had been turned upside down, I don't believe you knew just how true it was. It's not only upside down; it's non-existent. Our chief prop is knocked to blazes. Damn the rotten, impossible . . . !" He stared at the sheet of paper as though he meant to crush it into a ball. "A phone-call just came through from the Yard. They've heard from Bucharest."

"I'm afraid I know what you're going to say," Dr. Fell nodded. "You're going to say that brother Henri—"

"*There is no brother Henri,*" said Hadley. "*The third of the three Horváth brothers died over thirty years ago.*"

The faint reddish light had grown muddy; in the cold, quiet study they could hear from far away the mutter of London awaking towards nightfall. Walking over to the broad desk, Hadley spread out the crumpled sheet on the desk so that others could read. The shadow of the yellow jade buffalo lay across it sardonically. Across the room they could see the slashes gaping in the picture of the three graves.

"There's no possibility of a mistake," Hadley went on. "The case is a very well-known one, it seems. The whole cablegram they sent was very long, but I've copied the important parts verbatim from what they read over the phone. Take a look."

No difficulty about information desired [it ran]. Two men now in my personal service were at Siebenturmen as warders in 1900, and confirm record. Facts: Károly Grimaud Horváth, Pierre Fley Horváth, and Nicholas Revéi Horváth were sons of Professor Károly Horváth (of Klausenburg University) and Cécile Fley Horváth (French) his wife. For robbery of Kunar Bank at Brasso, November, 1898, the three brothers were sentenced, January,

236 · JOHN DICKSON CARR

1899, to twenty years' penal servitude. Bank watchman died of injuries inflicted, and loot never recovered; believed to have been hidden. All three, with aid of prison doctor during plague scare of August, 1900, made daring attempt at escape by being certified as dead, and buried in plague-ground. J. Lahner and R. Gorgei, warders, returning to graves an hour later with wooden crosses for marking, noticed disturbance had taken place on earth at grave of Károly Horváth. Investigation showed coffin open and empty. Digging into other two graves, warders found Pierre Horváth bloody and insensible, but still alive. Nicholas Horváth had already suffocated to death. Nicholas reburied after absolute certainty made the man was dead; Pierre returned to prison. Scandal hushed up, no chase of fugitive, and story never discovered until end of war. Pierre Fley Horváth never mentally responsible afterwards. Released January, 1919, having served full term. Assure you no doubt whatever third brother dead.

—ALEXANDER CUZA, Policedirector, Bucharest

"Oh yes," said Hadley, when they had finished reading. "It confirms the reconstruction right enough, except for the little point that we've been chasing a ghost as the murderer. Brother Henri (or brother Nicholas, to be exact) never did leave his grave. He's there yet. And the whole case . . ."

Dr. Fell rapped his knuckles slowly on the paper.

"It's my fault, Hadley," he admitted. "I told you this morning that I'd come close to making the biggest mistake of my life. I was hypnotized by brother Henri! I couldn't think of anything else. You see now why we knew so remarkably little about that third brother, so little that with my cursed cocksureness I put all kinds of fantastic interpretations on it?"

"Well, it won't do us any good just to admit the mistake. How the devil are we going to explain all those crazy remarks of Fley's now? Private vendetta! Vengeance? Now that that's swept away, we haven't a lead to work on. Not one lead! And, if you exclude the motive of vengeance on Grimaud and Fley, what is there left?"

Dr. Fell pointed rather malevolently with his stick.

"Don't you see what's left?" he roared. "Don't you see the explanation of those two murders that we've got to accept now or retire to the madhouse?"

"You mean that somebody cooked up the whole thing to make it look like the work of an avenger?—I'm at the state now," explained the superintendent, "where I could believe nearly anything. But that strikes me as being a good bit too subtle. How would the real murderer ever know we could dig so far into the past? We'd never have done it if it hadn't been, saving your presence, for a few lucky shots. How would the real murderer know we should ever connect Professor Grimaud with a Hungarian criminal, or connect him with Fley or any of the rest of it? It strikes me as a false trail far *too* well concealed." He paced up and down, driving his fist into his palm. "Besides, the more I think of it the more confusing it gets! We had damned good reason to think it was the third brother who killed those two . . . and, the more I think of that possibility, the more I'm inclined to doubt that Nicholas is dead. Grimaud *said* his third brother shot him!—and when a man's dying, and knows he's dying, what earthly reason would he have for lying? Or . . . Stop a bit! Do you suppose he might have meant *Fley?* Do you suppose Fley came here, shot Grimaud, and then afterwards somebody else shot Fley? It would explain a lot of the puzzles—"

"But," said Rampole, "excuse the interruption, I mean, but it wouldn't explain why Fley kept talking about a third brother as well! Either brother Henri is dead or he isn't. Still, if he is dead, what reason have both victims got to lie about him all the time? If he's really dead, he must be one hell of a live ghost."

Hadley shook the briefcase. "I know. That's exactly what I'm kicking about! We've got to take somebody's word for it, and it seems more reasonable to take the word of two people who were shot by him, rather than this cablegram which might be influenced or mistaken for several reasons. Or—h'm! Suppose he really is dead, but the murderer is pretending to be that dead brother come to life?" He stopped, nodded, and stared out of the window. "Now I think we're getting warm. That would explain all the inconsistencies, wouldn't it? The real murderer assumes the rôle of a man neither of the other brothers has seen for nearly thirty years; well? When the murders are committed, and we get on his track—if we do get on his track—we put it all down to vengeance. How's that, Fell?"

Dr. Fell, scowling heavily, stumped round the table.

"Not bad . . . no, not bad, as a disguise. But what about the motive for which Grimaud and Fley were really killed?"

"How do you mean?"

"There has to be a connecting thread, hasn't there? There might be any number of motives, plain or obscure, why a person would kill Grimaud. Mills or Dumont or Burnaby or—yes, anybody *might* have killed Grimaud. Also, anybody might have killed Fley: but not, I must point out, anybody in the same circle or group of people. Why should Fley be killed by a member of

Grimaud's group, none of whom had presumably ever seen him before? If these murders are the work of one person, where is the connecting link? A respected professor in Bloomsbury and a tramp actor with a prison record. Where's the human motive that ties those two together in the murderer's mind, unless it is a link that goes back into the past?"

"I can think of one person who is associated with both from the past," Hadley pointed out.

"Who? You mean the Dumont woman?"

"Yes."

"Then what becomes of somebody impersonating brother Henri? Whatever else you decide on, you must decide that she's not doing that. No, my lad. Dumont is not only a bad suspect; she's an impossible suspect."

"I don't see that. Look here, you're basing your whole belief that Dumont didn't kill Grimaud on the grounds that you think she loved Grimaud. No defence, Fell—no defence at all! Remember that she told the whole fantastic story to begin with . . ."

"In coöperation with—Mills," boomed Dr. Fell, with a sardonic leer. He was puffing again. "Can you think of any two less likely conspirators to band together at the dark of the moon and hoodwink the police with their imaginative fairy-tales? She might wear a mask; I mean a figurative mask in life. Mills might wear a mask. But the combination of those two masks, and their activities, is too much. I prefer the one literal false face. Besides, bear in mind that as the double killer Ernestine D. is absolutely O-U-T. Why? Because, at the time of Fley's death sworn to by three good men and true, she was here in this room, talking to us." He pondered, and a twinkle began to appear in his eye. "Or will you drag in the second generation? Rosette is Grimaud's daughter; suppose the mysterious Stuart Mills is really the son of the dead brother Henri?"

About to reply, Hadley checked himself and studied Dr. Fell. He sat down on the edge of the desk.

"I know this mood. I know it very well," he asserted, with the air of one who confirms a sinister suspicion. "It's the beginning of some more blasted mystification, and there's no use arguing with you now. Why are you so anxious for me to believe the story?"

"First," said Dr. Fell, "because I wish to force it into your head that Mills told the truth. . . ."

"You mean, as a point in the mystification, in order to prove later that he didn't? The sort of low trick you played me in that Death Watch case?"

The doctor ignored this with a testy grunt. "And, second, because I know the real murderer."

"Who is somebody we've seen and talked to?"

"Oh yes; very much so."

"And have we got a chance of—?"

Dr. Fell, an absent, fierce, almost pitying expression on his red face, stared for some time at the desk.

"Yes, Lord help us all," he said, in a curious tone, "I suppose you've got to. In the meantime, I'm going home. . . ."

"Home?"

"To apply Gross's test," said Dr. Fell.

He turned away, but he did not immediately go. As the muddy light deepened to purple, and dust-coloured shadows swallowed up the room, he remained for a long time staring at the slashed picture which caught the last glow with its turbulent power, and the three coffins that were filled at last.

19
THE HOLLOW MAN

THAT NIGHT Dr. Fell shut himself up in the small cubbyhole off the library which was reserved for what he called his scientific experiments and what Mrs. Fell called "that horrible messing about." Now, a liking for messing about is one of the best of human traits, and Rampole and Dorothy both offered to assist. But the doctor was so serious, and so unwontedly troubled, that they left off with an uncomfortable feeling that to make a joke would be bad taste. The tireless Hadley had already gone off to check alibis. Rampole left the matter with only one question.

"I know you're going to try to read those burnt letters," he said, "and I know you think they're important. But what do you expect to find?"

"The worst possible thing," replied Dr. Fell. "The thing that last night could have made a fool of me."

And with a sleepy shake of his head he closed the door.

Rampole and Dorothy sat on opposite sides of the fireplace, looking at each other. The snow was whirling outside, and it was not a night to venture far. Rampole at first had an idea that he ought to invite Mangan out to dinner, to renew old times; but

Mangan, when he telephoned, said that obviously Rosette could not go, and he had better remain with her. So the other two, Mrs. Fell being at church, had the library to themselves for argument.

"Ever since last night," commented her husband, "I've been hearing about Gross's method for reading burnt letters. But nobody seems to know what it is. I suppose you mix chemicals or something?"

"I know what it is," she told him, with an air of triumph. "I looked it up while you people were dashing about this afternoon. And what's more, I bet you it won't work even if it is simple. I bet you *anything* it won't work!"

"You read Gross?"

"Well, I read it in English. It's simple enough. It says something like this. It says that anybody who has thrown letters on the fire will have noticed that the writing on the charred fragments stands out quite clearly, usually white or grey against a black background, but sometimes with the colours reversed. Did you ever notice that?"

"Can't say I have. But then I've seen very few open fires before I came to England. Is it true?"

She frowned. "It works with cardboard boxes that have printing on them, boxes of soap flakes or things like that. But regular writing. . . . Anyway, here's what you're supposed to do. You get a lot of transparent tracing-paper and pin it to a board with drawing-pins. As you pick up each of the charred pieces of paper you cover a place on the tracing-paper with gum, press the charred paper down on it. . . ."

"When it's crumpled up like that? It'll break, won't it?"

"Aha! That's the trick, Gross says. You have to soften the fragments. You arrange over and around the tracing-paper a frame two or three inches high, with all the bits under it. Then you stretch across a damp cloth folded several times. That puts the papers in a damp atmosphere, and they straighten out. When they're all flattened out and fixed, you cut out the tracing-paper round each separate fragment. Then you reconstruct them on a sheet of glass. Like a jig-saw puzzle. Afterwards you press a second sheet of glass over the first, and bind the edges, and look through both against the light. But I'll bet you anything you like—"

"We'll try it," said Rampole, impressed and afire with the idea.

The experiments at burning paper were not a complete success. First he got an old letter out of his pocket and touched a match to it. Despite his frantic manœuvring, it soared up into flame, twitched round, sailed out of his hand, and shrank to rest on the hearth as not more than two inches of shrivelled blackness rolled up like an umbrella. Though they got down on their knees and scrutinized it from every angle, no writing was visible. Rampole burnt several more pieces, which sailed apart like gentle skyrockets and powdered the hearth. Then he began to get mad and burn everything within reach. And, the madder he got, the more convinced he grew that the trick could be worked somehow if he did it properly. Typewriting was tried; he tapped out "Now is the time for all good men to come to the aid of the party" a number of times on Dr. Fell's machine and presently the carpet was littered with floating fragments.

"Besides," he argued, with his cheek against the floor and one eye closed as he studied them, "these aren't charred—they're burnt to hell. They're too far gone to fulfill the conditions. Aha! Got it! I can see 'party' as plain as day. It's much smaller than the actual typing; it seems to be indented on the black; but here it is. Have you got anything out of that handwritten letter?"

Her own excitement was growing as she made a discovery.

The words "East 11th Street" stood out in dirty grey letters. With some care, but much powdering of the brittle pieces, they at last deciphered plainly the words, "Saturday night," "ginch," "hangover," and "gin." Rampole got up with satisfaction.

"If those pieces can be straightened out by dampness, then it works!" he declared. "The only thing is whether you could get enough words out of any letter to make sense of it. Besides, we're only amateurs; Gross could get the whole thing. But what does Dr. Fell expect to find?"

This was the subject of an argument which was carried on far into the night.

"And with the case turned upside down," Rampole pointed out, "where do we go now for a motive? That's the crux of the whole business. There's no motive that could connect both Grimaud and Fley with the murderer! By the way, what's become of your wild theories last night, that the guilty person must be either Pettis or Burnaby?"

"Or the funny-faced blonde," she corrected, with a certain emphasis on the term. "I say, you know, what bothers me most is that overcoat changing colour and disappearing and all the rest of it. It seems to lead straight back to that house, or does it?" She brooded. "No, I've changed my mind altogether. I don't think Pettis or Burnaby can be implicated. I don't even think the blonde is. The possible murderer, I'm certain now, can be narrowed down to two other people."

"Well?"

"It's either Drayman or O'Rourke," she said, firmly, and nodded. "You mark my words."

Rampole stifled a strong protest. "Yes, I'd thought of O'Rourke," he admitted. "But you're picking him for just two reasons. First because he's a trapeze man, and you associate a flying escape of some sort with the way this thing was done. But, so far as I can see, it's impossible. Second and more important, you're picking him for the reason that he doesn't seem to have any connection with this case at all; that he's standing around for no good reason, and that's always a suspicious sign. Isn't that so?"

"Maybe."

"Then Drayman . . . yes, Drayman might have been the only one who could now be associated with both Grimaud and Fley in the past. That's a point! H'm. Also, nobody saw him during the whole evening from dinner time until a much later hour— eleven o'clock, anyhow. But I don't believe he's guilty. Tell you what: let's make a rough time-table of last night's events to get this thing straightened out. We'll put in everything, from before dinner on. It'll have to be a very rough time-table, with a lot of guessing on smaller points. We don't know much definitely except the time of the actual murders and a few statements leading up to them, but we can make a stab at it. Our times before dinner are vague too. But let's say . . ."

He took out an envelope and wrote rapidly.

(About) 6:45 Mangan arrives, hangs his coat in the hall closet, and sees a black overcoat hanging there.

(About) 6:48 (give her three minutes) Annie comes from the dining-room, switches off the light in the hall closet left burning by Mangan, and sees no overcoat at all.

(About) 6:55 (this is not specified, but we know it was before dinner), Mme Dumont looks into the hall closet and sees a yellow overcoat.

"I arrange it like that," said Rampole, "because presumably in the very brief time between Mangan's hanging up his own coat and going away with the light left on, Dumont didn't rush out to look in there before Annie came to turn the light off."

The girl's eyes narrowed. "Oo, wait! How do you know that? I mean, if the light wasn't on, how did she see a yellow coat at all?"

There was a pause while they looked at each other. Rampole said:

"This is getting interesting. And, if it comes to that, why did she look in there, anyhow? The point is this: If the sequence of times can be established at what I've written, that's reasonable. First, there's a black coat, which Mangan sees. Well, then somebody swipes the black coat just after Mangan goes—for what reason we don't know—and Annie sees nothing. Later the coat is replaced with a light tweed one. That sounds all right. *But,*" he cried, stabbing out with his pencil, "if it worked the other way around, then either somebody is lying or the whole thing is impossible. In that case it doesn't matter what time Mangan arrived, because the whole business must have taken place in a matter of minutes or even seconds. See it? Boyd gets there, hangs his coat up, and walks away. Out comes Dumont, looks in, and walks away. Along comes Annie immediately afterwards, turns out the light, and *she* goes. In that short flash a black overcoat has first turned yellow and then disappeared. Which is impossible."

"Well done!" said the other, beaming. "Then which one was lying? I suppose you'll insist it wasn't your friend—"

"I certainly will. It's the Dumont woman, I'll bet you anything you like!"

"But she's not guilty. That's been proved. Besides, I like her."

"Don't mix me up, now," Rampole urged. "Let's go on with this time-table and see if we can discover anything else. Haa! Where were we? Yes. Dinner we'll put at seven o'clock, because we know it was over at seven-thirty. Hence—

"7:30 Rosette G. and Mangan go to drawing-room.

7:30 Drayman goes upstairs to his room.

7:30 E. Dumont—where she goes is not known, except that she remains in the house.

7:30 Mills goes to downstairs library.

7:30 Grimaud joins Mills in downstairs library, tells him to come upstairs about 9:30, since he expects a visitor then.

"Whoa! Here's a snag. I was just going to write that then Grimaud goes on to the drawing-room, and tells Mangan the visitor is expected at ten o'clock. But that won't do, because Rosette knew nothing about it, and yet she was with Mangan! The trouble is, Boyd didn't say exactly when he was told that. But it isn't important—Grimaud might have taken him aside or something like that. Similarly, we don't know when Madame Dumont was told to expect the visitor at nine-thirty; probably earlier. It amounts to the same thing."

"Are you sure it does?" enquired Dorothy, searching after cigarettes. "H'm! Well, carry on."

"(About) 7:35 Grimaud goes up to his study.

7:35 to 9:30 no developments. Nobody moves. Heavy snow.

(About) 9:30 snow stops.

(About) 9:30 E. Dumont collects coffee-tray from Grimaud's study. Grimaud remarks that visitor will probably not come that night. E. Dumont leaves study just as—

9:30 Mills comes upstairs.

"I don't think anything noticeable happened in the next interval. Mills was upstairs, Drayman in his room, and Rosette and

Boyd in the front room with the radio on. . . . Wait! I'm forgetting something. A little while before the door-bell rang, Rosette heard a thud from somewhere out in the street, as though somebody had fallen off a high place. . . ."

"How did she hear that if they had the radio on?"

"Apparently it wasn't playing loudly enough to— Yes, it was, though. It made such a racket they could hardly hear the fake 'Pettis's' voice. But put that in order:

"9:45 Door-bell rings.

9:45 to 9:50 E. Dumont goes to answer door; speaks to visitor (failing to recognize voice). She receives card, shuts the door on him, examines card and finds it blank, hesitates, and starts upstairs. . . .

9:45 to 9:50. Visitor, after E. D. has started upstairs, gets inside somehow, locks Rosette G. and Boyd M. in front room, answers their hail by imitating the voice of Pettis—"

"I don't like to keep on interrupting you," cut in Dorothy. "But doesn't it seem to have taken them a terribly long time to sing out and ask who the caller was? I mean, would anybody wait so long? If I were expecting a visitor like that, I know I should have piped up, 'Hullo! who is it?' as soon as I heard the door open."

"What are you trying to prove? Nothing? Sure of that? Don't be so hard on the blonde! It was some time before they expected anybody, remember—and that sniff of yours indicates prejudice. Let's continue, with the still inclusive times of nine forty-five to nine-fifty, the interval between the moment X entered the house and the moment he entered Grimaud's study:

"9:45 to 9:50. Visitor follows E. Dumont upstairs, overtakes her in upper hall. He takes off cap and pulls down coat collar, but does not remove mask. Grimaud comes to the door, but does not recognize visitor. Visitor leaps inside and door is slammed. (This is attested by both E. Dumont and S. Mills.)

9:50 to 10:10. Mills watches door from end of hall; Dumont watches same door from staircase landing.

10:10 Shot is fired.

10:10 to 10:12. Mangan in front room finds door to hall locked, on the inside.

10:10 to 10:12. E. Dumont faints or is sick, and gets to her room. (N. B. Drayman, asleep in his room, does not hear shot.)

10:10 to 10:12. Mangan in front room finds door to hall locked, attempts to break it and fails. He then jumps out window, just as—

10:12 We arrive outside; front door unlocked; we go up to study.

10:12 to 10:15. Door is opened with pliers, Grimaud found shot.

10:15 to 10:20. Investigation, ambulance sent for.

10:20 Ambulance arrives. Grimaud removed. Rosette goes with him in ambulance. Boyd M., at orders from Hadley, goes down stairs to telephone police.

"Which," Rampole pointed out with some satisfaction, "absolutely clears both Rosette and Boyd. I don't even need to set down minute times there. The ambulance-men coming upstairs, the doctor's examination, the body taken down to the ambulance—all that in itself would have taken at least five minutes if they'd moved fast enough to slide down the banisters with that stretcher. By God! it's as plain as print when you write it out! It would have taken a good deal longer before they could get to the nursing-home . . . and yet Fley was shot in Cagliostro Street at just ten twenty-five! Now, Rosette did ride over with the ambulance. Boyd was in the house when the ambulance-men arrived, because he came upstairs with them and went down after them. There's a fairly perfect alibi."

"Oh, you don't need to think I'm so anxious to convict them!—especially Boyd, who's rather nice what little I've seen of him." She frowned. "That's always granting your guess that the ambulance didn't arrive at Grimaud's before ten-twenty."

Rampole shrugged. "If it did," he pointed out, "then it flew over from Guilford Street. It wasn't sent for before ten-fifteen, and even so it's something like a miracle that they had it at Grimaud's in five minutes. No, Boyd and Rosette are out of it. Besides, now that I remember, she was at the nursing-home—in the presence of witnesses—when she saw the light in the window of Burnaby's flat at ten-thirty. Let's put the rest into the record and exonerate anyone else we can.

"10:20 to 10:25. Arrival and departure of ambulance with Grimaud.

10:25 Fley shot in Cagliostro Street.

10:20 to (at least) 10:30. Stuart Mills remains with us in study, answering questions.

10:25 Madame Dumont comes into study.

10:30 Rosette, at nursing-home, sees a light in the window of Burnaby's flat.

10:25 to 10:40. Madame Dumont remains with us in the study.

10:40 Rosette returns from nursing-home.

10:40 Arrival of police at Hadley's call."

Rampole, sitting back to run his eye down the scrawl, drew a long flourish under the last item.

"That not only completes our time-table as far as we need to go," he said, "but it unquestionably adds two more to our list of innocents. Mills and Dumont are out. Rosette and Boyd are out. Which accounts for everybody in the house except Drayman."

"But," protested Dorothy, after a pause, "it's getting even worse tangled up. What happens to your brilliant inspiration about the overcoat? You suggested somebody was lying. It could only have been either Boyd Mangan or Ernestine Dumont; and both are exonerated. Unless that girl Annie— But that won't do, will it? Or it shouldn't."

Again they looked at each other. Wryly he folded up his list and put it into his pocket. Outside, the night wind whirled by in a long blast, and they could hear Dr. Fell blundering round his cubbyhole behind the closed door.

Rampole overslept the next morning, partly from exhaustion and partly because the following day was so overcast that he did not open his eyes until past ten o'clock. It was not only so dark that the lights were on, but a day of numbing cold. He had not seen Dr. Fell again last night, and, when he went downstairs to breakfast in the little back dining-room, the maid was indignant as she set out bacon and eggs.

"The doctor's just gone up to have a wash, sir," Vida informed him. "He was up all night on them scientific things, and I found him asleep in the chair in there at eight o'clock this morning. I don't know what Mrs. Fell will say, indeed I don't. Superintendent Hadley's just got here, too. He's in the library."

Hadley, who was impatiently knocking his heels against the fender as though he were pawing the floor, asked for news with some eagerness.

"Have you seen Fell?" he demanded. "Did he go after those letters? And if so—?"

Rampole explained. "Any news from you?"

"Yes, and important news. Both Pettis and Burnaby are out. They've got cast-iron alibis."

Wind whooped past along Adelphi Terrace, and the long window-frames rattled. Hadley continued to paw the hearth rug. He went on: "I saw Burnaby's three card-playing friends last night. One, by the way, is an Old Bailey judge; it'd be pretty difficult to drag a man into court when the judge on the bench can testify to his innocence. Burnaby was playing poker on Saturday night from eight o'clock to nearly half-past eleven.—And this morning Betts has been round to the theatre where Pettis said he saw the play that night. Well, he did. One of the bar-attendants at the theatre knows him quite well by sight. It seems that the second act of the show ends at five minutes past ten. A few minutes afterwards, during the interval, this attendant is willing to swear he served Pettis with a whisky-and-soda in the bar. In other words, he was having a drink at just about the exact moment Grimaud was shot nearly a mile away."

"I expected something like that," said Rampole, after a silence. "And yet, to hear it confirmed. . . . I wish you'd look at this."

He handed over the time-table he had made last night. Hadley glanced over it.

"Oh yes. I sketched out one of my own. This is fairly sound; especially the point about the girl and Mangan, although we can't swear too closely to time in that respect. But I think it would hold." He tapped the envelope against his palm. "Narrows it down, I admit. We'll have another go at Drayman. I phoned the house this morning. Everybody was a bit hysterical because they've brought the old man's body back to the house, and I couldn't get much out of Rosette except that Drayman was still only half-conscious and under morphia. We—"

He stopped as they heard the familiar, lumbering step with the tap of the cane, which seemed to have hesitated just outside the door as though at Hadley's words. Then Dr. Fell pushed open the door. There was no twinkle in his eye when he wheezed in. He seemed a part of the heavy morning, and a sense of doom pervading that leaden air.

"Well?" prompted Hadley. "Did you find out what you wanted to know from those papers?"

Dr. Fell fumbled after, found, and lit his black pipe. Before he answered he waddled over to toss the match into the fire. Then he chuckled at last, but very wryly.

"Yes, I found out what I wanted to know.—Hadley, twice in my theories on Saturday night I unintentionally led you wrong. So wrong, with such a monstrous and dizzying stupidity, that if I hadn't saved my self-respect by seeing the truth of this thing yesterday, I should have deserved the last punishment reserved for fools. Still, mine wasn't the only blunder. Chance and circumstance made an even worse blunder, and they've combined to make a terrifying, inexplicable puzzle out of what is really only a commonplace and ugly and petty murder-case. Oh, there was shrewdness to the murderer; I admit that. But—yes, I've found out what I wanted to know."

"Well? What about the writing on those papers? What was on those papers?"

"Nothing," said Dr. Fell.

There was something eerie in the slow, heavy way he spoke the word.

"You mean," cried Hadley, "that the experiment didn't work?"

"No, I mean that the experiment did work. I mean that there was *nothing* on those papers," boomed Dr. Fell. "Not so much as a single line or scrap or shred of handwriting, not so much as a whisper or pothook of the deadly secrets I told you on Saturday night we might find. That's what I mean. Except—well, yes. There were a few bits of heavier paper, rather like thick cardboard, with one or two letters printed there."

"But why burn letters unless—?"

"Because they weren't letters. That's just it; that's where we went wrong. Don't you see even yet what they were? . . . Well, Hadley, we'd better finish this up and get the whole mess off our minds. You want to meet the Invisible Murderer, do you? You want to meet the damned ghoul and hollow man who's been walking through our dreams? Very well; I'll introduce you. Got your car? Then come along. *I'm going to see if I can't extract a confession.*"

"From—?"

"From somebody at Grimaud's house. Come on."

Rampole saw the end looming, and was afraid of it, without an idea in his whirling head as to what it might be. Hadley had to spin a half-frozen engine before the car would start. They were caught in several traffic blocks on the way up, but Hadley did not even curse. And the quietest of all was Dr. Fell.

All the blinds were drawn on the house in Russell Square. It looked even more dead than yesterday, because death had come inside. And it was so quiet that even from outside they could hear the ringing of the bell when Dr. Fell pressed it. After a long interval Annie, without her cap or apron, answered it. She looked pale and strained, but still calm.

"We should like to see Madame Dumont," said Dr. Fell.

Hadley jerked his head round to look, even though he remained impassive. Annie seemed to speak out of the darkness in the hall as she moved back.

"She is in with the—she's in there," the girl answered, and pointed towards the drawing-room door. "I'll call—" She swallowed.

Dr. Fell shook his head. He moved over with surprising quietness and softly opened the drawing-room door.

The dull brown blinds were drawn, and the thick lace curtains muffled what little light filtered through. Although the room looked vaster, its furniture was lost in shadow; except for one piece of furniture, of gleaming black metal lined with white satin. It was an open coffin. Thin candles were burning around it. Of the dead face Rampole afterwards remembered that from where he stood he could see only the tip of a nose. But those candles alone, or the faint thickness of flowers and incense in the air, moved the scene weirdly from dun London to some place of crags and blasts among the Hungarian mountains: where the gold cross loomed guard against devils, and garlic wreaths kept off the prowling vampire.

Yet this was not the thing they first noticed. Ernestine Dumont stood beside the coffin, one hand gripping its edge. The high, thin candle-light above turned her greying hair to gold; it softened and subdued even the crumpled posture of her bent shoulders. When she turned her head slowly round, they saw that her eyes were sunken and smeared—though she still could not weep. Her breast heaved jerkily. Yet round her shoulders she

had wound a gay, heavy, long-fringed yellow shawl, with red bro-
cade and bead embroidery that burnt with a shifting glitter under the light. It was the last touch of the barbaric.

And then she saw them. Both hands suddenly gripped the
edge of the coffin, as though she would shield the dead. She remained a silhouette, one hand outspread on either side, under
the unsteady candles.

"It will do you good, madame, to confess," said Dr. Fell, very
gently. "Believe me, it will do you good."

For a second Rampole thought she had stopped breathing,
so easy was every motion to follow in the unearthliness of that
light. Then she made a sound as though she were half-coughing,
which is only grief before it becomes hysterical mirth.

"Confess?" she said. "So that is what you think, all you fools?
Well, I do not care. Confess! Confess to murder?"

"No," said Dr. Fell.

His voice, in that one quiet monosyllable, had a heavy note
across the room. And now she stared at him, and now for the
first time she began to stare with fright as he moved across towards her.

"No," said Dr. Fell. "You are not the murderer. Let me tell you
what you are."

Now he towered over her, black against the candle-light, but
he still spoke gently.

"Yesterday, you see, a man named O'Rourke told us several
things. Among them was the fact that most illusions either on
or off the stage are worked with the aid of a confederate. This
was no exception. You were the confederate of the illusionist and
murderer."

"The hollow man," said Ernestine Dumont, and suddenly began to laugh hysterically.

"The hollow man," said Dr. Fell, and turned quietly to Hadley, "in a real sense. The hollow man whose naming was a terrible and an ironic jest, even if we did not know it, because it was the exact truth. That is the horror and in a way the shame. Do you want to see the murderer you have been hunting all through this case?—The murderer lies *there*," said Dr. Fell, "but God forbid that we should judge him now."

And with a slow gesture he pointed to the white, dead, tight-lipped face of Dr. Charles Grimaud.

20
THE TWO BULLETS

DR. FELL continued to look steadily at the woman, who had again shrunk against the side of the coffin as though to defend it.

"Ma'am," he went on, "the man you loved is dead. He is beyond the reach of the law now, and, whatever he has done, he has paid for it. Our immediate problem, yours and mine, is to hush this thing up so that the living may not be hurt. But, you see, you are implicated, even though you took no actual hand in the murder. Believe me, ma'am, if I could have explained the whole thing without bringing you into it at all, I should have done so. I know you have suffered. But you will see for yourself that such a course was impossible if I were to explain the entire problem. So we must persuade Superintendent Hadley that this affair must be hushed up."

Something in his voice, something of the unweary, unchanging, limitless compassion that was Gideon Fell, seemed to touch her as gently as sleep after tears. Her hysteria had gone.

"Do you know?" she asked him, after a pause, and almost eagerly. "Do not fool me! Do you really know?"

"Yes, I really know."

"Go upstairs. Go to *his* room," she said in a dull voice, "and I will join you presently. I—I cannot face you just now. I must think, and— But please do not speak to anybody until I come. Please! No, I will not run away."

Dr. Fell's fierce gesture silenced Hadley as they went out. Still in silence they tramped up the gloomy stairs to the top floor. They passed no one, they saw no one. Once more they came into the study, where it was so dark that Hadley switched on the mosaic lamp at the desk. After he had made sure the door was closed, Hadley turned round rather wildly.

"Are you trying to tell me that Grimaud killed Fley?" he demanded.

"Yes."

"While he was lying unconscious and dying under the eyes of witnesses in a nursing-home, he went to Cagliostro Street and—!"

"Not then," said Dr. Fell quietly. "You see, that's what you don't understand. That's what's led you wrong. That's what I meant by saying that the case had been turned not upside down, but *the wrong way round.* Fley was killed before Grimaud. And, worst of all, Grimaud was trying to tell us the exact, literal truth. He did tell us the exact truth, when he knew he was dying beyond hope—it's one of the good gleams in him—but we chose to misinterpret it. Sit down, and I'll see if I can explain it. Once you have grasped the three essential points, you will need no deduction and very little elucidation from me. The thing will explain itself."

He lowered himself, wheezing, into the chair behind the desk. For a little time he remained staring vacantly at the lamp. Then he went on:

"The three essential points, then, are these. (1) There is no brother Henri; there are only two brothers. (2) Both these broth-ers were speaking the truth. (3) A question of time has turned the case wrong way round.

"Many things in this case have turned on a matter of brief spaces of time, and how brief they are. It's a part of the same irony which described our murderer as the hollow man that the crux of the case should be a matter of mistaken time. You can easily spot it if you think back.

"Now remember yesterday morning! I already had some oc-casion to believe there was something queer about that business in Cagliostro Street. The shooting there, we were told by three (truthful) witnesses who agreed precisely and to a second, took place at just ten twenty-five. I wondered, in an idle sort of way, why they corroborated each other with such startling exactitude. In the case of the usual street accident, even the most cool wit-nesses don't usually take such notice, or are careful to consult their watches, or (even if they do) agree about the time with such uncanny precision. But they were truthful people, and there must have been some reason for their exactitude. The time must have been thrust on them.

"Of course there was a reason. Just across from where the murdered man fell there was a lighted show-window—the only lighted window thereabouts—of a jeweller's shop. It was the most noticeable thing in the foreground. It illuminated the mur-dered man; it was the first place to which the constable rushed in search of the murderer; it quite naturally focussed their at-tention. And, facing them from that window, there was an enor-mous clock of such unusual design that it immediately took the eye. It was inevitable that the constable should look for the time, and natural that the others should also. Hence their agreement.

"But one thing, not apparently important at that time, both-

ered me a little. After Grimaud was shot, Hadley summoned his
men to this house, and instantly dispatched one of them to pick
up Fley as a suspect. Now, then, those men arrived here . . . about
what time?"

"About ten-forty," said Rampole, "according to a rough calcu-
lation. I've got it in my time-table."

"And," said Dr. Fell, "a man was sent immediately to get Fley.
This man must have arrived in Cagliostro Street—when? Between fifteen and twenty minutes after Fley was presumed to
have been killed. But in the space of that brief time what has
happened? An incredible number of things! Fley has been carried down to the doctor's house, he has died, an examination has
been made, a fruitless effort undertaken to identify Fley; and
then, 'after some delay' in the words of the newspaper account,
the van is sent for and Fley removed to the mortuary. All this!
For, when Hadley's detective arrived in Cagliostro Street to pick
up Fley, he found the whole business finished—and the constable back making inquiries from door to door. The entire excitement had died down. Which seemed incredible.

"Unfortunately, I was so dense that I didn't see the signifi-
cance of this even yesterday morning when I saw the clock in the
jeweller's window.

"Think back once more. Yesterday morning we had breakfast at my house; Pettis dropped in, and we talked to him—until
what time?"

There was a pause.

"Until exactly ten o'clock," Hadley answered, suddenly, and
snapped his fingers. "Yes! I remember, because Big Ben was
striking just as he got up to go."

"Quite right. He left us, and afterwards we put on our hats
and coats and drove *straight* to Cagliostro Street. Now, allow any

reasonable margin of time you like for our putting on our hats, going downstairs, driving a short distance on deserted roads Sunday morning—a drive that took us only ten minutes when there was Saturday-night traffic. I think you'll say the whole process can hardly have taken twenty minutes in all. . . . But in Cagliostro Street you showed me the jeweller's shop, and that fancy clock was just striking *eleven.*

"Even then in my musing density it never occurred to me to look at that clock and wonder, just as in their excitement it never occurred to the three witnesses last night. Just afterwards, you recall, Somers and O'Rourke summoned us up to Burnaby's flat. We made quite a long investigation, and then had a talk with O'Rourke. And while O'Rourke was speaking, I noticed that the earlier dead quiet of the day—the quiet when in the street we heard only the wind—had a new sound. I heard church bells.

"Well, what time *do* church bells begin to ring? Not after eleven o'clock; the service has begun. Usually before eleven, for a preparatory bell. But, if I accepted the evidence of that German clock, it must then be a very long time past eleven o'clock. Then my dull mind woke up. I remembered Big Ben and our drive to Cagliostro Street. The combination of those bells and Big Ben— against (hem!) a trumpery foreign clock. Church and State, so to speak, couldn't both be wrong. . . . In other words, *the clock in that jeweller's window was more than forty minutes fast. Hence the shooting in Cagliostro Street the night before could not have taken place at twenty-five minutes past ten. Actually it must have taken place a short time previous to a quarter to ten. Say, roughly, at nine-forty.*

"Now, sooner or later somebody would have noticed this; maybe somebody has noticed it already. A thing like that would be bound to come out in a coroner's court. Somebody would come forward to dispute the right time. Whether you'd have instantly seen the truth then (as I hope), or whether it would have confused you even more, I don't know. . . . But the solid fact remains that the affair in Cagliostro Street took place some minutes before the man in the false face rang the bell of this house at nine forty-five."

"But I still don't see—!" protested Hadley.

"The impossible situation? No; but I have a clear course now to tell you the whole story from the beginning."

"Yes, but let me get this straightened out. If Grimaud, as you say, shot Fley in Cagliostro Street just before nine forty-five—"

"I didn't say that," said Dr. Fell.

"*What?*"

"You'll understand if you follow my patient elucidation from the beginning. On Wednesday night of last week—when Fley first appeared out of the past, apparently out of his grave, to confront his brother with rather a terrible threat at the Warwick Tavern—Grimaud resolved to kill him. In the whole case, you see, Grimaud was the only person with a motive for killing Fley. And, my God! Hadley, but he did have a motive! He was safe, he was rich, he was respected; the past was buried. And then, all of a sudden, a door blows open to admit this thin grinning stranger who is his brother Pierre. Grimaud, in escaping from prison, had murdered one of his brothers by leaving him buried alive; he would have murdered the other except for an accident. He could still be extradited and hanged—and Pierre Fley had traced him.

"Now, bear in mind exactly what Fley said when he suddenly flew in to confront Grimaud that night at the tavern. Study *why* he said and did certain things, and you will see that even shaky-minded Fley was very far from being as mad as he liked to pretend. Why, if he were intent merely on private vengeance, did he choose to confront Grimaud in the presence of a circle of friends and speak in just the innuendoes he used? He used his *dead* brother as a threat; and it was the only time he did speak of that *dead* brother. Why did he say, 'He can be much more dangerous to you than I can'? Because the dead brother could hang Grimaud! Why did he say, 'I don't want your life; he does'? Why did he say, 'Shall I have him call on you'? And then why, just afterwards, did he hand Grimaud his card on which his own address was carefully written? The giving of that card, combined with his words and later actions, is significant. What Fley really meant, veiled so that he could throw a scare into Grimaud before witnesses, was just this: 'You, my brother, are fat and rich on the proceeds of a robbery we both committed when we were young. I am poor—and I hate my work. Now will you come and call on me at my address, so that we can arrange this matter, or shall I set the police on you?'"

"Blackmail," said Hadley, softly.

"Yes. Fley had a bee in his bonnet, but Fley was far from being a fool. Now mark how he twisted round his meaning in his last threatening words to Grimaud. 'I also am in danger when I associate with my brother, but I am prepared to run that risk.' And in that case, as always afterwards, he was referring in strict truth to *Grimaud*. 'You, my brother, might also kill me as you killed the other, but I will risk it. So shall I call on you amiably, or will my other dead brother come to hang you?'

"For think of his behaviour afterwards, on the night of his murder. Remember the glee he had of smashing up and getting rid of his illusion-properties? And what words did he use to O'Rourke? Words which, if you look at them squarely in the light of what we now know, can have only one explanation. He said:

" 'I shall not need them again. My work is finished. Didn't I tell you? I am going to see my brother. He will do something that will settle an old affair for both of us.'

"Meaning, of course, that Grimaud had agreed to come to terms. Fley meant that he was leaving his old life for good; going back to his grave as a dead man with plenty of money; but he couldn't be more specific without blowing the gaff. Still, he knew that his brother was tricky; he'd had good reason in the past to know it. He couldn't leave behind him a big warning when he spoke with O'Rourke, in case Grimaud really meant to pay; but he threw out a hint:

" 'In case anything happens to me, you will find my brother in the same street where I myself live. That is not where he really resides, but he has a room there.'

"I'll explain that last statement in just a moment. But go back to Grimaud. Now, Grimaud never had any intention of coming to terms with Fley. Fley was going to die. That wily, shrewd, theatrical mind of Grimaud's (who, as you know, was more interested in magical illusions than anybody else we have met) was determined not to suffer any nonsense from this inconvenient brother of his. Fley must die—but this was more difficult than it looked.

"If Fley had come to him in private, without anybody in the world ever being able to associate Fley's name with his, it would have been simple. But Fley had been too shrewd for that. He had blazoned forth his own name and address, and hinted at mysterious secrets concerning Grimaud, before a group of Grimaud's friends. Awkward! Now if Fley is found obviously murdered, somebody is likely to say, 'Hullo! Isn't that the same chap who—?' And then presently there may be dangerous enquiries; because Lord knows what Fley may have told *other* people about Grimaud. The only thing he isn't likely to have confided to somebody else is his last deadly hold over Grimaud; and that is the thing about which he must be silenced. Whatever happens to Fley, however he dies, there are likely to be enquiries concerning Grimaud. The only thing to do is frankly to pretend that Fley is after his life; to send himself threatening letters (not too obviously); to stir up the household in an ingenious way; finally, to inform everybody that Fley has threatened to call on him on the night he himself intends to call on Fley. You will see very shortly just how he planned to work out a very brilliant murder.

"The effect he intended to produce was this: The murderous Fley should be seen calling on him on Saturday night. There should be witnesses to this. The two should be together alone when Fley goes into his study. A row is heard, the sound of a fight, a shot, and a fall. The door being opened, Grimaud should be found alone—a nasty-looking but superficial wound from a bullet scratched along his side. No weapon is there. Out of the window hangs a rope belonging to Fley, by which Fley is assumed to have escaped. (Remember, it had been predicted that there would be *no* snow that night, so it would have been impossible to trace footprints.) Grimaud says: 'He thought he killed me; I pretended to be dead; and he escaped. No, don't set the police on him, poor devil. I'm not hurt.'—And the next morning Fley would have been found dead in his own room. He would have been found, a suicide, having pressed his own gun against his chest and pulled the trigger. The gun is beside him. A suicide note lies on the table. In despair at thinking he has killed Grimaud, he has shot himself. . . . That, gentlemen, was the illusion Grimaud intended to produce."

"But how did he do it?" demanded Hadley. "And, anyway, it didn't turn out like that!"

"No. You see, the plan miscarried badly. The latter part of the illusion of Fley calling on him in his study when actually Fley would already have been dead in the Cagliostro Street house— I'll deal with in its proper place. Grimaud, with the aid of Madame Dumont, had already made certain preparations.

"He had told Fley to meet him at Fley's room on the top floor over the tobacconist's. He had told Fley to meet him there at nine o'clock on the Saturday night, for a cash settlement. (You recall that Fley, gleefully throwing up his job and burning his properties, left the theatre in Limehouse at about eight-fifteen.)

"Grimaud had chosen Saturday night because that night, by inviolable custom, he remained alone all evening in his study without anyone being allowed to disturb him for any reason whatsoever. He chose that night because he needed to use the areaway door, and go and come by way of the basement; and Saturday night was the night out for Annie, who had her quarters there. You'll remember that, after he went up to his study at seven-thirty, nobody *did* see him until, according to the evidence, he opened the study door to admit the visitor at nine-fifty. Madame Dumont claimed to have spoken to him in the study at nine-thirty, when she gathered up the coffee things. I'll tell you shortly why I disbelieved that statement—the fact is, he was not in the study at all: he was in Cagliostro Street. Madame Dumont had been told to lurk round the study door at nine-thirty, and to come out for some excuse. Why? Because Grimaud had ordered Mills to come upstairs at nine-thirty, you see, and watch the study door from the room down the hall. Mills was to be the dupe of the illusion Grimaud meant to work. But if—as he came upstairs near the study door—Mills had for any reason taken it into his head to try to speak with Grimaud, or see him, Dumont was there to head him off. Dumont was to wait in the archway, and keep Mills away from that door if he showed any curiosity.

"Mills was chosen as the dupe of the illusion: why? Because, although he was so meticulously conscientious that he would carry out his instructions to the tick, he was so afraid of 'Fley' that he would not interfere when the hollow man came stalking up those stairs. It was not only that he must not attack the man in the false face in those dangerous few moments before the man got into the study (as, for instance, Mangan or even Drayman might have done), but also that he must not even venture out of his room. He had been told to stay in that room, and he would. Finally, he had been chosen because he was a very short man, a fact which will presently became clear.

"Now, he was told to go upstairs and watch at nine-thirty. This was because the hollow man was timed to make his appearance only a little afterwards; although, in fact, the hollow man was late. Mark one discrepancy. Mills was told nine-thirty—but Mangan was told ten o'clock! The reason is obvious. There was to be somebody downstairs to testify that a visitor had really arrived by the front door, confirming Dumont. But Mangan might be inclined towards curiosity about this visitor; he might be inclined to challenge the hollow man . . . unless he had first been jokingly told by Grimaud that the visitor would probably not arrive at all, or, if he did arrive, it could not possibly be before ten o'clock. All that was necessary was to throw his mind off, and make him hesitate long enough, for the hollow man to get upstairs past that dangerous door. And, if the worst came to the worst, Mangan and Rosette could always be locked in.

"For everybody else: Annie was out, Drayman had been supplied with a ticket to a concert, Burnaby was unquestionably playing cards, and Pettis at the theatre. The field was clear.

"At some time before nine o'clock (probably about ten minutes) Grimaud slipped out of the house, using the area door up to the street. Trouble had already started. It had been snowing heavily for some time, contrary to rules. But Grimaud did not regard it as serious trouble. He believed he could do the business and return by half-past nine, and that it would still be snowing heavily enough to gloss over any footprints that he would make, and cause no comment on the absence of any footprints the visitor later *should* have made when the visitor would be supposed to have swung down from his window. In any case, his plans had been carried too far for him to back out.

"When he left the house he was carrying an old and untraceable Colt revolver, loaded with just two bullets. The sort of hat he wore I don't know, but his overcoat was a light yellow, glaring tweed with chicken-pox spots. He bought this coat several sizes too large. He bought it because it was the sort of coat he had never been known to wear and because nobody would recognize him in it if he were to be seen. He—"

Hadley intervened.

"Stop a bit! What about that business of the overcoats changing colour? That would come earlier in the evening. What had happened there?"

"Again I've got to ask you to wait until we get to the last illusion he worked; that's a part of it.

"Well, Grimaud's purpose was to call on Fley. There he would speak with Fley amiably for a time. He would say something like: 'You must leave this hovel, brother! You will be comfortably off now; I will see to that. Why not leave these useless possessions behind and come to my house? Let your landlord have the damned things in place of notice!"—Any sort of speech, you see, the purpose being to make Fley write one of his ambiguous notes for the landlord. 'I am leaving for good.' 'I am going back to my grave.' Anything *that could be understood as a suicide note when Fley was found dead with a gun in his hand.*"

Dr. Fell leaned forward. "And then Grimaud would take out his Colt, jam it against Fley's chest, and smilingly pull the trigger.

"It was the top floor of an empty house. As you have seen, the walls are astonishingly thick and solid. The landlord lived far down in the basement, and was the most incurious man in Cagliostro Street. No shot, especially a muffled shot with the gun held against Fley, could have been heard. It might be some time before the body was discovered; it would certainly not be before morning. And in the meantime, what will Grimaud do? After killing Fley he will turn the same gun on himself to give himself a slight wound, even if he has to imbed the bullet—he had, as we know from that little episode of the three coffins years before, the constitution of an ox and the nerve of hell. Then he would leave the gun lying beside Fley. He would quite coolly clap a handkerchief or cotton wool across this wound, which must be *inside* the coat and across the shirt; bind it with adhesive tape until the time came to rip it open—and go back home to work his illusion, which should prove that Fley came to see him. That Fley shot him, and then returned to Cagliostro Street and used the same gun for suicide, no coroner's jury would afterwards doubt. Do I make it clear so far? It was crime turned the wrong way round.

"That, as I say, was what Grimaud *intended* to do. Had he performed it as he intended, it would have been an ingenious murder; and I doubt whether we should ever have questioned Fley's suicide.

"Now, there was only one difficulty about accomplishing this plan. If anybody—not anybody recognizable as himself, but anybody at all—were seen visiting Fley's house, the fat would be in the fire. It might not appear so easily as suicide. There was only one entrance from the street—the door beside the tobacconist's. And he was wearing a conspicuous coat, in which he had reconnoitred the ground before. (By the way, Dolberman, the tobacconist, had seen him hanging about previously.) He found the solution of his difficulty in Burnaby's secret flat.

"You see, of course, that Grimaud was the likeliest person of all to have known of Burnaby's flat in Cagliostro Street? Burnaby himself told us that, some months before when Grimaud suspected him of having an ulterior motive in painting that picture, Grimaud had not only questioned him—he had *watched* him. From a man who was in such fancied danger, it would have been real watching. He knew of the flat. He knew from spying that Rosette had a key. And so, when the time came and the idea occurred to him, he stole Rosette's key.

"The house in which Burnaby had his flat was on the same side of the street as the house where Fley lived. All those houses are built side by side, with flat roofs; so that you have only to step over a low dividing wall to walk on the roofs from one end of the street to the other. Both men, remember, lived on the top floor. You recall what we saw when we went up to look at Burnaby's flat—just beside the door to the flat?"

Hadley nodded. "Yes, of course. A short ladder going to a trap-door in the roof."

"Exactly. And, on the landing just outside Fley's room, there is a low skylight also communicating with the roof. Grimaud had only to go to Cagliostro Street by the back way, never appearing in the street itself, but going up the alley which we saw from Burnaby's window. He came in the back door (as we saw Burnaby and Rosette do later), he went up to the top floor and thence to the roof. Then he followed the roofs to Fley's lodgings, descended from the skylight to the landing, and could both enter and leave the place without a soul seeing him. Moreover, he knew absolutely that that night Burnaby would be playing cards elsewhere.

"And then everything went wrong.

"He must have got to Fley's lodgings before Fley arrived there himself; it wouldn't do to make Fley suspicious by being seen coming from the roof. But we know that Fley had some suspicions already. This may have been caused by Grimaud's request for Fley to bring along one of his long conjuring-ropes. . . . Grimaud wanted that rope as a piece of evidence to use later against Fley. Or it may have been caused by Fley's knowledge that Grimaud had been hanging about in Cagliostro Street for the past couple of days; possibly seeing him duck across the roofs towards Burnaby's after one reconnoitering, and thereby making Fley believe he had taken a room in the street.

"The two brothers met in that gaslit room at nine. What they talked about we don't know. We may never know. But evidently Grimaud lulled Fley's suspicions; they became pleasant and amiable and forgot old scores; Grimaud jocularly persuaded him to write that note for the landlord. Then—"

"I'm not disputing all this," said Hadley, quietly, "but how do you happen to know it?"

"Grimaud told us," said Dr. Fell. Hadley stared.

"Oh yes. Once I had tumbled to that terrible mistake in times, I could understand. You'll see. But to continue:

"Fley had written his note. He had got into his hat and coat for departure—because Grimaud wished it to be assumed that he had killed himself just after having returned from a journey *outdoors:* his return from the phantom visit to Grimaud, in other words. They were all ready to go. And then Grimaud leaped.

"Whether Fley was subconsciously on his guard; whether he twitched round to run for the door, since he was no match for the powerful Grimaud; whether it happened in the twisting and scuffle—this we do not know. But Grimaud, with the gun against Fley's coat as Fley wrenched round from him, made a hellish mistake. He fired. And he put the bullet in the wrong place. Instead of getting his victim through the heart, he got him under the left shoulder blade: a wound of almost the same sort, although at the back, as the one from which Grimaud later died himself. It was a fatal wound, but far from instantly fatal. The poetic ironies were working to kill these brothers, with interchangeable methods, in precisely the same way.

"Of course Fley went down. He could do nothing else; and it was the wisest course, or Grimaud might have finished him. But Grimaud, for a second, must have lost his nerve in sheer terror. This might have wrecked his whole plan. *Could* a man shoot himself in that spot? If not, God help the murderer. And worse—Fley, not caught quickly enough, had screamed out before the bullet went home, and Grimaud thought he heard pursuers.

"He had sense enough, and guts enough, even in that hellish moment, to keep his head. He jammed the pistol into the hand of the motionless Fley, lying on his face. He picked up the coil of rope. Somehow, in spite of crash and fuddlement, the plan must go on. But he had more sense than to risk the noise of another shot to be heard by people possibly listening, or to waste more time. He darted out of the room.

"The roof, do you see! The roof was his only chance. He heard imaginary pursuers everywhere; maybe some grisly recollection came back to him of three graves in a storm below the Hungarian mountains. He imagined that they would hear him and track him across those roofs. So he dashed for the trap door at Burnaby's, and down into the dark of Burnaby's flat.

"It was only then that his wits began to recover themselves. . . .

"And, meantime, what has happened? Pierre Fley is fatally hurt. But he still has the ribs of that iron frame which once enabled him to survive being buried alive. The murderer has gone. And Fley will *not* give in. He must get help. He must get to—

"*To a doctor,* Hadley. You asked yesterday why Fley was walking towards the other end of the street, towards the end of a blind alley. Because (as you saw in the newspaper) a doctor lived there: the doctor to whose office he later was carried. He is mortally hurt and he knows it; but he will not be beaten! He gets up, still in his hat and overcoat. The gun has been put into his hand; he rams it in his pocket, for it may be useful. Down he goes, downstairs as steadily as he can, to a silent street where no alarm has been raised. He walks on. . . .

"Have you asked yourself why he was walking in the middle of the street and kept looking so sharply round? The most reasonable explanation is not that he was going to visit anybody; but that he knew the murderer to be lurking somewhere, and he expected another attack. He thinks he is safe. Ahead of him, two men are walking rapidly. He passes a lighted jeweller's, he sees a street lamp ahead on the right. . . .

"But what has happened to Grimaud? Grimaud has heard no pursuit, but he is half-insane with wondering. He does not dare go back to the roof and risk investigation. But stop a moment! If there has been any discovery, he will be able to know by looking for a second out into the street. He can go down to the front door, look out, and peer up the street, can't he? No danger in that, since the house where Burnaby lives is deserted.

"He goes softly downstairs. He opens the door softly, having unbuttoned his coat to wind the coil of rope round him inside that overcoat. He opens the door—full in the glow of a street lamp just beyond that door—and facing him, walking slowly in the middle of the street, is the man he left for dead in the other house less than ten minutes ago. And for the last time those brothers come face to face.

"Grimaud's shirt is a target under that street lamp. And Fley, driven mad with pain and hysteria, does not hesitate. He screams. *He* cries the words, 'The second bullet is for *you!*'—just before he whips up the same pistol and fires.

"That last effort is too much. The hemorrhage has got him, and he knows it. He screams again, lets go of the gun as he tries to throw it (now empty) at Grimaud; and then he pitches forward on his face. That, my lads, is the shot which the three witnesses heard in Cagliostro Street. It was the shot which struck Grimaud in the chest just before he had time to close the door."

21
THE UNRAVELLING

"And then?" prompted Hadley, as Dr. Fell paused and lowered his head.

'The three witnesses did not see Grimaud, of course," said Dr. Fell, wheezing, after a long pause, "because he was never outside the door; never on the steps at all; never within twenty feet of the man who seemed to have been murdered in the middle of a snow desert. Of course Fley already had the wound, which jetted blood from the last convulsion. Of course any deduction from the direction of the wound was useless. Of course there were no fingerprints on the gun, since it landed in snow and in a literal sense had been washed clean."

"By God!" said Hadley, so quietly that he seemed to be making a statement. "It fulfills every condition of the facts, and yet I never thought of it. . . . But go on. Grimaud?"

"Grimaud is inside the door. He knows he's got it in his chest; but he doesn't think it's very serious. He's survived worse things than bullets, and other things (he thinks) *are* more serious.

"After all, he's only got what he was going to give himself—a wound. He could bark out that chuckle of his at such a thing.

But his plan has crashed to hell! (How is he to know, by the way, that the clock at the jeweller's will be fast? He doesn't even know that Fley is dead, for there is Fley walking in the street with fire and sting still in him. Luck—by reason of the jeweller's clock—is with him when he thought it had deserted him, but how is he to know it?) All he is sure of is that Fley will never now be found, a suicide, up in that little room. Fley—probably dangerously wounded, yes, but still able to talk—is out in that street with a policeman running towards him. Grimaud is undone. Unless he can use his wits, he's on his way to the hangman, for Fley will not keep silent now.

"All this comes an instant after the shot, the rush of fancies crowding in. He can't stay here in this dark hall. He'd better have a look at that wound, though, and make sure he doesn't leave a trail of blood. Where? Burnaby's flat upstairs, of course. Up he goes, gets the door open, and switches on the lights. Here's the rope wound round him . . . no use for *that* thing now; he can't pretend Fley came to call on him when Fley may now be talking with the police. He flings the rope off and leaves it.

"A look at the wound next. There's blood all over the inside of that light tweed overcoat, and blood on his inner clothes. But the wound is of small consequence. He's got his handkerchief and his adhesive tape, and he can plug himself up like a horse gored in the bull-ring. Károly Horváth, whom nothing can kill, can afford to chuckle at this. He feels as steady and fresh as ever. But he patches himself up—hence the blood in the bathroom of Burnaby's flat—and tries to collect his wits. What time is it? Good God! he's late; it's just on a quarter to ten. Got to get out of here and hurry home before they catch him. . . .

"And he leaves the lights on. When they burnt up a shilling's worth and went out in the later course of the night, we don't know. They were on three-quarters of an hour afterwards, anyhow, when Rosette saw them.

"But I think that his sanity returns as he hurries home. *Is* he caught? It seems inevitable. Yet is there any loophole, any ghost of a fighting chance, however thin? You see, whatever else Grimaud is, he's a fighter. He's a shrewd, theatrical, imaginative, sneering, common-sense blackguard: but don't forget that he's also a fighter. He wasn't all of a black colour, you know. He would murder a brother, but I question whether he would murder a friend or a woman who loved him. In any case, *is* there some way out? There's one chance, so thin that it's almost useless; but the only one. That's to carry through his original scheme and pretend that Fley has called on him and given him that wound *in his own house.* Fley still has the gun. It will be Grimaud's word, and his witnesses' word, that he never left the house all evening! Whereas they can swear that Fley did come to see him—and then let the damned police try to prove anything! Why not? The snow? It's stopped snowing, and Fley won't have left a track. Grimaud has thrown away the rope Fley was supposed to have used. But it's a toss-up, a last daring of the devil, the only course in an extremity. . . .

"Fley shot him at about twenty minutes to ten. He gets back here at a quarter to ten or a little after. Getting into the house without leaving a footprint? Easy! for a man with a constitution like an ox, and only slightly wounded. (By the way, I believe he was really wounded only slightly, and that he'd live now to hang, if he hadn't done certain things; you'll see.) He'll return by way of the steps down to the areaway, and the area door, as arranged. —How? Well, there is a coating of snow on the areaway steps, of course. But the entrance to the areaway steps is beside the next house, isn't it? Yes. And, at the foot of the area steps, the basement door is protected from snow by a projection: the projection of the main front steps overhanging. So that there is no snow exactly in front of the area door. If he can get down there without leaving a mark—

"He can. He can approach from the other direction, as though he were going to the house next door, and then simply jump down the area steps to the cleared patch below. . . . Don't I seem to remember a *thud*, as of some one falling, which some one heard just before the front-door bell rang?"

"But he didn't ring the front-door bell!"

"Oh yes, he did—but from inside. After he'd gone into the house by way of the area door, and up to where Ernestine Dumont was waiting for him. Then they were ready to perform their illusion."

"Yes," said Hadley. "Now we come to the illusion. How was it done, and how do you know how it was done?"

Dr. Fell sat back and tapped his finger tips together as though he were marshalling facts.

"How do I know? Well, I think my first suggestion was the weight of that picture." He pointed sleepily at the big slashed canvas leaning against the wall. "Yes, it was the weight of the picture. That wasn't very helpful, until I remembered something else. . . ."

"Weight of the picture? Yes, the picture," growled Hadley. "I'd forgotten that. How does *it* figure in the blasted business, anyhow? What did Grimaud mean to do with that?"

"H'mf, ha, yes. That's what I wondered, you see."

"But the weight of the picture, man! It doesn't weigh very much. You yourself picked it up with one hand and turned it round in the air."

Dr. Fell sat up with an air of some excitement. "Exactly. You've hit it. I picked it up with one hand and swung it round. . . . Then why should it take two husky men, the cabman and one extra, to carry it upstairs?"

"What?"

"It did, you know. That was twice pointed out to us. Grimaud, when he took it from Burnaby's studio, easily carried it downstairs. Yet, when he returned here with that same painting late in the afternoon, two people had a job carting it up. Where had it picked up so much weight all of a sudden? He didn't have glass put in it—you can see that for yourself. Where was Grimaud all that time, the morning when he bought the picture and the afternoon when he returned with it? It's much too big a thing to carry about with you for pleasure. Why was Grimaud so insistent on having the picture all wrapped up?

"It wasn't a very far-fetched deduction to think that he used that picture as a blind to hide something that the men were carrying up, unintentionally, along with it. Something in the same parcel. Something very big . . . seven feet by four . . . h'm . . ."

"But there couldn't have been anything," objected Hadley, "or we'd have found it in this room, wouldn't we? Besides, in any case the thing must have been almost absolutely flat, or it would have been noticed in the wrappings of the picture. What sort of object is it that's as big as seven feet by four, and yet thin enough not to be noticed inside the wrappings of a picture; what's as huge a business as that picture, which can nevertheless be spirited out of sight whenever you wish?"

"A mirror," said Dr. Fell.

After a sort of thunderous silence, while Hadley rose from his chair, Dr. Fell went on sleepily: "And it can be spirited out of sight, as you put it, merely by being pushed up the flue of that very broad chimney—where we've all tried to get our fists, by the way—and propped up on the ledge inside where the chimney turns. You don't need magic. You only need to be damnably strong in the arms and shoulders."

"You mean," cried Hadley, "that damned stage trick . . ."

"A new version of the stage trick," said Dr. Fell, "and a very good one which is practical if you care to try it. Now, look round this room. You see the door? What do you see in the wall directly opposite the door?"

"Nothing," said Hadley. "I mean, he's had the bookcases cleared away in a big space on either side. There's blank panelled wall, that's all."

"Exactly. And do you see any furniture in a line between the door and that wall?"

"No. It's cleared."

"So if you were out in that hall looking in, you would see only black carpet, no furniture, and to the rear an expanse of blank oak-panelled wall?"

"Yes."

"Now, Ted, open the door and look out into the hall," said Dr. Fell. "What about the walls and carpet out there?"

Rampole made a feint of looking, although he knew. "They're just the same," he said. "The floor is one solid carpet running to the baseboards, like this one, and the panelling is the same."

"Right! By the way, Hadley," pursued Dr. Fell, still drowsily, "you might drag out that mirror from behind the bookcase over there. It's been behind the bookcase since yesterday afternoon, when Drayman found it in the chimney. It was lifting it down that brought on his stroke. We'll try a little experiment. I don't think any of the household will interrupt us up here, but we can head off anybody who does. I want you to take that mirror, Hadley, and set it up just inside the door—so that when you open the door (it opens inwards and to the right, you see, as you come in from the hall) the edge of the door at its outermost swing is a few inches away from the mirror."

The superintendent with some difficulty trundled out the object he found behind the bookcase. It was bigger than a tailor's swinging mirror; several inches, in fact, higher and wider than the door. Its base rested flat on the carpet, and it was supported upright by a heavy swing-base on the right-hand side as you faced it. Hadley regarded it curiously.

"Set it up inside the door?"

"Yes. The door will only swing open a short distance; you'll see an aperture only a couple of feet wide at the most. . . . Try it!"

"I know, but if you do that . . . well, somebody sitting in the room down at the end of the hall, where Mills was, would see his own reflection smack in the middle of the mirror."

"Not at all. Not at the angle—a slight angle, but enough; a poor thing, but mine own—not at the angle to which I'm going to tilt it. You'll see. The two of you go down there where Mills was while I adjust it. Keep your eyes off until I sing out."

Hadley, muttering that it was damned foolishness, but highly interested in spite of that, tramped down after Rampole. They kept their eyes off until they heard the doctor's hail, and then turned round.

The hallway was gloomy and high enough. Its black-carpeted length ran down to a closed door. Dr. Fell stood outside that door, like an overfat master of ceremonies about to unveil a statue. He stood a little to the right of the door, well back from it against the wall, and had his hand stretched out across to the knob. "Here she goes!" he grunted, and quickly opened the door—hesitated—and closed it. "Well? What did you see?"

"I saw the room inside," returned Hadley. "Or at least I

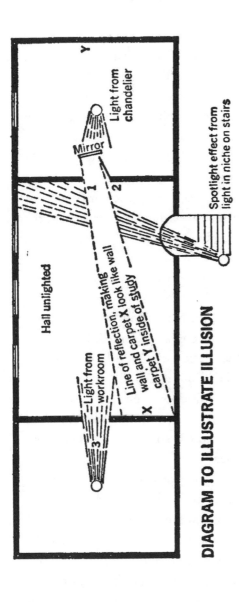

DIAGRAM TO ILLUSTRATE ILLUSION

1. Man whose own reflection is seen by watcher, but appearing three inches taller than reflection because watcher, thirty feet away, is sitting down on a much lower level of observation.

2. Confederate who opens and shuts door.

3. Watcher.

In testing this illusion, one important point must be observed. No light must fall directly *on* the mirror, else there will be a reflected dazzle to betray its presence. It will be seen that a spotlight from the niche on the stairs has been caused to fall *across* the line of the door, but not in a position to catch any reflection. No light is in the hall, and the workroom light does not penetrate far. In the study itself, the light comes from the chandelier in a very high ceiling, thus coming almost directly over the top of the mirror. It will throw, therefore, very little shadow of this mirror into the hall; and such throw will be obscured by the counter-shadow of the man standing before the door.

thought I did. I saw the carpet, and the rear wall. It seemed a very big room."

"You didn't see that," said Dr. Fell. "As a matter of fact, you saw the reflection of the panelled wall immediately to the right of the door where you're standing, and the carpet going up to it. That's why it seemed so big a room: you were looking at a double length of reflection. This mirror is bigger than the door, you know. And you didn't see a reflection of the door itself because it opens inwards to the right. If you looked carefully, you might have seen a line of what looks like a shadow just along the top edge of the door. That's where the top edge of the mirror inevitably reflects, being taller, an inch or so of the *inner* top edge of the door. But your attention would be concentrated on any figures you saw. . . . Did you see me, by the way?"

"No; you were too far over. You had your arm across the door to the knob, and kept back."

"Yes. As Dumont was standing. Now try a last experiment before I explain how the whole mechanism worked. Ted, you sit down in the chair behind that desk—where Mills was sitting. You're very much taller than he is, but it will illustrate the idea. I'm going to stand outside, with this door open, and look at myself in the mirror. Now, you can't mistake ME, either from the front or the rear; but then I'm more distinguishable than some people. Just tell me what you see."

In the ghostly light, with the door partly open, the effect was rather eerie. A figure of Dr. Fell stood inside the door, peering out at another figure of Dr. Fell standing on the threshold and confronting himself—fixed and motionless, with a startled look.

"I don't touch the door, you see," a voice boomed at them. By the illusion of the moving lips Rampole would have sworn that the Dr. Fell inside the door was speaking. The mirror threw the voice back like a sounding-board. "Somebody obligingly opens and closes the door for me—somebody standing at my right. I don't touch the door, or my reflection would have to do likewise. Quick, what do you notice?"

"Why—one of you is very much taller," said Rampole, studying the images.

"Which one?"

"You yourself: the figure in the hall."

"Exactly. First because you're seeing it at a distance, but the most important thing is that you're sitting down. To a man the size of Mills I should look like a giant. Hey? H'mf. Hah. Yes. Now if I make a quick move to dodge in at that door (supposing me to be capable of such a manœuvre), and at the same time my confederate at the right makes a quick confusing move with me and slams the door, in the muddled illusion the figure inside seems to be—?"

"Jumping in front of you to keep you out."

"Yes. Now come and read the evidence, if Hadley has it."

When they were again in the room, past the tilted mirror which Hadley moved back, Dr. Fell sank into a chair, sighing wheezingly.

"I'm sorry, gents. I should have realized the truth long before, from the careful, methodical, exact Mr. Mills' evidence. Let me see if I can repeat from memory his exact words. Check me up, Hadley. H'm." He rapped his knuckles against his head and scowled. "Like this:

"'She [Dumont] was about to knock at the door when I was startled to see the tall man come upstairs directly after us. She turned round and saw him. She exclaimed certain words. . . . The tall man made no reply. He walked to the door, and without haste turned down the collar of his coat and removed his cap, which he placed in his overcoat pocket. . . .'

"You see, gents? He had to do that, because the reflection couldn't show a cap and couldn't show a collar turned up when the figure inside must appear to be wearing a dressing-gown. But I wondered *why* he was so methodical about that, since apparently he didn't remove the mask—"

"Yes, what about that mask? Mills says he didn't—"

"Mills didn't see him take it off; I'll show you why as soon as we go on with Mills:

"'Madame Dumont cried out something, shrank back against the wall, and hurried to open the door. Dr. Grimaud appeared on the threshold—'

"Appeared! That's precisely what he did do. Out methodical witness is uncomfortably exact. But Dumont? There was the first flaw. A frightened woman, looking up at a terrifying figure while she's standing before the door of a room in which there's a man who will protect her, doesn't *shrink back*. She rushes towards the door to get protection. Anyhow, follow Mills' testimony. He says Grimaud was not wearing his eye-glasses (they wouldn't have fitted behind that mask). But the natural movement of a man inside, I thought, would have been to raise his glasses. Grimaud—according to Mills—stands *stock-still* the whole time; like the stranger, with his hands in his pockets. Now for the damning part. Mills says: 'I am under the impression that Madame Dumont, although she was shrinking back against the wall, closed the door after him. I recall that she had her hand on the knob.'

Not a natural action for her, either! She contradicted him—but Mills was right." Dr. Fell gestured.

"No use going on with all this. But here was my difficulty: if Grimaud was alone in that room, if he simply walked in on his own reflection, what became of his clothes? What about that long black overcoat, the brown peaked cap, even the false face? They weren't in the room. Then I remembered that Ernestine's profession had been the making of costumes for the opera and ballet; I remembered a story O'Rourke had told us; and I knew—"

"Well?"

"That Grimaud had burnt them," said Dr. Fell. "He had burnt them because they were made of paper, like the uniform of the Vanishing Horseman described by O'Rourke. He couldn't risk the long and dangerous business of burning real clothes in that fire; he had to work too fast. They had to be torn up and burnt. And bundles of loose, blank sheets of writing-paper—perfectly blank!—had to be burned on top of them to hide the fact that some of it was coloured paper. Dangerous letters! Oh, Bacchus, I could murder myself for thinking such a thing!" He shook his fist. "When there was no blood-trail, no bloodstain at all, going to the drawer in his desk where he did keep his important papers! And there was another reason for burning papers . . . they had to conceal the fragments of the 'shot.'"

"Shot?"

"Don't forget that a pistol was supposed to have been fired in that room. Of course, what the witnesses really heard was the noise of a heavy firecracker—pinched from the hoard Drayman always keeps, as you know, for Guy Fawkes night. Drayman discovered the missing thunderbolt; I think that's how he tumbled to the scheme, and why he kept muttering about 'fireworks.'

Well, the fragments of an exploding firecracker fly wide. They're heavy reënforced cardboard, hard to burn, and they had to be destroyed in the fire or hidden in that drift of papers. I found some of them. Of course, we should have realized no bullet had really been fired. Modern cartridges—such as you informed me were used in that Colt revolver—have smokeless powder. You can smell it, but you can't see it. And yet there was a *haze* in this room (left by the firecracker) even after the window was up.

"Ah, well, let's recapitulate! Grimaud's heavy crêpe-paper uniform consisted of a black coat—black like a dressing-gown, long like a dressing-gown, and having at the front shiny lapels which would show like a dressing-gown when you turned down the collar to face your own image. It consisted of a paper cap, to which the false face was attached—so that in sweeping off the cap you simply folded both together and shoved 'em into your pocket. (The real dressing-gown, by the way, was already in this room while Grimaud was out.) And the black 'uniform,' early last evening, had been incautiously hung up in the closet downstairs.

"Mangan, unfortunately, spotted it. The watchful Dumont knew that he spotted it, and whisked it out of that cupboard to a safer place as soon as he went away. She, naturally, never saw a yellow tweed coat hanging there at all. Grimaud had it upstairs here with him, ready for his expedition. But it was found in the closet yesterday afternoon, and she had to pretend it had been there all the time. Hence the chameleon overcoat.

"You can now make a reconstruction of just what happened when Grimaud, after killing Fley and getting a bullet himself, returned to the house on Saturday night. Right at the start of the illusion he and his confederate were in dangerous trouble.

You see, Grimaud was late. He'd expected to be back by nine-thirty—and he didn't get there until a quarter to ten. The longer he delayed, the nearer it got to the time he had told *Mangan* to expect a visitor, and now Mangan would be expecting the visitor he had been told to watch. It was touch-and-go, and I rather imagine the cool Grimaud was fairly close to insane. He got up through the basement entrance, where his confederate was waiting. The tweed coat, with the blood inside it, went into the hall closet to be disposed of presently—and it never was, because he died. Dumont eased open the door, rang the bell by putting her hand out, and then went to 'answer' it while Grimaud was getting ready with his uniform.

"But they delayed too long. Mangan called out. Grimaud, with his wits still not functioning well, grew a little panicky and made a blunder to ward off immediate detection. He'd got so far; he didn't want to fail then from the nosiness of a damned penniless kid. So he said that he was Pettis, and locked them in. (You notice that Pettis is the only one with a voice of the same bass quality as Grimaud's?) Yes, it was a spur-of-the-moment error, but his only wish was to writhe like a footballer down a field and *somehow* escape those hands for the moment.

"The illusion was performed; he was alone in his room. His jacket, probably with blood on that, had been taken in charge by Dumont; he wore the uniform over his shirtsleeves, open shirt, and bandaged wound. He had only to lock the door behind him, put on his real dressing-gown, destroy the paper uniform, and get that mirror up into the chimney. . . .

"That, I say again, was the finish. The blood had begun to flow again, you see. No ordinary man, wounded, could have stood the strain under which he had already been. He wasn't killed by

Fley's bullet. He ripped his own lung like a rotted piece of rubber when he tried to—and superhumanly did—lift that mirror into its hiding-place. That was when he knew. Then was when he began to bleed from the mouth like a slashed artery; when he staggered against the couch, knocked away the chair, and reeled forward in his last successful effort to ignite the firecracker. After all the hates and dodgings and plans, the world was not spinning in front of him: it was only slowly going black. He tried to scream out, and he could not, for the blood was welling in his throat. And at that moment Charles Grimaud suddenly knew what he would never have believed possible, the breaking of the last and most shattering mirror-illusion in his bitter life. . . ."

"Well?"

"He knew that he was dying," said Dr. Fell. "And, stranger than any of his dreams, he was glad."

The heavy leaden light had begun to darken again with snow. Dr. Fell's voice sounded weirdly in the chill room. Then they saw that the door was opening and that in it stood the figure of a woman with a damned face. A damned face and a black dress, but round her shoulders was still drawn a red-and-yellow shawl for the love of the dead.

"You see, he confessed," Dr. Fell said in the same low, monotonous tone, "he tried to tell us the truth about his killing of Fley, and Fley's killing of him. Only we did not choose to understand, and I didn't understand until I knew from the clock what must have happened in Cagliostro Street. Man, man, don't you see? Take first his final statement, the statement made just before he died:

"'It was my brother who did it. I never thought he would shoot. God knows how he got out of that room—'"

"You mean Fley's room in Cagliostro Street, after Fley had been left for dead?" demanded Hadley.

"Yes. And the horrible shock of coming on him suddenly, as Grimaud opened the door under the street light. You see:

"'One second he was there, and the next he wasn't . . . I want to tell you who my brother is, so you won't think I'm raving. . . .'

"For, of course, he did not think anybody knew about Fley. Now, in the light of that, examine the tangled, muddled, half-choked words with which—when he heard the statement that he was sinking—he tried to explain the whole puzzle to us.

"First he tried to tell us about the Horváths and the salt-mine. But he went on to the killing of Fley, and what Fley had done to him. *'Not suicide.'* When he'd seen Fley in the street, he couldn't make Fley's death the suicide he pretended. *'He couldn't use the rope.'* Fley couldn't, after that, be supposed to use the rope that Grimaud had discarded as useless. *'Roof.'* Grimaud did not mean this roof; but the other roof which he crossed when he left Fley's room. *'Snow.'* The snow had stopped and wrecked his plans. *'Too much light.'* There's the crux, Hadley! When he looked out into the street, there was too much light from the street lamp; Fley recognized him, and fired. *'Got gun.'* Naturally, Fley had got the gun then. *'Fox.'* The mask, the Guy Fawkes charade he tried to work. But finally, *'Don't blame poor—'* Not Drayman; he didn't mean Drayman. But it was a last apology for the one thing, I think, of which he was ashamed; the one piece of imposture he would never have done. 'Don't blame poor Pettis; I didn't mean to implicate him.'"

For a long time nobody spoke.

"Yes," Hadley agreed, dully. "Yes. All except one thing. What about the slashing of that picture, and where did the knife go?"

"The slashing of the picture, I think, was an extra touch of the picturesque to help the illusion; Grimaud did it—or so I imagine. As for the knife, I frankly don't know. Grimaud probably had it here, and put it up the chimney beside the mirror so that the invisible man should seem to be doubly armed. But it isn't on the chimney ledge now. I should suppose that Drayman found it yesterday, and took it away—"

"That is the one point," said a voice, "on which you are wrong."

Ernestine Dumont remained in the doorway, her hands folded across the shawl at her breast. But she was smiling.

"I have heard everything you said," she went on. "Perhaps you can hang me, or perhaps not. That is not important. I do know that after so many years it is not quite worth while going on without Charles. . . . I took the knife, my friend. I had another use for it."

She was still smiling, and there was a blaze of pride in her eyes. Rampole saw what her hands were hiding. He saw her totter suddenly, but he was too late to catch her when she pitched forward on her face. Dr. Fell lumbered out of his chair and remained staring at her with a face as white as her own.

"I have committed another crime, Hadley," he said. "I have guessed the truth again."

DISCUSSION QUESTIONS

- Were you able to predict any part of the solution to the case?

- Aside from the solution, did anything about the book surprise you? If so, what?

- Did any aspects of the plot date the story? If so, which ones?

- Would the story be different if it were set in the present day? If so, how?

- What role did the setting play in the narrative?

- What sort of detective is Dr. Gideon Fell? What special skills make him a great investigator?

- Can you think of any contemporary mystery authors who seem to be influenced or inspired by John Dickson Carr's writing?

MORE JOHN DICKSON CARR FROM
═══ AMERICAN MYSTERY CLASSICS ═══

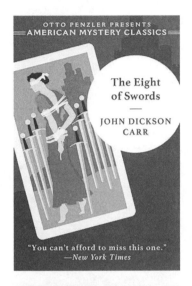

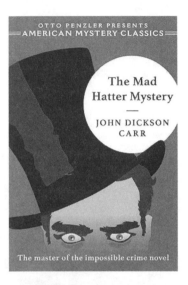

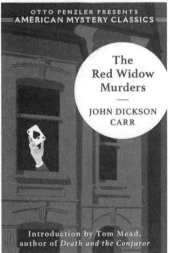